THE TOWN UPSTAIRS

Frank Jamison

In Memory

of

Elbert Williams

*In June 1940, in Haywood County, Tennessee, a man named Elbert
Williams was the victim of the last documented lynching to occur in
the state. It was the direct result of his efforts to register to vote.
No one was ever charged with the crime.*

Acknowledgments

There is a Celtic phrase, Anam Cara, which means something like Soul Friend. There are many such in my life, both family and friends. You know who you are.

Thanks to the Orr Mountain Writers who critiqued portions of the early drafts. Darnell Arnoult urged me to launch this project and provided insightful advice all along the way. Thank you, Darnell.

Thanks to Kate Winter for your editing and design work.

There are fragments of two of my own poems embedded in the text. Thanks to *River Oak Review* for publishing "Deviations and Detours," and to *Chrysalis Reader* for publishing "Finishing."

Thanks especially to the following journals which published short story excerpts:
    Arkana, Issue 8, "Catfish"
    The Penmen Review, March 8, 2022, "The Funeral"

Prologue

Griffin Wynne
June 15, 1940
Hatchie Landing, TN

"THIS WILL BE MY LAST MONUMENT," Griffin Wynne whispered to himself. The stone was a deep gray granite, almost blue in certain lights, and the afternoon sunlight slanting through the roll-up door at the end of the cutting shed made a myriad of sparkles on the carving. Griffin's fingers glided over the delicate scrollwork like a blind man's, and little flecks of stone glinted away like meteors. Satisfied that it was perfect, he positioned the hoist over the stone and grappled thick lifting bands around it, and then raised it off the floor. He walked the stone into the sandblaster. After settling it into place for the final polishing, he removed the straps, closed the compartment, loaded the hopper with a fine grit, and started the blaster. The thick dust was like the fog that had settled over Parham's field the night before and the awfulness that followed there. It seemed he could see Bennie Hoskins's image fading in and out and white-robed men circling a burning cross, their eyes dark and indiscernible behind their peaked masks. He recalled their laughter and jeers as Bennie tried to hoist the unconscious body that finally took four men to heave into the air.

Wynne shut down the blaster and watched the enclosure's settling dust and thought of the body in the fog, the way it had twirled when the little breezes came up, and the small hope that sprang in his own breast that the poor man might still be alive.

When the dust had settled in the chamber, Griffin gently wiped the stone with a rag. A clean, smooth surface interrupted by beautiful scrolls and an angel with open wings appeared from beneath the dust, and then a name and date came forth. Josiah Tolliver, Born 1895 – Died June 8, 1940.

Griffin ran the straps beneath the stone once again, moved it out onto its cradle in the cutting shed, and knelt before it to finish wiping it down. He didn't notice the man silhouetted in the doorway with the late sun at his back.

"You look like you might be praying," the man said.

Wynne looked up, startled. He couldn't see the face, but knew Malcolm Oakes's voice.

"I just dropped by to let you know we'll meet tomorrow night in Parham's field."

Wynne ran his rag over the monument. "I won't be there, Malcolm. I'm finished with this business."

For a long moment, the only sound was a mockingbird in the hackberry tree outside.

"You're in it, Griffin. You worked with us."

Wynne looked at the stone in front of him and thought about Josiah Tolliver's hanging. "I'm leaving," was all he said, and began brushing the stone.

"You'd best be there," Oakes said, and turned back toward his car.

Wynne followed as far as the doorway and watched the big black-and-gold Sheriff's Department emblem on the cruiser pivot in the sunlight as the car drove away.

The mockingbird went quiet in the hackberry tree as Wynne turned to go back inside. He finished brushing the dust from the monument, backed his truck into the shed, and hoisted a different monument into the bed, scotched and tied it down. This one, too, was full of scrollwork and had two angels in relief at the top, but no name or birth or death dates. He pulled the truck out and closed the shed.

The stone was for Norman Parker's mortuary over in Paradise, and as he drove eastward across the levees, he thought about his declaration to Malcolm Oakes and the predicament he had put himself in. He was certain of his decision, but he had no idea how to accomplish the break. His monument business was all he knew and all he had.

As he pulled to a stop in the rear of Parker's mortuary, Norman came out of the back door. The two men knew each other from frequent business.

"Where do you want this stone, Norman?"

"Just over there beside those two small ones." He pointed. "We're having a service tomorrow, and the family wants to choose a monument right away. If they like this one, you can put a name and dates on it later."

"Sure. Just let me know and I'll take it back to the shop and finish it."

Parker leaned into the bed of the truck and looked at the stone. "You're an artist, Wynne. I don't know how you do it."

"I may not be doing it much longer."

"No? How come?"

Wynne evaded the question. "Monument work is changing, Norman. It won't be long before all this artwork will be done by machines. I've lived in Hatchie Landing all my life, but it's time to leave, maybe try to get into something different somewhere else."

"I understand. I'm getting too old for this myself." He waved to the building behind him. "Are you really serious about leaving? I'd hate to see you quit, Wynne. I've told you. You're an artist. I'd take you into this business in a heartbeat. I've been at it for forty years. I'm ready for somebody to take it over."

"I'm serious, Norman. I've got to move on."

"Come in with me." He swung his arm again back toward the mortuary.

"Norman, I don't know anything about your business. I've never even seen it done. Embalming somebody, I mean."

"Well, that stone you've got there?" He pointed to the unfinished monument. "I'm about to prepare the body of the man whose family may take it. Why don't you come in and watch?"

They stood in the twilight, silent for another moment. A truck trundled by, unseen on the street out front. A street lamp winked on.

"I guess I could," Wynne said. "Let me unload first, before the light's completely gone." He turned the truck in the small lot and maneuvered it into position, then hooked the stone to the small hoist in the bed and lowered it to the ground.

Inside, as Parker prepared the body, Wynne took note of each action and the order in which it was performed. He leaned in close as Parker applied makeup to the face. When he was finished, Parker looked at Wynne. "Well, what do you think?"

"He looks like he's sleeping."

"Good. That's the effect I shoot for. It helps the family. I could teach you."

"Maybe so. I don't know, Norman. I appreciate the offer, but I'll have to think about it."

Wynne pondered the offer on the way home to Hatchie Landing. He needed to get away from the likes of Malcolm Oakes and decided this might at least be an interim step toward the future. When Parker called a couple of days later to say the family wanted the monument, Griffin drove back to Paradise to reload the stone and told Norman he would accept his offer of a job.

"Not a job, Griffin. A partnership. This is wonderful. I'll teach you everything, get you licensed, and you can take over this business and buy me out with the proceeds. You'll need a place to live. Why don't you take the little apartment upstairs until you find something better?" They discussed other details then and there, shook hands, and the deal was done.

PART I

1975

"Often the hands will solve a mystery that the intellect has struggled with in vain."

– Carl Gustav Jung

Chapter 1

Jesse Wickham
April 1, 1975
Paradise, TN

WEST TENNESSEE IS A LOVELY PART of the earth. The Tennessee River has made its great bend out of Alabama and turned north to the Ohio. The land to the west of it rolls gently down to the delta in front of the great Mississippi River, and on this land live some of the gentlest people on earth. In the middle of this land is a place called Paradise, a place that struggles to live up to its name, often failing, but always rising up again to struggle with the impossible. Jesse Wickham grew up in Paradise but left to become a journalist in another place, knitting together the fragments of other people's stories. He intended to venture out, to cover the world, to report from far-flung places, but at age thirty-five, he was sitting at a desk in the *Paradise Sun* newsroom, as quiet as a funeral home at this hour.

He had left Paradise after college, believing there is no such thing as paradise on earth or in heaven. He had returned, still harboring doubts, to report on the town's shortcomings and successes. He was surprised how close to him those early years still stood when he was a child of six in 1946, the trains going north and south, the winter's chill, birds' feet on cold wires, coal smoke settling heavily in the air like time, his parents' house on Institute Street, their wooden kitchen table, and suppers cooking on the stove; the lovely stillness of summer evenings, soft and sultry after the war, that dull and lovely town before the last passenger trains rumbled their couplings down the line and pulled out north and south, those few years when there seemed to be no weight to be borne and street lamps lit a few corners here and there, a time when he knew nothing of the trouble that soon would rumble into town.

He slit open the envelope in front of him and began to read.

Dear Mr. Wickham,

I was pleased to finally meet you the other day at Griffin Wynne's funeral. It's fortuitous that you recently returned to Paradise to work for the Sun. Griffin often mentioned your name when you lived here years ago. He would have been delighted that you have returned to Paradise. He was as proud of you as if you were the son he never had.

As I mentioned, I am the executor of his will. His sister and my sister married brothers, so Wynne and I were close friends for many years. He left the funeral home to his sister, Lula Bartlett, who lives here in town. It's impossible for her to operate it, so she has accepted an offer of sale. The new owners will take possession at closing, which should occur within the month. They plan to consolidate the Griffin Wynne business with their own. As a result, the Griffin Wynne home will no longer be staffed full-time. All the administrative work and sales are to be handled at the other location, and Griffin Wynne will only be opened and used when there is to be a funeral. Consequently, they want to begin some renovations right away.

As executor, I will assist his sister in disposing of the contents that don't accompany the sale. In that regard, Mr. Wynne's will states that one item is to go to you and another to you and me jointly. I hope the joint ownership won't create a problem, though I have no real interest in the item, which is a large replica of the town of Paradise upstairs in the funeral home. It was Mr. Wynne's hobby for many years. It is done in incredible detail, including the railroads and railyards. A Mr. Allison got him interested in model railroading, I believe, but he is dead, and I can't find his heirs, or we could offer it to them. Perhaps the railroad museum would like to have it.

Griffin Wynne willed to you a small trunk containing several things clearly belonging to one individual named Nathan Hanks. In the trunk is a box of old notebooks of the Blue Horse brand, like we used in school. They seem to be a set of diaries kept by this same Nathan Hanks. Also inside the box are instructions in Mr. Wynne's handwriting to contact you if you could be found. You are to have the notebooks and also the trunk and its other contents if you want the entire lot. Otherwise, we are to destroy the notebooks and dispose of the trunk and its other contents. There is similar language in the will itself.

I took the liberty of reading the first few pages of one of the notebooks. They're very well written. There is some sadness in them, but some joy also. You might want to get them to his family. I'm not sure why Griffin did not do so. It was a strange time. I remember when Nathan Hanks died. Curiously, on top of the notebooks, there was an envelope addressed "To Whom It May Concern." I'm enclosing it here since it is among the remaining items for you to handle. As executor, I'd appreciate it if you would share its contents, provided you are comfortable doing so.

Please call me at the number below to discuss a time for us to meet at the funeral home and determine the disposition of these items. Wynne's former secretary, Vivian Paxton, will meet us and let us in.

Please let me know if I can be of further service.

Cordially,
Loyal Hall, Esq.

Jesse leaned back and recalled those childhood days when he would visit the funeral home to watch the model trains run through "The Town Upstairs" as Griffin Wynne had referred to it. He remembered a black man named Nathan who used to work in their neighborhood and who would tell him stories. That Nathan had died in a house fire on Tanyard Street, and could be the same Nathan as the man named in Loyal Hall's letter. If they were the same person, there might be a good human interest story.

He opened the envelope and read…

I left Hatchie Landing and settled in Paradise to begin a new life, but the images of what happened in Hatchie Landing in the summer of 1940 have never left me. I see myself dressed in all my faults and shortcomings. I feel diminished. Some might counsel that I should forgive myself, but it isn't possible. One can only make allowance and keep on living. So I do the only thing I can, which is to turn to whatever work is before me. Attention to detail is a penance I proffer as I serve both the dead and the living who come into my care. My only extravagance is the replica of Paradise I am constructing above me.

Griffin Wynne, Paradise, TN, June 8, 1948.

"Curious is hardly the word for it," thought Jesse. He recalled his college years working for Griffin Wynne and living in the small apartment upstairs in the funeral home, where he had discovered a cache of notebooks as he rummaged around in a closet one night. Mr. Wynne told him not to disturb things in the closets and took away the notebooks. It was the only time Jesse could remember him being agitated. He thought to himself, we write our stories in bits and pieces, strewn behind us like elm leaves in autumn, small yellowed fragments, jagged outlines, traces of ourselves like signposts along the paths we followed to now.

He picked up the phone and called Loyal Hall.

"So good to hear from you, Jesse. I hoped you would contact me right away."

"As a matter of fact, I think the information you've come across might make a human interest story. The Nathan you mention in your letter is likely the same man I knew when I was a child. I'd like to find out more about him."

"I see. Well, in that case, I'll be glad to help as much as I can. But understand the new owners of Griffin Wynne are anxious to have their space."

They agreed to meet the next day.

Chapter 2

Jesse Wickham and Loyal Hall
April 2, 1975
Paradise, TN

JESSE DROVE TO MEET LOYAL HALL at eleven o'clock at the old Griffin Wynne Funeral Home *to view his inheritance;* he chuckled. He drove around the square, noting where the old newspaper had once stood, where he liked to think he had begun his writing career. Where he had delivered papers, worked the mail room, and written a weekly article about college life. He could almost hear the sound of the old hot lead press, smell the ink, and hear the rhythmic tattoo as sections of print rolled off. He drove the three short blocks to the funeral home. A black sedan waited at the curb. He recognized Vivian Paxton as she got out, and he held out his hand to greet her. Instead, she took it and pulled him to her and hugged him.

"Jesse, it's so good to see you." She was diminutive, with clear blue eyes and gray showing in her hair. She took the keys from her purse and led the way up the front steps.

"Come inside. Let me show you around. Loyal should be along shortly."

Jesse thought how things become smaller over time, our minds expanding with added geography and experience, or is it something else? He didn't know. Vivian opened the door, and they entered a cool and quiet place. She flipped on the lights. "The things are still upstairs."

Jesse stopped in the small lobby, taking in the rush of long-ago events. "Do you remember when I was once a paid mourner here?" he asked.

"No, I had forgotten. We did use paid mourners a number of times, though. And of course, I remember when you worked for us and lived upstairs." She turned to face him with her hand on the banister.

He looked around. Here was Mr. Wynne's little office, and over there was the equally small room where Vivian had handled the myriad administrative chores pertaining to the dead. The place even smelled the same, a funeral smell of flowers and eucalyptus. The walls were papered differently, and there were new light fixtures and drapes. The floor was fully carpeted. He wondered if the beautiful wooden floors were still underneath.

"Trapped in a memory?" Vivian asked quietly and smiled.

He looked up at her and grinned. "Yes. Yes, I was. You know, sometimes memories of a place you haven't visited for decades come rushing back to fill your mind. There's a loneliness with it and the realization that something from the past has been lost forever."

"I've experienced a goodly share of that feeling as I've worked to clear out the upstairs. Come on, let's go get this over with and get out of here. It's too pretty outside today to be shut up in a dusty old funeral parlor like this." She continued up the steps.

Just then, Loyal Hall came bustling in the door. "Sorry I'm late."

"Jesse, you met Loyal at the funeral, did you not? Loyal, we're just about to go upstairs and have a look," Vivian spoke in a hurried voice and motioned them to come.

"As executor and also as Wynne's sister's attorney," Loyal said, "I've had a quick look at the items Wynne left in his will, but not in detail."

Jesse remembered the staircase being wide and leading to a high place, but now it looked modest and perfectly normal in its ascent. At the top was a small landing with doorways to the right and left. "This room over here to the right is where the train was, wasn't it?"

"And it's still in there," said Loyal. "Do you want to see it?"

"Yes! Absolutely! I helped him work on it sometimes, but it was late in the game. He was almost finished with it by then. When I was a little boy, I lived just a block from here on Institute Street, and I'd come up here to see it. He was a generous man and always let me go up to admire it. If there wasn't a funeral or other work going on, he'd operate it for me. He was an artist."

"Yes, he was. But first, let's take a look at the trunk and get that bit of business out of the way. If I let you in there with that train, we may never get our real task done today." Loyal's eyes twinkled when he said it. The keys jangled as Vivian opened the door to the left, and they entered the little apartment Jesse had occupied when he worked there. "The whole second floor was Griffin's sanctuary," she said. "I rarely came up here. I tried to grant him his peace. He was at times such an introspective man."

The room was full of clutter, but her attempt to bring order into the chaos showed. Things were arranged in clumps. The trunk sat on the floor along with articles of clothing and some books in stacks. "Do all these things go together?" Jesse asked.

"No, not necessarily," Vivian said, "I've just tried to group things according to similarity of object. I don't know. The trunk seemed to be in a class all its own, so I left it there where you see it. I've never seen anything quite like it. It's not fine furniture or anything, but it is old, I'll bet."

"Antique, I'd say, whatever the word means these days," Jesse said. "You know, I've seen this before when I worked here. It was over there behind that little door in the attic crawl space. I told Mr. Wynne about finding it, and he told me to leave it alone. He took it away, and I never saw it again. Strange that he's leaving it to me now. Where did you find it, Vivian?"

"It was among Mr. Wynne's things in the closet in his office. I brought it up here until I could go through everything. Everything is still in there, the notebooks, a pencil or two, and a few other things."

The trunk was more like a little steamer trunk, but handmade of walnut. There were seams between the little planks in one or two places where the wood had shrunk with age. There was a brass latch on the front and leather handles on each end that looked like they had been fashioned from pieces of an old belt. It looked as if there might have been different handles at one time, but they had been replaced by these.

Jesse knelt and lifted the lid. On top was the handwritten instruction from Griffin Wynne written on an unfolded sheet of paper, with instructions to contact Jesse Wickham and give him this trunk or otherwise destroy the contents. The address given for Jesse was one where he had first lived after leaving home.

Next were four Blue Horse notebooks; he removed them. On the front of the first three was penciled a date, a dash, and another date. He took this to be the beginning and ending dates of the entries in them. The notebooks began in August 1947. The fourth notebook only had what appeared to be accounting for work performed at various places.

He set them aside and looked at the other articles. Vivian was right about the trunk being unique. He had never seen anything quite like it either. Further inside was a wooden ruler, a small bone-handled pocketknife, two yellow No. 2 pencils, a packet of envelopes tied with a thin, faded pink ribbon, and a framed picture of a black family dressed in their Sunday best. There was a ledger book and a single envelope addressed to Jesse Wickham. The word "*PERSONAL*" in all capital letters was written slantwise beside his name.

"Have you read any of these?" he asked Vivian and Loyal.

"No, I haven't opened anything else," Vivian said. "I only read a few notebook pages. I've had too much stuff to go through up here, and most days it was either too warm or too cool in here to stay long.

The building was fitted out with central air much later after it was built, and they didn't do such a good job of ducting up here."

"Oh, I'm sure of it," said Loyal. "This building, which was actually a house, was old before it became the funeral home."

"Yes, I know," said Vivian, "and frankly, I was overwhelmed with the magnitude of junk stored up here. You know, you can't just plow through this kind of thing. Each item triggers a memory. Some days, I'd be in tears half the time. It has been a hard job. I was alone with no one for a prop." There was a catch in her voice. "Would you like to see the train layout now?"

"Of course." Jesse replaced the contents of the trunk and stood. "Do you mind if I look around in here first?"

"No, go ahead and take your time. If you need to come back later, I can manage that too. We will have the run of the place until the closing takes place."

"Which will be soon," Loyal reminded them.

"How soon?"

"Within three weeks, I'd say."

There wasn't much territory to cover on this side of the upstairs. There was the larger room they stood in, and off that were a small bathroom and another small room. He walked around the piles and opened that door.

The cabinets were still in place, but the stove and sink were gone. He stepped inside and opened one of the cabinets. There was a ceramic coffee mug on one shelf. He picked it up. The inscription on the side read Alpha Tau Omega 1960. "This was my little kitchen when I lived here," he said. "My old fraternity mug."

"Then take that, too," Vivian said.

Jesse put the mug into the little trunk, picked it up, and followed Vivian and Loyal across the landing at the top of the stairs and into the other room. It was his turn to be overwhelmed. Griffin Wynne's train layout had progressed enormously since he had last seen it, and now it almost covered the entire room wall to wall with only a narrow passage around the perimeter. They had to turn sideways to move around it. There was a plywood skirt around the entire layout with doors in a couple of places so that a person could crawl underneath to one of four access hatches located strategically about the model. The detail was phenomenal. The whole town of Paradise, as it was in 1960, lay before them.

"This needs to be in a museum," Jesse whispered.

"Remarkable, isn't it?" Loyal said.

"It's incredible. You know, this gives me an idea for a series of stories for the Sunday paper about Paradise and its development over the years. I could use Wynne's model, take pictures of different locations, and write a story about it. In fact, the model is a story in itself. People would love to know about it, and it deserves to be known about."

"You'd better arrange for the pictures right away," Loyal said, "We don't have much time. The alternative is to find a new home for it."

"That will take some doing and considerable time, I'm sure," Jesse said.

"The railroad museum in the old N. C. and St. L. station might take it," Loyal suggested. "I'll ask them."

"That'll be great. Meantime, I'll get a photographer over here right away. Do you think the new owners would consider delaying their renovations? I'd even be willing to pay a nominal rent if they would."

"I doubt it, but I'll call and ask. I'll let you know."

"Thanks. I'll take the trunk back with me if that's okay."

"By all means, do so. It's yours per the will."

They made their way back downstairs, saying their goodbyes as Vivian locked the door. Jesse sat in his car, jotting notes in one of the little spiral notebooks he kept with him at all times, then set it aside. He decided to take a long loop back to the newspaper and cruise the old neighborhoods.

Chapter 3

Jesse Wickham
April 2, 1975
Paradise, TN

JESSE DROVE TO ROYAL STREET and turned left at the Jay Hawk restaurant, then right onto Main and crossed the railroad tracks. He was immediately in his old neighborhood, the place where he had lived from age ten until his parents died, when he had gone to live with his brother in Gibson. Much had changed, and much had not. The magnolia tree out front was huge. The yard was not kept like his father had kept it. The azaleas in front were gone. A white picket fence had been installed but needed paint, and pickets were missing. The Delano apartment building across the street was gone. Other houses were still there, some in good repair, but he thought, it's true that you can't go home again. You may encounter the nostalgia, but home is only a memory of the musty smells, the heard voices, freight trains plowing the midnight darkness, their lamps washing the tracks ahead of them, the child's struggle to understand what he or she is, the sudden knowledge that, after all is said and done, you are alone. He made his way back across town and carried the little chest up to the newsroom.

For the next half hour, he set down his impressions of the morning's events.

Then he pulled a chair over to his desk and lifted the little trunk onto it. He removed the letter addressed to him and the four notebooks. Beneath those four was a ledger book. He opened the letter first and read.

Dear Jesse,

I want you to have this trunk and its contents. Please do with it whatever you wish. It came into my hands when Nathan Hanks died. Never mind how. I should have given it and at least some of its contents to his family, but I couldn't do that. There is too much unnecessary history in it.

You should contact Mr. Loyal Hall, the executor of my estate. I asked him to also draw up the will, but he sent me to another attorney since he would be the executor. Loyal will be interested in the contents also, but they are for you to dispose of as you wish. I enjoyed our many hours together working on the model train. Do you remember we called it "the town upstairs?" You are a sensitive and meticulous young man, much like me in that way. I was pleased when you came to work for me while you were in college. I would have liked to have had a son like you.

There are hints of a story in the items in this trunk, and if our little town upstairs still exists as you read this, there are bits of the story in there as well. The story brushed against me again and again like a soft breeze rustles the leaves in the morning, then lies down in the burning heat of the day, only to return to whisper in the low places in the evening. It was a constant memory touching my shoulder, reminding me that what is real and what is dreamed are inseparable. Even so, I could never let myself tell the whole story in words.

I am sure you will ferret out the narrative and handle it more than adequately. I could never bring myself to be the one to tell it.

With much remembered affection,

Griffin Wynne

Odd, Jesse thought. Unnecessary history? What's that about?

He set the letter aside. Three of the notebooks were composition books, side-bound. One of them was spiral wire-bound, and the other two were tape-bound. The fourth notebook was bound with tape at the top, the sort usually called a tablet when he was in elementary school. The covers on the first three notebooks were creased and worn at the edges, and it was clear someone's hand had opened them often.

There were light stains where fingers had lifted the covers at the same places time after time.

He opened the first one. The handwriting was well-formed and legible, though the ink had faded in places. A few entries were in pencil, but even these were neatly made. The pencil lead was soft, and you could tell when the writer had paused now and then to sharpen his pencil. He noted that three of the notebooks had a date followed by a dash and an end date on the front, and one had only a beginning date followed by a dash. He flipped pages in the first one and saw that most of the entries were also dated. A few undated entries might have been continuations of dated entries made on or about the same date, but he would have to read them all to tell.

The first book was dated August 8, 1947, to December 14, 1947. Jesse read the first entry.

August 8, 1947 —

I have failed my best friend. I have failed my whole family. I am in exile in a place called Paradise, but it is no such thing.

I met with Galt today at his church. He promises to see what he can do to get me back with my family in Hatchie Landing, but most likely, even if he can do that, I'll not be able to teach again, and the Paradise High School for Negroes has no opening for a teacher of English.

June, I wish you were here with me. I'm so very lonesome without you.

I dream every night of what Mani and I saw in the darkness over in Hatchie Bottom. Was it only two months ago? It seems longer. I hope he doesn't have such dreams. He's just a child, and maybe God will be kind to him and not let the awfulness rest in his memories, though I doubt He can do that any more than Galt can help me get back to you, my dear family. I would come back to you in a minute if I had only myself to think of, but I cannot put you in danger. I dream of you day and night.

I found a little bit of work today, and Galt has helped me get this place to live for a while. I'm tired. I'm lonely, but I'm not without hope.

Nathan

Jesse wondered what the incident was. The entry was cryptic, but whatever this Nathan's child saw, it sounded pretty awful. What about being an exile and the danger to his family? What did he mean? He was living here in Paradise when he made this entry. This Galt person might still be alive and living here.

The next entry was short, not cryptic, and more or less uninformative. It told of Nathan's day doing manual labor. It did, however, mention two names that rang a bell. It said he had worked all afternoon for Miss Emily and Miss Lula.

Jesse remembered that Griffin Wynne had a sister named Lula Bartlett. She was also an acquaintance of his mother when he was a child. He remembered she and another woman lived together in the old Georgian house on Chester Street just down from the Griffin Wynne Funeral Home. She might be the Emily in the notebook. If Griffin Wynne's sister was the same as the Lula in the Blue Horse notebook, then the Nathan of the notebooks was likely the Nathan he had known as a child. He pulled out a phone book and looked up the names. Both ladies were listed at the same address on Chester. He made a note to ask Vivian or Loyal about them.

He pondered what to do next. He could go to Hatchie Landing, but at this point, he had no idea what to look for there other than to inquire about Nathan and his family, and they very likely were not there either.

The phone jangle interrupted his thoughts. It was Vivian.

She launched right in. "I just hung up the phone from talking to the new owners. They're willing to give you some time with the train layout side of the upstairs, but they want to stay on schedule with the other side. I have agreed. You have some time."

"Thank you so much, Vivian. I'll tell Loyal, and we'll try not to hold them up long. Between the town upstairs and the notebooks and letters in this trunk, there's a story. I can feel it."

"It was my pleasure, and maybe it'll buy you some time too to find a new home for the train and all. I need to go now, but call me if

I can help more. I'll have an extra key made for you. They said that would be all right. I'll bring it to you. Let's meet over there tomorrow morning, say about eleven o'clock."

"That will be fine, and if you are free, I'll treat you to lunch. I have some more questions if you don't mind. Meantime, one quick question, do you remember or know the whereabouts of an Emily or a Lula Bartlett?"

"Oh, yes, I do. Emily Hall and Lula Wynne married brothers named Bartlett. Both men died years ago. Lula is Mr. Wynne's sister, and Emily is Loyal's sister. They live together now on Chester Street. Loyal and Wynne would often meet at their house for lunch or supper. Loyal still does."

"I'd like to talk to them."

She agreed to help him make the contacts. "But I'll have to decline your offer of lunch tomorrow. Maybe another time. I've got too much on my plate."

Jesse chuckled at the unintended pun. They said their goodbyes and hung up. He mulled over this information, then he opened the first notebook again.

August 18, 1947

Took the Greyhound to Hatchie this morning. June, Bibi, and Mani met me at the station. Buster and his wife, Millie, brought them in his old Ford. We all packed into his car and went to Buster's old home place over toward Nutbush. Nobody bothered us, and we had a fine time at his house. Buster's momma made a big dinner for us. I thought I'd died and gone to heaven. I told June I should just come back home and forget about all the trouble with Ellis, but she won't hear of it. She says it's still there underneath the surface. She says Mani hasn't been hurt or threatened, and he'll go back to school in September. The cotton fields look good this year. Buster's daddy says his crop will be a good one, but so will everybody else's, so he doesn't expect to get paid as much for it. They took me back to the bus station at 5 o'clock and I caught the 8 o'clock to Paradise.

Jesse read the rest of the first notebook. They all seemed to be written by Nathan. Though the incident in the night was referred to more than once, there were no details about it. He was more convinced than ever that this Nathan was the same man he knew as a child, and if that was true, then he died in the house fire Jesse had witnessed when he was only ten years old. The fourth tablet appeared to be blank.

He took up the bundle of letters. They were written in a delicate hand from June to Nathan, mostly newsy pieces telling about the goings-on at home in Hatchie Landing. In one letter, she told him that the child, Mani, had dreamed about the "incident" as she called it. She assured Nathan that the child was fine and hadn't had the dream anymore.

He found the notebook entry Nathan wrote about that letter. Nathan was worried about Mani, and for the first time, Jesse could feel Nathan's rage. "Why do we live apart like this, exiled? It's inhuman. It's wrong, I won't do it any longer. I'm coming home,"

Nathan at least felt forced to live in Paradise. Why was that, Jesse wondered?

He picked up the ledger and thumbed pages filled with entries of purchases and sales, delivery dates, and an occasional reminder note, all seeming to pertain to the monument business. The entries were in a different hand than Nathan Hanks's notebooks. Toward the back, the business entries ceased, and there were instead a handful of diary entries in the same hand as the earlier entries, with dates from 1940 until 1964. He read the first one.

June 15, 1940

Malcolm Oakes came to see me this afternoon as I was preparing to deliver a monument to Norman Parker. It was unsettling. He stood in the doorway the whole time. Thank goodness he couldn't see the monument I had just finished for JT.

Who were Malcolm Oakes and JT? Why the initials, and why did Griffin seem to be relieved that Oakes hadn't seen the monument? Strange. He wondered if Loyal had seen these entries and might know.

Another entry read:

I left Hatchie Landing in 1940 and settled in Paradise to begin a new life, but the images of what happened that summer of 1940 have never left me. I wish I could forgive myself, but it isn't possible.

Griffin Wynne, June 8, 1946

Some of the same words that were in Griffin's letter to me, thought Jesse. It was a revelation to find this side of the man he had known as a child. He remembered that Griffin had been in the monument business before becoming a mortician. What had happened in 1940 that weighed so heavily on the man? It's as if the model town was for him a petition for forgiveness.

The next entry was dated 1964, and in spite of the eighteen-year hiatus, it seemed to take up where the earlier one left off.

Of course, there were others in the warp and weft of it, Nathan Hanks's family, my own sister, Loyal Hall and his sister, the boy Jesse Wickham, and those men I ran away from and whose actions you might say were the first thread in the story. But who can ever say when and where a story begins; who can tell the whole story of a life?

Like me and all the rest, Nathan Hanks came to Paradise with a dream, an exile nurturing a small hope.

~ Griffin Wynne, Paradise, Tennessee, 1964

Jesse pondered this for a minute. Why did Griffin write this so many years after Nathan Hanks's death? Why did he write it at all? Was he mainly talking about his own exile—which turned out to be pretty comfortable, by the way—or was he thinking about Nathan Hanks and events long past?

Chapter 4

Jesse Wickham
April 3, 1975
Paradise, TN

THE NEXT MORNING, there was a message on Jesse's desk to call Vivian.

"Good morning. I'm returning your call."

"I called Lula and Emily. Remarkably, it turns out that they stay in touch with June Hanks. She visits them occasionally. I'll bring their contact information when I come with the key today. I will work upstairs for two or three hours beginning around eleven o'clock. I'll leave the front door unlocked. Just come on in. Yell before coming up. I don't want to be startled."

Jesse was at the funeral home at eleven thirty. When he called out to Vivian, she met him at the top of the stairs with an envelope. "These are the contacts I promised and the key."

"I'll go see them right away. Hopefully, they can help me contact June and find the others. Do you mind if I have a look at the train layout while I'm here?"

"No, of course not. Go on in and take all the time you want. I'll be working through these remaining boxes for at least another hour today. I suppose I could just dump them all, but then something valuable might get lost. I can't bring myself to do that. Sing out if you need me."

Jesse crossed over to the train layout and admired the completeness of it. The whole town was there. The figures, automobiles, and delivery vehicles were in perfect harmony and scale. There were even horse-drawn wagons here and there, just as they were when he was a child on Institute Street.

He began locating specific places he had known: Chester Street, the funeral home, and here was Institute Street. The National Guard Armory was there on the corner of Chester and Institute as it had been then. Even the houses down the street were all there, almost exactly as he remembered them. Down a slight hill at the foot of Institute was Tanyard Street.

It came to him that this was the street where Nathan's house had burned. He opened one of the access doors below the layout and crawled under and lifted the nearest hatch. Just to his left was Tanyard running toward Royal Street, and midway down Tanyard was a little fire truck and a crew of firemen in front of a house. An ambulance was just beyond that. He bent closer. The ambulance was white with gold-and-green lettering on the side, "Griffin Wynne Ambulance."

Jesse was astounded that Wynne had duplicated the scene—a conscious act, he sensed, not artistic coincidence. There was a tiny gurney behind the ambulance, and the back door to the vehicle was open. Two figures were beside the gurney as if to lift it into the vehicle. The gurney was covered in black cloth, but it was clear the intent was to convey the presence of a body beneath. The house the firemen were attending had little wisps of gray-colored cotton lifting up from beneath the eaves.

He heard a sound behind him and turned. "My goodness, you look like you've seen a ghost," Vivian said.

"I think I have." He told Vivian what was in the scene. He pointed out all the details. "This is too much detail. Look here at the shape underneath the gurney cloth. It's a body. Why would he intentionally replicate this little scene? Was he leaving a message?"

She chuckled. "I wouldn't read more into it than is there. He was a meticulous man. He spent hours up here."

"You're probably right. But this work is almost too perfect and in such detail."

"But don't you think all of his modeling is nearly perfect?"

"Yes, but why would a model train enthusiast go to so much trouble to create a scene of death?" He stared awhile longer and said, "The only thing that would make it any more perfect would be if one of the figures beside the gurney looked like Mr. Wynne."

"Well, does it?" she asked.

He bent for a closer look, knowing as he did that it would not be the case. He shook his head. "Not as I remember him, it doesn't." He smiled at Vivian and turned again. He took one more look at the miniature scene and stopped altogether.

"Now what is it?"

Jesse pointed his forefinger close to two little figures sitting on the curb opposite the smoking house. "Here, these two little boys. These could be my friend Campo and me. I remember we heard the fire trucks that day and the ambulance. We were only about ten years old. We ran from Campo's backyard down here"—he pointed to what would have been Campo's house—"to Tanyard Street here, where the fire trucks pulled up." He pointed again. "We watched the whole thing that day. We saw the firemen bring a stretcher out of the house. It was covered in a black cloth. We knew someone was dead beneath it. We never saw Nathan again after that."

"But Mr. Wynne couldn't have known any of that. And I doubt he would have remembered two little boys sitting on a curb watching all this happen and been impressed enough to include it in his train layout."

"Vivian, he did know all that. He came to our house afterward to talk to my mother. He was afraid we were traumatized by it all. He told her it was all right for me to come up here and see the trains anytime I wanted. I did come after that, many times. You remember. Then, later, when I was older and working here and found the trunk, I asked him if I could read the papers. He told me they were private and had belonged to a man named Nathan, but he told me not to meddle about in the closets and to please not do that anymore. I apologized. I told him I had known a black man named Nathan who told me stories when I was a child, and that my friend Campo and I had seen his house burn. Mr. Wynne had been very stern with me until that moment. Suddenly, he was his kind self again. He said, 'Unfortunate things happen to good people sometimes.' I remember all that as clearly as if it had happened yesterday, Vivian."

Vivian was quiet. She looked at the model of the town, at the trains, the houses, and the people on the streets. She turned toward him, her eyes moist. "He was a good man. I believe you."

Chapter 5

———◆———

Jesse Wickham, June Hanks, Lula and Emily Bartlett
April 4, 1975
Paradise, TN

JESSE PARKED AT THE CURB in front of Emily and Lula's house the next day. The exterior of the old house was in need of some repairs, but it was largely as Jesse remembered it. The round tower with the onion dome was still its singular feature. He mounted the steps and was about to knock when a woman opened the front door.

"I'm Jesse Wickham. I think Vivian Paxton called to introduce me?"

Emily took him by the hand and led him inside. "I'm pleased to meet you, Mr. Wickham. Lula and June are just here in the parlor. June has come over to visit. Let me introduce you."

Jesse had expected a musty-smelling old house, but there was only the warmth of a place well lived in and cared for. Everything was immaculately clean. A window was open, and curtains shifted slightly in the little breeze that entered, unusual in this day of air-conditioned and enclosed houses. They could hear birds in the trees outside.

"We read your daily articles in the paper, Mr. Wickham," Emily said. "Vivian tells us we may be of some help to you."

"What sort of help is it you think we can give?" Lula asked.

Jesse looked from one to the other. "Thank you for seeing me." He paused, and Lula finished for him, "It's awkward with two Mrs. Bartletts, so why don't you use our first names. Emily, Lula, and June. June is family as far as we're concerned. She looks in on us often. She and her mother live over in Hatchie Landing, and she comes by whenever she's in Paradise. We couldn't live without her. We're all friends here with some shared experiences, so let's go by first names."

"All right, but only if you call me Jesse."

"Agreed." Lula smiled brightly at him, and June seemed uncertain whether to say anything or not. "We really are pleased to have you and to help in any way we can. We love to have company. Vivian tells us that you've come into some information that may be connected to us, information left to you by my brother."

Jesse hesitated again before answering. The grandfather clock in the hall struck the half hour as if to urge him on. He leaned forward, elbows on his knees, and his fingers knit together. "I used to live near here when I was growing up. I knew Mr. Wynne, your brother, and I knew this house, and I remember the two of you, Emily and Lula. Both of you were acquainted with my mother."

"Edna Wickham? Oh my lord. Yes, we were friends and had some church activities in common."

"Through Vivian's diligence, I have some documents and things that Griffin Wynne left to me. They belonged to a person I'm almost certain I once knew when I was a child here in Paradise. His name was Nathan Hanks." He looked over at June. "Would that be any relation to you?"

June sat forward in her chair. "Nathan was my husband's name." Her voice was mellow and refined.

"Tell me some things about him, if you don't mind," he asked.

"Oh, I could tell you lots of things, but they don't matter anymore. All of that is in the past. It's done and gone. He died a long time ago."

"How did he die?"

"In a house fire. Smoke, they told me. Smoke filled up his lungs and poisoned him in the old house he was living in."

"Were you with him then?"

"No, I wasn't living with him then. We were living apart. Not because we chose to, but because we were made to do it. We didn't like it." She looked down at her lap and shook her head side to side as if she was remembering a bad thing. Lula interrupted, "After Nathan died, June stayed on in Hatchie Landing. She was a teacher over there. For a long while after the funeral, Wynne would drive over there to check on June and her mother and Mani, her son. He never said what compelled him to go out of his way to do that, but I'm glad he did, or else we wouldn't have this lovely friendship. After that, June always came by whenever she could, and now that she's retired, she drives over from Hatchie Landing at least once a week, sometimes more. Nathan used to do some work for us when he was living here in exile."

"Exile?"

"Well, that's what it was, exile. He was forced out of his home and made to leave his family. What else would you call it? Those were bad times, and we were glad we could help, even just a little. And when he died, we felt we ought to help out his family. Loyal knew something about the troubles they had been through, and he thought we ought to do something too. He knew some people over in Hatchie Landing and tried to help Nathan out before he died, during their troubles, but it wasn't any use."

When she didn't continue, Jesse asked, "In what way was Loyal trying to help Nathan out?"

"The trouble—that's what we call it—was a long time ago," Emily said. "It was a time when folks were afraid to do what was right, and a lot of folks even worked at doing what was wrong. A few people doing what is wrong can poison a whole society if the rest keep quiet. Poor June and Nathan were caught up in it. Loyal was trying to help because of his job back then. He was working for the FBI. Later, when he got his years in, he retired from the Bureau and started up a private law practice here in town. That was in about 1955. He's a good man."

June looked at her and said softly, "We weren't caught up in anything. We were in it because we wanted to be, at least Nathan wanted to be, and we became its victims."

This story was turning out to be more than Jesse had expected. It was as if he were walking slowly into swampy shadows, tangled and musty, with no paths and no firm ground.

He wanted details. He wanted to know the source and cause of "The Trouble," as they called it. And he wanted all of it quickly, but he could tell that these kind women were not to be hurried. They had lived a lifetime with the knowledge of something that had affected them all. "I'd like to understand this trouble as you call it, if you care to tell me about it."

"My Nathan died, and I lost my boy because of it. I don't need to live that all over again." June stood, but she didn't move away from her chair.

"June, dear, please don't be angry. Mr. Wickham, Jesse, is just trying to learn your story. If he wants to write about it, then maybe it will help to end it all at last. Let's try. Let's try, sweetheart. You've been so good to us, and you're still carrying that burden around after all these years. You need to lay it down. Let's tell Jesse what happened."

"June, I'm sorry. I don't want to cause you pain, but you may be the only person left who can help me understand."

The mellow tones in her voice took on an edge. "You are a writer and you don't know what you are writing about? Lord, that sounds like everybody else who came along and tried to help. Just about everybody said they'd try to help. They'd say they could try. They'd say they were going to do their best for me, but it always came to nothing. Mr. Wickham, I know what I'm talking about when I talk about the trouble. I lived it, and I know who caused the trouble, and that trouble hurt a lot of people. White people and black people, and it's still hurting people. Do you know what I'm saying? Can you even imagine?"

Jesse was taken aback and didn't say anything at first. How could he possibly know what they went through? Was he just dredging up the past and hurting them all over again? Could he be putting them in danger all over again? He had no idea what was at stake here. "Miss June, I can't imagine your trouble or the hurting, but I hear what you are saying. I recognize that I may never fully understand, but I want to try if you'll help me."

"You don't need to 'Miss June' me. Just call me June. I've been here too long to be a 'Miss' anybody." She sat back down and began to smooth her skirt. Several times she looked up and then back at her hands. Lula took her hand, but she drew it back. Finally, she looked up at them and said, "How can I tell it? I lived through it. I've told it over and over, and nobody can do a thing about it. What good will telling it again do anybody? What good will it do for Mani? Mr. Wickham, if I tell you about the trouble, what will you do about it? Tell me what you'll do about it. Tell me how you're any different from all the other people who wanted to know."

"June, Mr. Wynne left me some items he had kept over the years. I didn't know what they were at first, but in them I have discovered a mystery that is connected somehow to me. And now I've learned it's close to you, too. There is a letter to me from him charging me with putting the pieces of this story together. I can't possibly figure it out without your help. I only want to learn the truth and to tell it the best I can. Maybe if I can do that, it will help you too." Jesse almost held his breath while June looked at him. Then she looked at Emily and Lula and said, "All right, just one more time. I'm going to tell this man all about it. There are things even you two don't know, and I'm now going to tell it. It may take a while, Mr. Wickham, but if you've got time, I will tell it to you."

Jesse reached into his briefcase, took out a small recorder, and showed it to her. "June, will it be all right to record what you have to tell me?"

"You can do what you want to. I'm going to tell it all and not leave out a thing. You can write it or record it. It doesn't matter to me, and it might take me two, three sittings to tell it all, but I'm going to do it. Not for you. No, I'm going to do it for my Nathan, now, after all this time. And the other thing is, Mr. Wickham, there are some other people who can tell their parts of it to you if you're willing to hear them out, and I can tell you who they are. You need to come to my house and talk to my momma. Everybody calls her Bibi. She's getting old. Even she doesn't know how old she is. She must be a hundred. She and these two women are all I've got except for my boy, who is lost and locked up. We've all got to have somebody while we are on this earth, Mr. Wickham. We've all got to have somebody, or we are lost. You plan on coming back tomorrow. Come in the morning. Eleven o'clock and I'll bring the food. We'll have some dinner on the porch, and then we can talk as long as you want. All afternoon will be all right with me.

"It's a hard story to tell, but living it has been harder," June said. "I'll tell it one more time and for the last time. Maybe you can find the missing pieces and put things to rest. Sounds like Mr. Wynne had faith in you doing that."

Chapter 6

Jesse Wickham and June Hanks
April 5, 1975
Paradise, TN
June Hanks's Version of Events of May 1946 to April 1948

THE NEXT MORNING, Jesse arrived at Emily and Lula's house promptly at eleven. Much had changed since he was a child in the neighborhood. Houses had been demolished to make room for a viaduct that rose up to cross over Royal Street just to the east. The old National Guard Armory had stood just up from his house on Institute Street. It was gone, as was most of the old neighborhood, to make room for a civic center parking lot. The space between his old house at 206 and Campo's was an empty field. He stood on the sidewalk musing over the past and admiring the house in front of him. The house was an old two-and-a-half-story Georgian house with gables cut into the roof line in the upper half-story and a round tower cut into the right front corner.

The front door opened, and Lula called out to him. "Come on in, Jesse. Lunch will be ready in a little while." He waved to her and retrieved his briefcase and recorder, then followed Lula to the side porch overlooking the little garden. Everywhere he looked, something was blooming: hollyhocks, roses, and cleomes. The house belonged to Emily, but after her husband Art died, Lula came to live with Emily. They needed each other. They each had a void to fill and needed someone to care for. The house had a covered porch that wrapped from the tower across the front and down the side to the rear. A wide hallway bisected the house from the front door to the rear door, and rooms opened right and left off it. The living room was the first room to the left off the hallway; the parlor was set against the round tower, so the wall on one side was convex. There were bookshelves built into the concave walls on the other side. The inward curvature and the warm wood tones in the shelves with their books made the room feel the way a comfortable library feels. A couch and chairs were set out from the shelves to create a sitting area. A stairway inclined along the left side of the hall to the upper stories. Another porch secluded from the street extended from the tower to the kitchen at the rear. Access to this porch was from the tower and the kitchen. Lula led them here.

"Have a seat, Jesse. Anywhere you like." Lula indicated with a sweep of her hand. "Make yourself comfortable."

June came out onto the porch, and Emily followed her with a tray of iced-filled glasses and a sweating pitcher of amber tea. He stood to greet them. "It's nice to have a gentleman in the house," Emily said. "Sit down. Please, Jesse. Be at home." She poured glasses of tea.

"Thank you."

He laid his recorder on the table in front of him and took out his notebook and a pencil. A hummingbird zipped among the hollyhocks and cleomes. June sipped her tea. "I hope you don't object to me recording this, June."

"That's all right with me. I'll just sit here and talk, and you can write it down or record it. Whatever you want to do is all right with me."

"Well, I want you to be comfortable telling me all this."

"Don't you worry a bit about me being comfortable. I've made up my mind to do this thing with you, but there's nothing comfortable about any of it."

"Tell me about Nathan's being away, his exile."

Nathan was hiding in Paradise from August 1947 to May 1948, when he died. When he came home the first time, I didn't know whether to laugh or cry when I saw him hiking up the street. It was hot and dusty. It hadn't rained in days. Let's see, that was in September. School was turned out for the next two weeks, so I was off from work. You know, in those days, we still let school out for two weeks in September for cotton picking. Well, I couldn't contain myself. I ran out the door yelling Nathan's name at the top of my lungs. Bibi, that's my momma, came out on the porch when she heard all my screeching. Nathan just stopped at the gate and opened his big arms, and I leaped into them. I have never pressed another body into mine that felt like that in my whole life. If I never had another second to live, that would've made it all right.

I was scared, too, though. I wanted him back with me, with us, as a family again, but I was afraid of what might happen if those men heard he was back. They'd already killed one man, and they wouldn't hesitate to kill again. I was pretty sure I knew who some of them were, but I'd never let on like I did. Everybody at school knew what had happened, and they knew Nathan had been run out of town like the leper in the Bible, like some criminal, when he wasn't even the one who committed the crime. But here he was, back in our front yard, in my arms.

I jabbered like a schoolgirl and told him to come on inside. Bibi had been cooking all morning. I don't know what all. I let him know that I had been afraid, though, afraid he might not make it. Nathan just laughed and hugged me close again, and then he hugged Mani.

Mani told him he'd been picking cotton over at Mr. Clifford's, and Nathan asked him if Mr. Clifford was treating him right. I told him how Mr. Clifford had come over after Nathan left and told us that what had happened wasn't right, and he knew something about it, but he said he couldn't do anything about it. He said he would help us any other way he could, though.

I appreciated that from Mr. Clifford. He didn't have to do anything like that at all, but he did, and when cotton-picking time came, he came over and asked Mani if he wanted to work. Of course, Mani wanted to have some spending money, so he said he would. Mani went over there every day when school let out for picking.

I try not to think about what happened to poor Ellis Wiggins out there in that swamp. Nathan always felt like it should have been him. He felt like Ellis wouldn't have gotten into the voter registration deal in the first place if Nathan hadn't been willing to join in, but I told Nathan he couldn't take on that weight; it would kill him, too. I told him that he and Ellis had been doing a good thing. They came after Ellis and killed him, but it could have been Nathan.

Still, Nathan felt like he failed Ellis. Ellis was a good friend. Nathan said he felt like he failed us, too, but I couldn't see that. Bibi fussed at him whenever she heard him talk that way. She said it didn't make any sense to think like that, but I know what he meant. He remembered the time when Mr. James Weldon Johnson came through Hatchie Landing on the way to Nashville and spoke at the church. He remembered Mr. Johnson talking about the NAACP.

Nathan meant that if he and Ellis had never heard him say those words, then this never would have happened. He took it all to heart. Later on, when Reverend Galt came over from Paradise and we all heard him preach that sermon about walking into the Promised Land, Ellis and Nathan decided they ought to do something. He said it was only because of hearing those words that he decided to go to work to get people set up to vote. He wasn't even trying to make them vote for anybody in particular.

Anyway, that day Nathan came back home, we were still out on the porch hugging and laughing and crying all at the same time when Bibi called us in to eat. We went in carrying on like we were just children again. The table was all set, and Bibi had food spread out like somebody had died. I never saw so much food. It's her way of celebrating. She's the glue that keeps this family together, even now that we are all separated so far away from each other. She talks about each and every one of us every day. That's how she keeps us alive to each other, telling her stories about us. Every family needs someone like Bibi to glue them together, to weave the thread that runs through everything they do. That's our Bibi, my momma.

I used to get put out with her sometimes, telling those outlandish stories, but Mani thrived on them, especially all those tales from Africa. It's like she wanted to make him into something other than what he was growing up to be. It's where we come from and who we are, she would argue back to me. She still does, and I suppose she's right, but somehow I'm afraid even to this day of the change it can lead to. Some of those stories are just plain wild, what with the lions and crocodiles and all. Mani loved them, though, and I didn't have any stories like those to give him. So I love her for loving him. I love her for giving him his Mani name. It's the only thing we call him now.

"June, what really happened to Ellis Wiggins?" Jesse asked.

"I'll get to that, and you'll have to hear it from Mani and Mr. Loyal Hall, too. They can tell you things I can't, but I'll get to it in a little bit. We never saw him again, and so we don't really know what happened, but we all know he was killed, killed out in that swamp by some old men and boys who didn't understand a thing about what was going on. They didn't know Ellis, and they didn't care that he was good and kind and loved his family every bit as much as they loved theirs. I guess you can say they loved theirs, but who knows what happens when one man decides to kill another man? Something breaks down when that happens, and when it does, the brokenness spreads to other people like sickness, and they get broken too. They can save themselves from it, but if they don't, if they don't run from it real hard, they catch it, and they get broken too. So many people, so many people to break down for so many years, it's a shame and a disgrace.

"They never found Ellis's body. You can turn that thing off," she motioned with a hand wave as if to dismiss the recorder. "It's almost dinnertime. Let's have something to eat and then I'll tell you some more of the story."

For a moment, June seemed to be miles away from this tidy spot on a porch in a garden in Paradise. Then she rose. Jesse remained on the porch while she went to the kitchen. He jotted down questions to ask later. There were more of them than answers. He closed his eyes and listened to the soft stirrings inside the house and the melodious birds in the garden. Just who were Buster, Galt, and Ellis? How did they come to be such good friends? What were their particular involvements in the trouble? How did Ellis die?

In a few minutes, all three women returned to the porch. Emily poured sweet tea over ice in their tall, cut-glass goblets. June brought out plates with fresh tomatoes stuffed with chicken salad and a basket with little corn muffins still fresh and warm from the oven.

"What a treat this is," Jesse said. "I think I never had a good tomato while I was away from Paradise."

"That would be a long time to go without a decent tomato," Lula said.

They ate with only small talk, asking him about what he had been doing all these years. Emily wanted to know why he left Paradise in the first place.

"I left mainly because I wanted to go to graduate school. I thought I wanted to write, but I wasn't sure if I could make a living at it. So I went off to the University of Tennessee and studied English. I got a master's degree in it and got a job working for the newspaper."

"But did you want to leave Paradise?" Lula asked. "We were talking about that last evening. You must have, because you didn't come back until recently, did you?"

"I did feel compelled to leave this place, but you know, now that so much time has passed, I'm really not sure why I had that feeling.

Somehow, I felt stifled by Paradise. Maybe it's just that it was my hometown and I was so familiar with all of its nooks and crannies and some of its secrets. I went to church here all through childhood, and that too was something that weighed heavily on me. The way we were taught to believe was too heavy-handed. There was too much fear and retribution involved. I remember thinking once that if God confined himself to worrying about the good and evil in people, then he couldn't be much more than us. I know that sounds blasphemous, but it's true. I had that thought even as a child. It wasn't very comforting to say the least. I think as I grew older, I began a long journey of questioning and felt I couldn't make that journey if I lived on in Paradise."

They didn't seem unduly alarmed at what he had just confessed. June looked at Jesse and said, "You don't know about doubting God until someone close to you dies."

Then she quoted, "*...perhaps it is better for God we do not believe in him...*"

"June?" Emily questioned. "I've never heard you say such a thing, Sweetheart?"

June completed the quotation, "*...and we fight with all our might against death, without raising our eyes heavenward where he keeps silent.*"

She smiled at them and said to Jesse, "I know some of what Albert Camus meant when he wrote that. I lived it over there in Hatchie Landing and here in Paradise. So I do know what you mean, Jesse. I do know."

Emily spoke up. "June has a good education, dear."

"Yes, I do. I graduated from Tuskegee, and so did Nathan." There was an edge to her voice—and, Jesse thought, deservedly so. Then she softened. "It's where we met each other. He was older than me by almost ten years, but he came back for a reunion while I was there. We had met before when I was only a child, but we were never out of touch after that. When I graduated, we married and came to Hatchie Landing, where he had a job teaching English in the colored high school. I took a job there, too, teaching first grade. Does it surprise you that black people read the likes of Albert Camus, Mr. Wickham? Don't answer that. It's an unfair question. Forgive me. Still, we were teaching and reading all the great philosophers, the great ideas, right here in the South. Nobody paid any attention. Nobody cared, as long as we kept to our place."

Jesse didn't quite know what to say to this tangential expedition of hers, so he turned it with a question. "Did anyone seem to care what happened to Ellis Wiggins and Nathan?"

"Well, let's clear the table and then we'll get back to that," she said.

Jesse helped carry the dishes to the kitchen.

"Just put them in the sink," Emily instructed. "I'll take care of washing them later." They went through the hallway to the little round parlor at the front of the house. It was like being in a small library. Jesse commented on it. Emily told him it was her husband Art's idea to build the round tower on the front of the house and to put an onion dome on top.

The women spent the afternoon with Jesse as he made notes and changed tapes now and then as June continued her story. She wound down finally. "Jesse, I have told you all of it, at least all that happened to me. You need to talk to Bibi, too, if she feels like it. Oh, and Mr. Loyal Hall, be sure to hear his side. They can both tell you things I don't know about. Later, if you want me to talk some more, I'll be glad to do it, but first, you go talk to them."

It was as if June had taken control and was guiding him through the whole set of incidents. She said, "I'll tell Bibi you want to come see her. I'll tell her to talk to you, but don't be surprised if she holds back at first. That thing that happened to Mani when he was a little boy out there in that swamp crippled him in some ways. You'll see for yourself if you ever meet him. She will tell you the whole story or all she knows of it, but don't rush her. Let her tell it in her way. She never quit believing that someone is likely to come after us someday, so she may be reluctant at first."

"Thank you."

"Give me your phone number and I'll call you." She gave him her address and phone number. "We still live in our same little house in Hatchie Landing. If she does it, you will have the time of your life, and you will learn about a lot of things that have nothing to do with this story, but you'll be glad of it. She loves an audience when she is feeling good. She's impossible not to love."

Jesse looked over at Emily and Lula, who had sat quietly throughout. Emily then surprised him. "I think maybe Lula and I can shed some important light on the matter, too. After all, Nathan was working for us when he died."

He put away his things and thanked them for the lunch and for June's efforts on his behalf. As a reporter, he had learned surprising things come when you ask an unexpected question. He hesitated at the door and asked Emily, "You didn't say, but I assume Art passed away?"

"Yes, he died shortly after Nathan died."

"When Nathan was hiding here in Paradise, what kind of work did Nathan do for you and Art?"

"He and Art built this round tower, and together they built the onion dome on top. Nathan was good with his hands and a smart man, educated. He helped Art figure out how to build the dome. I thought it was a remarkable thing they did. He never got to see it finished."

Chapter 7

Jesse Wickham with Bibi Durber
April 6, 1975
Hatchie Landing, TN
Bibi's Version of Events of May 1946 to April 1948

THERE WAS A MESSAGE FROM JUNE when Jesse got back to the newsroom telling him to come Sunday morning at eight o'clock.

He parked on the empty street in front of the address in Hatchie Landing she had given him. As he got out and stretched, June's voice called to him from the porch. "Come on up, Jesse."

She held open the door and led him to the kitchen. Bibi was frying eggs and bacon for breakfast and baking some cornbread for dinner after church. Bibi looked up. "Whooee, who is this, June? Why'nt you tell me we were having company? I'd have put on my dress. Oh, Lord, this is the man you told me about. Mr. Jesse, come on in and have a seat. I just didn't expect you so soon."

She beamed at Jesse, then at June. "Fine, y'all just going to stand there while I rave on? Y'all sit down and have some coffee, and I'll get some breakfast on plates. Then I've got to get dressed for church. June, you have to drive me over to the church. Buster is gonna preach this morning."

She shuffled in her slippers to the stove, picked up the coffee pot and two cups, and brought them to the table. She poured coffee for him and June.

Jesse sipped the coffee and glanced at Bibi. "You like some cream?" she asked. "Some sugar?"

"Bibi, Jesse would like to hear about the trouble," June said.

Bibi stirred the eggs and checked the biscuits in the oven. "Lord, son, there are a ton of things that happened years ago. A ton of them right here in Hatchie Landing, even. June told me you maybe knew our Nathan when you was a little boy living in Paradise same time as him. Is that right?"

"Yes, ma'am. And now I've come across some notebooks that he kept, a sort of diary. June, they really belong to you. You should have them, and I'll bring them to you." Jesse paused. He was uncertain about whether to tell this and how to tell it. It seemed so sensitive, especially to these good people. "But they don't tell the whole story. June has explained a great deal of it to me and offered to introduce me to you. She said you can tell me parts of it that she can't tell."

Silent seconds ticked away until Bibi spoke. "June can tell you all about everything, and I can too. I guess we tell it different, though."

"I want to hear your side of it, especially what happened to Mani."

"How did you come to have those notebooks?" Bibi sat down across from Jesse.

"It's a long story. But the short version is I worked at the Griffin Wynne Funeral Home in Paradise while I was in college. I had a small upstairs apartment there. One Saturday, I was browsing around in the attic and found them. I didn't know then who they belonged to. I told Mr. Wynne about them, and he took them away. I forgot about them until recently, when Mr. Wynne's executor contacted me. He said there were several things stored upstairs in the funeral home that Mr. Wynne had willed to me. The notebooks were among them. Naturally, I was interested, if for no other reason than that someone would keep them all these years."

"What's in those notebooks?" Bibi asked.

"Nathan wrote them. I'll bring them to June. They tell about him being in exile and a killing that occurred somewhere around here way back in 1947. It reads to me like maybe it was a lynching. Somehow,

Nathan was involved or affected by it. They don't tell any of the details. He writes about being in exile. I didn't understand that part until June told me her side of it."

You could hear a feather drop when he said that. "You've come to the right place to find out about that story, but I don't know whether I want to tell it. Sometimes things are best left alone."

June put her arms around Bibi. "Bibi, how long have we been wondering and hoping someday something would happen? Now here comes Jesse on a Sunday morning, innocent as Jesus's lamb, to help us find some answers. We should listen to him and help him. Who knows? Maybe he can help us."

Bibi looked at Jesse. "Tell us about the books. What do they say?"

"Well, it's like I said, I discovered them years ago, and Mr. Wynne must have kept them."

"Bring them to me," June said. "But I'm almost afraid to read them after all these years. Why didn't Mr. Wynne give them to me? He was here in our house. Why did he keep them secret from us?"

"I don't know the answer to that. He hints at history in his letter to me, history he believed shouldn't be reopened, unnecessary was the word he used."

"It's our history too. We have a right to decide as much as him. It wasn't his alone."

"June, I'm beginning to suspect he was afraid, like Nathan, for some reason. Could he have been connected somehow to Nathan's trouble?"

"I don't see how. He was too good to us."

"If there was a lynching," Jesse said, "who do you think would know and could tell me about it? How was Nathan involved?"

Bibi pulled herself up from the table and faced Jesse, hands on her hips. "Lord, son, we don't only know about it, we were in it." She turned back to the stove, shuffling and shoving skillets over the burners. Her cooking took on a ferocity. "Are y'all hungry? Have some more coffee. Eggs? Bacon?"

She brought food to the table and sat while Jesse and June ate.

Jesse addressed them both. "Tell me about it. What happened? How were you involved?"

Bibi told him about her, Nathan, and Mani going fishing, and about them catching some catfish before all the terror began so many years ago. When she finished, she said, "I know who some of those men were. I saw them in my dream. I saw their names on the foreheads of those wild dogs over there."

Jesse wasn't sure how to take this comment. "I don't understand. What wild dogs? What do you mean you *saw* them?"

"I saw them walking back and forth, the lions and the dogs, back and forth. The dogs had their names written on their foreheads. I saw Bennie Hoskins and I saw Malcolm Oakes and the High Sheriff and some others. The lions were Trouble and Death. I saw them all, but I didn't tell June or anybody else about it."

Jesse sipped his coffee and set down the cup. "I don't understand what you're saying. How were you able to see those names, Bibi? Where were the lions walking back and forth?"

"If Mani was here, he could tell you how much I like to sit out on the porch and think and dream. I still do it. June knows. That's when I say my prayers to Jesus, too, and that's when I see across to the other side. My own bibi told me that her momma told her about coming over. She told her that when she came across the ocean, she thought she was going to the other side to die. That's what her people believed. They believed that when you die, you go across Kakunga. That's the line that separates us from the spirit world. She thought the big ships had come to take them across.

"I dream about the spirit world sometimes, and I can see across. You probably wouldn't understand. Not many people can, but I knew who those men were after I dreamed and after I studied about it awhile. Who else could it be but them? You tell me that. Who else? They're the ones who came to talk to Nathan that night. They're the ones who told Buster and Ellis and Nathan they couldn't vote, not then, not ever. And they're the ones brought that old cross into the Quarter and burned it in front of Ellis and Arlene's house that night."

"How do you know it was them that burned the cross?" Jesse asked.

"I could see the things that made some of them who they were."

"What sort of things?"

"Things like how they stood and how they moved and how they sounded, and something else."

"What else?"

She looked at him and smiled a big smile. She said, "They trucks."

Jesse smiled back. "What about the truck?"

"Trucks got to be official, don't they? Got to have a license tag, don't they?"

"Well, sure, if they don't want to get pulled over."

"All right then. That's it. That's how I knew what the names written on those foreheads of those lions across Kakunga meant. That's how I knew who those wild dogs were. Some of them, anyway. I studied about it next day. That's what."

"What else?"

"What do you mean, what else? Ain't no what else. I just remembered those numbers like they were written across those men's foreheads and dreamed about it in the night, and next day I knew who they were."

"You mean the license tags? Did you ever tell anyone?"

"Yes, sir. I never thought anybody would believe me. It wasn't any use to tell, but one day I did."

"Who did you tell?"

"I told Mr. Griffin Wynne. That's who. He came back over to our house here, and he was sitting right out there in the front parlor, and we were talking about Nathan's funeral, and that's when I told him the names. He didn't ask or anything. I just said right out, I thought Ellis was dead, and I knew who killed him. He wanted to know who it was, but I wasn't so sure I should tell. He asked me if I thought whoever killed Ellis had anything to do with Nathan dying. I asked him if he thought Nathan dying was some kind of different trouble.

"He sat right up in his chair and looked a long time out the window before he said anything more to me. Then he said he thought maybe Nathan shouldn't have died unnecessarily. That's the way he put it."

"What did you say to that?"

"I told him, well, if that's so, then maybe it was some of the same people, but I couldn't see how it would be."

"Did you give him the names?"

"No, sir, I did not. I gave him something else, though. I told him the names on those foreheads were not the names they go by in this world. I told him I figured out what those names on those foreheads meant when I saw the trucks come into the Quarter with that old cross. I gave him those numbers that day, sitting right out there in the parlor. He wrote 'em all down, too. I gave him the numbers off the tags of three of those trucks out there. I did." She punctuated with an emphatic nod.

June had not spoken since Bibi began. She didn't speak now. She was looking at Bibi as if she had just experienced a revelation. Finally, she said, "Bibi, how come you never told me any of this?"

"Because, child, nothing ever came out of it, and you suffered more than any woman should have to. What good was that going to do? I told Mani one day. That boy like to pestered me to death when I told him about the dream and those lions with the names. He knew I knew something, but I wasn't going to tell him till he pestered me into it. I was afraid he would do something foolish, but I shouldn't have. Mani is sweet like you, his momma."

"Do you know whether Griffin Wynne ever did anything about those numbers?" Jesse asked.

"No, I don't. Far as I can tell, he never did a thing with them except write them down out there in that front parlor like I told you."

She pulled herself out of her chair and leaned on the table to steady herself. "I'd better get myself dressed for church now. Buster says he's going to preach through August, and then he's going to retire. He needs to. Poor soul can't hardly get up on the podium anymore. Sometimes one of the deacons got to help him up the steps, but he could still preach a good one. He can. Church ain't got nobody to take his place. It's starting to look like it'll just fold up and die when he does. He's been a good one, that Buster. He's helped us through a lot of trouble. June, I'm going to need you to drive me."

"I will, Bibi. I'll be ready."

Jesse thanked Bibi for the breakfast and the story. She put her hand on his face and said, "I can tell you're a good man, Mr. Jesse Wickham. You come back and I'll tell you some more."

She went into her room and closed the door. Jesse said goodbye to June and thanked her. They agreed for him to come back the next day and again as often as needed to hear the rest of Bibi's story.

Chapter 8

Jesse Wickham with Bibi Durber
April 7, 1975
Hatchie Landing, TN
Bibi's Version of Events of May 1946 to April 1948

JESSE ARRIVED AT TEN THE NEXT DAY. It was warm, and he and Bibi sat on the front porch, and June came out to join them.

"Everyone calls you Bibi. Is that your real name or a nickname? It's so unusual a name, I was just wondering."

"Most people just call me Bibi. It means Granny. My momma named me Melissa Shawl. My own bibi said my name was Dae. It meant 'dream,' and she always called me her little 'dream girl.' I married Polk Durber. He's dead now."

"What happened to Nathan? Why was he over there in Paradise when the rest of the family was here in Hatchie Landing?"

Well, I'll tell you this story because June wants me to, and I'll tell you some about Mani, but it won't do any good. I love to rock in the cool shade of the porch in the middle of the morning after the dishes are done and the beds all made up. The day Nathan came home, it was in May of 1946, I was rocking and thinking about what I dreamed in the night. In my dream, I looked across Kakunga. That's what my own bibi called the line that separates us from the other side. In the dream, it was like a river, heavy and thick with big brown gobs of water rolling up and spreading out into thick whorls that rolled and blended in the current. What I saw were lions and wild dogs walking back and forth over there, like they were hungry and looking across at something. I wasn't afraid. They weren't looking at me at all. They were looking at something else, maybe back over my shoulder, something in the dark coming up behind me. I wasn't afraid of that either in my dream. I knew it wasn't harm walking up on me, it was just something I couldn't see. But it was what the lions with their heads lowered down were staring at in the dark behind me that troubled me. I thought I knew some of those lions, too. One was named Trouble, and another one was named Death, but those two are always over there. Those wild dogs? I didn't know. I couldn't see their names plain yet.

Nathan and three of his friends, Ellis Wiggins, Buster Holt, and Joe Galt, had gone down to Tuskegee after high school. They graduated from Tuskegee and came back to Hatchie Landing expecting to take up their lives, even though clouds of war were forming. England was already in it, and it was understood that it was only a matter of time. Buster and Galt were preachers, Buster in Hatchie Landing and Galt over in Paradise. Nathan taught English at the black high school, and Ellis took over the grocery store and gas station up at the top of the Quarter toward town. When the war came, they answered the call to go back to Alabama to the college to be pilots. I was proud that they wanted to make a difference, but I was afraid when the four of them went over to Italy. I worried all through the war.

"Did something happen when they came home from the war that made Nathan move to Paradise?" asked Jesse.

I'll get to that, but first, you've got to know how it was with us. The day came when we figured Nathan would come home. I rocked at noontime when I was finished with my cooking and cleaning, and let the cool breeze fall on my face. I closed my eyes and dreamed a little bit more, and saw those wild dogs and those two lions again, with their names written on their faces right above their eyes. I never did tell June about the dream. No, I didn't.

Something told me to cook up some more food, and I was shuttling pots and pans from stove to sink and sink to stove when little Mani came home from school. I always got him something to eat when he came home, and we would sit down to talk about his day. That's when I saw Nathan turn onto the street up there at the top of the Quarter. At first, I couldn't believe it was him coming down this way. June was still at school, getting her classroom ready for her children the next day. We had Nathan's letter saying he was coming home, but we didn't know for sure when it would be. Lord, I was glad to see that man looking so good coming down the street. Walking straight and fine without a limp or anything, like he wasn't even touched by the war. No, sir.

He was wearing his uniform, and I ran out on the porch and held on to the banister. I couldn't help the tears coming into my eyes. They just came when I saw it was him. His letter said Buster and Ellis and Galt were coming home too, so everything was going to be all right again. Just like it used to be. Only when I remembered my dream, I thought maybe it wouldn't be exactly the same. So I put it out of my mind. Plenty of time to think about that later. Right now, here was June's man coming home.

I told little Mani to come see what's coming down the road, but he stayed inside and stood right over there behind that front screen looking out. *Bibi pointed to the front screen door.*

He said, "What's coming, Bibi?" He knew already what it was, but he didn't know how to act. I told him it's your daddy walking down the road, sure as we're standing here. Come on out here and see for yourself. You can run down and meet him. But the poor little thing couldn't bring himself to come out on the porch. It seemed like he, all of a sudden, was afraid. Fact is, he just didn't know his daddy. He'd been gone most of the child's life anyway, so that's why.

I opened the screen and picked him up. He was growing and getting heavy, but I carried him to the banister and we stood there, with him in my arms and his feet on top of the banister, both of us watching his daddy come down the street.

Nathan wasn't too sure of himself either, I could tell. He smiled a big smile and waved, and he started to say something, but he stopped in the middle of the street. I called out to him to come on up here and let us get a good look at you, but he only stood there, and then he smiled again and started up toward us.

Mani squirmed around in my arms and wanted to run away, but I held him up close and whispered in his ear that this was the man who loved him more than anybody else in the world. Mani wanted to know how his daddy could love him more than his momma? And I told him, child, your momma loves you more than anybody, too. So he asked me how two people can love him more than anybody? I told him when two people love each other as much as your momma and daddy love each other, then they're just like one person, and so they can both love their little child more than anybody else. He eased up then.

Nathan came up on the porch and knelt down on the top step. I stood Mani down, and Nathan looked his little boy in the eye and held out his arms. "My, my, how you have grown. You are a handsome man," Nathan said. He took off his cap and put it on Mani's head, and you should have seen that child. It was like he turned into something else right before their eyes. You can do that to a little boy. Put a hat on him and he'll be whatever the hat wants him to be. Mani stood up straight and saluted his daddy right then and there. Nathan saluted back and then reached out and grabbed him, and I thought he would squeeze the breath out of him, he held him so tight. When he looked up at me, I could see he was crying a little, but he didn't make any sound except to say to Mani he sure was glad to see him again. I couldn't imagine what it would be like when June got home and found Nathan back here in her house, all safe and sound. That was a reunion to watch, too.

I set about cooking up more food. I already had plenty, but didn't know what else to do. I was glad when Nathan came in the kitchen and said he hadn't had anything to eat since Knoxville except a couple of pecan pies at the bus station in Paradise, because I had a lot of food cooked up for him. That's when he put his arms around me, and that's when I broke down and bawled my eyes out, for all those boys who were finally coming home, for all those families like ours, and for all those families that would never see their boys again.

I thought a little about the dream I had and wondered if it had anything to do with Nathan coming home, but I couldn't figure it out yet. I wasn't worried, though. I had plenty of time to get to that. Right now, the war was over, and all the men coming home alive were hoping for good times.

June came running home early from school. Mr. Johnson, the principal, sent her home on account of he heard Nathan and some of the other young men had gotten home. It was like that in those days. Folks were just so glad to have the war over and their boys coming home, even if some of them were scarred. Mr. Johnson told June to go on home to see Nathan, and that's how she came to be running down the street. I saw her coming and told Nathan. He went to the front door and watched her through the screen.

I guess June couldn't see him there because when she got almost in front of the house, she stopped to catch her breath. She pushed her hair back from her face and tilted her head to dab her face with the puffed sleeve of her dress. She was combing her hair back with her fingers when Nathan stepped out into the sunlight.

"I nearly melted in the sunshine. I teared up," added June.

Her eyes were like stars. It was like something magic. She started toward Nathan, and he started down the steps toward her, but neither one of them moved fast. It was like they were drifting toward one another instead of doing it intentional. When they got to arm's length from each other, it was like they floated in light for an instant, and then you couldn't tell one from the other for two or three long minutes. Those two were meant for each other.

There was a fine reunion that night. Of course, it took some days to really get acquainted all over again, but we had a good time doing that part. We sure did. Later on, Nathan told us some about the war. It must have been awful at times, but I could tell he was proud of what they did—him, Buster, Galt, and Ellis. He showed us a leather billfold he carried with him in Italy. He kept June and Mani's pictures in it. An old man gave it to him one day. Out of kindness, he guessed it was. It was shiny where he had handled it so much during the last two years, shinier than when the old man thanked him and gave it to him. Nathan didn't even know where they were that day, only that they were on the way to an airfield somewhere in Italy. The town looked just like all the others they had come through: shells of houses, pocked walls, debris on the cobbled streets, and gaunt people glad, for the most part, to see the war moving on beyond them. The line of jeeps had been waiting to rendezvous with some others coming from the south. Nathan was slouched in the seat of the jeep with his leg stuck out around the windshield when that old man came out of a house that was pocked with bullet marks and handed him the leather case. It was empty except for a single picture of a young girl. Nathan held up the picture for the man to see, and the old man took it back and pressed it to his chest, and spoke in Italian. Of course, Nathan understood none of the words, but he understood perfectly what he meant. Dead. She was his daughter. The old man pushed the leather folder against Nathan's chest, and when Nathan put his hand on it, the old man turned away and went back into the scarred house. War is an awful thing, and it makes people do strange things.

I studied about those two lions and those wild dogs walking about in my dream, but I still wasn't sure what it meant.

Chapter 9

Jesse Wickham with Bibi Durber
April 7, 1975
Hatchie Landing, TN
Bibi's Version of Events of May 1946 to April 1948

"YOU KEEP MENTIONING THE TROUBLE. How did it all begin? What started it?"

We thought things would just go back to the way they were before the war, but that didn't happen. It couldn't. Those boys who went over there came back as men with new ideas and the feeling they had sacrificed and now they had some rights. Nathan got his old position back at the high school, but he farmed for Mr. Clifford until school started in the fall. The farm was large and just outside of Hatchie Landing, not too far from the Quarter. Once in a while, Nathan took Mani with him. The boy loved those days when his daddy teased him unmercifully. One time, Nathan asked him if he heard the world turn over last night. I wish you could have heard that one. You'd know how special Nathan was, and Mani too. He's special, and he'll get to his high place someday. Live up to his name. He will.

Mani told him, "The world doesn't make a sound," and Nathan said, "Oh yes, it does. It makes all kinds of sounds, but you have to listen closely to know what they mean." He said, "You can even hear the stars twinkle if you know how to listen. Imagine yourself way up high somewhere looking down. Close your eyes and listen. Your name,

Mani, the one Bibi gave you, means *from the mountain*, so just imagine yourself up on that mountain."

Mani wanted to know if that was the way it was when he was flying in the war. Could he see people and things? Even the black water Nathan would talk about down in the Hatchie Bottom, where he and Ellis would go fishing?

Nathan told him it's beautiful up there, except you can't see everything that's happening down where people live. He took Mani's face in his big hands and said, "Mani, you can see clearly from anywhere if you just imagine yourself up above everything. You'll always be able to see what's right. And that's what I'm talking about."

"Did something happen that summer?"

It was a careless time, in the beginning of that summer, a restful time, soft breezes on the summer nights, and bullbats circling through the night air, the summer storms yet to arrive, only heat lightning and distant thunder beyond the Quarter. No sign of the trouble that was coming.

I rocked on my porch, letting my dream unroll like a scroll. That lion I called Trouble was about to come across. For a while, that was my only trouble, and then Buster invited Reverend Galt to come over from Paradise to preach to all of us about rising up and walking into the Promised Land, the land of Moses and Joshua and the Children of Israel. How they wandered around outside the Promised Land for all those many years and still didn't have a thing to show for it until finally one day they went looking to see what it was the Lord had promised, and the Lord told them to go on in and see it for themselves, and they saw it. Galt preached a good one that Sunday, and it fired up all the Brothers and Sisters. It surely did, and Ellis and Nathan got fired up, too.

"How did they get fired up? What did they do?"

I'm coming to that. There is something people need to know about getting fired up. The Brothers get fired up, and the Sisters get fired up, but on something like this, it's different between them. The Sisters think on things a while and move along slow and let things happen a little bit at a time. They do. A woman has patience. God made women and men that way so they would be a help to each other, one balancing the other all the time.

Me and my husband, Polk, bless his soul. We would get fired up time to time, but that's a different kind of fired up, coming in from the fields on Saturday and cleaning up. Put on some clothes and go jukin'. Lord, that'll get you fired up. I remember the fine times, the children, June and Michael, who died of the scarlet fever when he was just a little thing. I loved them both, and they both came out of one of those fired-up Saturday nights.

The Brothers, though, they get fired up and anxious to move on. They want to go on into the Promised Land right away, like the Lord told Moses, Joshua, and the Children. It's what started the trouble. That old lion walked back and forth, and I knew.

What the Reverend Galt told us that Sunday afternoon in October of '46 was we had a right to the Promised Land, and in that land was privilege. He told us we should go on over and take up our privilege, but be ready to bear the burden of privilege. Your privilege is you are a citizen already of *this* Promised Land, the United States of America, and your privilege is you can vote. Only thing is, nobody wants to sign up to vote. Won't nobody go on over into this Promised Land. You have to sign up to go into the Promised Land, he said. And like the Children of Israel, you have to take up the burden of your responsibility, too. You have to be a part of all of it, the good and bad. You have to love this country like you do your own family, and you might have to die for it, but the burden, great as it is, is worth the privilege of walking upright in the Promised Land, and Nathan and Ellis and Buster got fired up.

Nathan and Ellis even took the Greyhound over to Paradise to see the Reverend Galt again, and came home with a plan to get people to sign up to vote in the election that was coming up in 1948. They commenced to go around the Quarter to people's houses, and that part was all right. That wasn't the trouble. Trouble, that old lion, roared out the first time when Nathan, Buster, and Ellis decided it was time to meet at the Hatchie Courthouse to sign up. June said she would go with them, but I said no, I'd go. I said if there was trouble, they wouldn't hurt an old woman. Y'all think things are different, but they're not, I told them. The others didn't like that, but I stood firm.

Chapter 10

—————◆—————

Jesse Wickham with Bibi Durber
April 7, 1975
Hatchie Landing, TN
Bibi's Version of Events of May 1946 to April 1948

THE DAY WAS BRIGHT AND CLEAR when Nathan, Ellis, Buster, and I went to the courthouse to register to vote. I remember it was in early November of '46. It was still warm, and the huge elm trees on the courthouse lawn were shedding their leaves, and the breeze blew them into little piles against the stone monument to the county's war dead.

I told them to let me go first, and I shuffled up the steps.

Bennie Hoskins, a wiry little deputy sheriff with a pocked face, was on duty at the entrance. He looked back and forth from one of us to the other with his mouth open like he wanted to say something. Finally, he asked us what we wanted. Ellis looked over my shoulder and asked, "Where do we go to sign up to vote?" Hoskins stammered it was right down the hall, but he didn't think we could do it.

Ellis said, "Sure, we can. We're citizens like anybody else. We aren't here to cause any problems. We just want to be good citizens of this land because it's been good to us, and we do have the right."

All three of them fought in the war, I said. They just want to keep on serving our country. We don't want to tell people how to vote or who to vote for, but to stand up and be counted like good citizens.

Just then, there was some noise from down the hall, and Malcolm Oakes and some other men came toward us. Oakes was a deputy sheriff. Everybody knew him and kept out of his way. Around the

Quarter, folks would shift their eyes and laugh and call Malcolm "the High Deputy" and Bennie "the Low Deputy" on account of Malcolm is the type who can get somebody else to do his work for him, and he always had Bennie Hoskins around to do it. He was yelling and pointing toward the front door, "Miss Bibi, you and these boys, get on out of here. There isn't going to be any voter registration today. The office is closed down for the day."

Ellis asked when they could come back, and Oakes said he didn't know, but Ellis persisted, and finally one of the others said the registration office wouldn't ever be open for them. "That's just the way it's going to be, so you boys get on out of here. You too, Miss Bibi."

We were backing away when Ellis, as calm as you please, looked at Oakes and the other men and said, "Gentlemen, I know you are in a difficult situation. I know that all of you are, but just so you'll know, we will come back, and we will bring more people every chance we get until we're allowed to sign up to vote."

We went on back home, but the next Saturday, Ellis, Nathan, and I drove to the courthouse. No one from the Quarter went with us. Who could blame them for being afraid? Everybody was afraid.

When we got there, Oakes and Hoskins were at the front again.

Ellis went first this time, and Bennie stepped in front of him and looked up at him. He poked him in the chest with his knuckle and told him to turn around and walk on out of there. Ellis smiled down at Bennie and repeated what he'd said the last time, that he just wanted to sign up to vote, to register like he had the right to do. I said, Mistuh Hoskins, these men just want to vote like other people. They're not here to cause any trouble. I tell you, the silence felt like something bad was about to happen. That Hoskins fellow, he relaxed a little like maybe he'd let us go by, but Ellis spoke up again.

"I have got to pay my taxes like everybody else," Ellis said, "so why can't I vote like anybody else?" And Bennie said, "Because you are colored and no damned colored is ever going to vote in this courthouse. That's just the way it is. Now go on home, all of you."

We moved back toward the steps, and Nathan said, "It's just us against two deputies with pistols and the whole house of law behind them. Let's just turn around and leave." Ellis agreed, but said, "It's not over."

A little crowd of people was gathered on the sidewalk outside. They were curious mostly, but some of them yelled at us to go on home. A couple of them came in close, and one woman said, "The niggers is going to take us over." Bennie came down the steps and got in front of me and Ellis with his back to the crowd. He told them to get on out of there or there would be trouble. I could almost smell the folks gathered around our car, but they parted and let us get in and drive off.

I said, "I'm afraid we've stirred up something big. We'd better let it go for a little while." The three men kept on trying to get folks to register, though.

They did get some to join the new chapter of the NAACP. For some, it was just a social thing, but for others, it was for real. Ellis was the organizer, always talking about it, showing up at somebody's door after supper, inviting himself in and talking about how the colored people were going to have to stand up if they were going to enter the Promised Land, and one way to stand up was to join in the cause, get educated, join the NAACP, which they most often did when he was finished. Ellis was a persuasive salesman and as good a friend as anyone could have, but my dream was telling me there would be trouble for all of them and especially for Ellis if he kept it up.

Chapter 11

Jesse Wickham with Bibi Durber
April 7, 1975
Hatchie Landing, TN
Bibi's Version of Events of May 1946 to April 1948

They did keep it up, and it was along about April of '47 when Nathan and the others began to have some luck with 'the campaign,' as they called it. They didn't get themselves signed up to vote yet, but some other folks said they would go sign up if any one of the three men could get signed up. So on a Saturday morning, Nathan, Buster, and Ellis showed up again at the courthouse. I wasn't with them that time. It had been a while since they'd tried, and when they showed up, there was nobody at the front door to stop them. They went straight to the election office and told the woman behind the window they wanted to sign up to vote.

Nathan said that woman went paler than she really was and called out for Mr. Henderson, the registrar, and he came running. He kept repeating, "I'm sorry, I'm sorry, I can't allow you to do this. It isn't right. It's highly irregular."

And that's when Ellis told Mr. Henderson it was the most regular thing any true and upstanding citizen can do. But Mr. Henderson said, "Maybe so, but not now. Not for you folks. It just isn't the time. Maybe someday, but not now. I can't allow it."

A commotion came from down the hall, and Malcolm Oakes, Bennie Hoskins, and the sheriff caught them from behind, swinging their clubs. Nathan went down holding his shoulder, and Oakes shoved him to the floor and cuffed him. Hoskins's club caught Ellis just above his right ear. Blood streamed down his face onto his shirt. The sheriff pushed him against the wall and cuffed him. Buster ducked and ran to the door. Nobody blamed Buster for running. He did the only thing he could do. Nobody stopped him, and he got away.

Ellis and Nathan ended up in jail. I couldn't believe it. That old lion named Trouble had stepped over the line, and he was hungry, too. Those wild dogs with their names written on their faces were coming too.

Nathan and Ellis stayed locked up for the rest of the day, then Oakes and Hoskins drove them over to Ellis's grocery and dropped them off. Ellis's wife, Arlene, went crazy when she saw his bloody shirt. She thought he was dying.

That night, around ten o'clock, cars came into the street. People peeped out their windows to see what was coming.

It was awful. The cars stopped all along the road, and a truck came up loaded with a huge cross, all wrapped in burlap soaked in coal oil. The smell filled the night and came all the way into the houses. They planted it in front of Ellis's house and set it afire. It lit up the night like some hellish conflagration, making the movements of the men's shadows seem ghostly. The leaves in the magnolia tree rustled with a harsh sound as roosting birds fluttered up into the darkness away from the heat and the brightness. A wind came in close to the ground and carried the smoke and smell over the Quarter. Men, some in hoods, but most in ordinary clothes, stood around, and one threw a rock onto Ellis's porch. Someone told him to cut it out and wait. They waited there watching to see if anyone would come out, ready to say or do something if they did. It was impossible to imagine what it would be. I couldn't tell if any of them had guns, but they weren't yelling or saying anything. Just low talk now and then as they stood around the burning cross with hoods and faces all aglow.

I grabbed Mani and whispered for them to hurry to the back of the house. I put him under my bed and waited. Nathan stood at the front door, right where those men could see him. I was afraid that they would come to the door any minute and take my family away, but they didn't, and they didn't get Ellis or his family either. The crowd fell silent before the burning cross, and the quiet was more frightening than the fiery cross, throwing shadows into the dark corners of the yard, shapes moving in and out, back and forth, like they were in search of something until they drove away.

Now, what do you think about burning a cross like that? Doesn't make any sense at all, does it? Jesus wouldn't like to see his cross burning in some poor soul's front yard. He wouldn't put up with it for a minute, but sometimes he doesn't show up when you think he will.

"Bibi, don't talk like that," said June.

Well, that's just the thing about Jesus. Sometimes, it seems like he's gone and left us to deal with trouble alone and by ourselves. And sometimes it seems like everybody with a belief at all believes Jesus is behind their own way of believing. Now, if you ask me, I say Jesus knows there is more than one way to get to God. If God is big enough to make Jesus, then He's too big to say the only way to find Him is to go to Jesus. If He wanted the only way to be Jesus, then He'd have to let Jesus show up a little more often. That's what I think. He would, but He was nowhere around that night, no sir, He was nowhere around.

"What did people do after that night? Did things settle back down?"

People all over the Quartet were afraid after that, and Ellis and his wife talked about leaving town. Ellis had a good business up on the edge of the Quarter, his little service station and grocery up there where everybody went for gas and bread and milk, even some white folks. But Arlene thought they'd better go to Paradise and get away from all of it for a while, pick up and leave all they'd worked for to go to nothing at all. Others talked about it too, even Nathan and June, but they didn't think it would last. Nathan stopped trying to get signed up to vote for the time being, hoping it would all quiet down, but it didn't.

Chapter 12

Jesse Wickham with Bibi Durber
April 7, 1975
Hatchie Landing, TN
Bibi's Version of Events of May 1946 to April 1948

IT WAS RIGHT AFTER THAT, in June of '47, that Ellis disappeared. The same night he went missing was when Mani, Nathan, and I saw what we saw in the Hatchie Swamp. I saw what it was going to do to that child. Those lions and those wild dogs were already across.

"What did you see?" asked Jesse.

I'm coming to that. You see, school was out the first week in June, and things had been quiet since the cross burning. Nathan and the others had stopped trying to get folks to register until things calmed down. Nathan came home one evening with a bright new tackle box for Mani. There were red and white bobbers, fishing line, and hooks in little compartments on a foldout tray inside. Mani was so excited, he ran upstairs and came down with his fishing rod bumping the steps behind him, begging his daddy to go fishing over in the Hatchie River.

That child didn't know what the Hatchie River was like, but he'd heard his daddy tell about it. Nathan was in one of his teasing moods, and he stared off into the distance as if contemplating some further idea. Mani yanked on his arm until he finally said, "I think maybe we can. Yes, I think it's time we did just that, and you know what? Let's go night fishing."

I wasn't for the idea. I didn't like the two of them going off down there, especially at night after what just happened right here.

I looked at Mani. His eyes were shining, and it would break his little heart if they didn't go. He'd be so disappointed. So, I said, let's all go. I thought it would be all right. Won't nobody bother two women, I said, especially an old woman like me. But June didn't want to. Said she didn't like to fish anyway.

Nathan whirled Mani around and said, "We'll go night fishing because we can catch some big catfish at night." Then he grabbed June and swung her around and kissed her, all the while bragging to Mani about Hatchie Bottom catfish. The best eating, the biggest, and on and on. He made it seem like an adventure, and he got a far-off look like he was gone to some other world. And that's the way it turned out— me, Nathan, and Mani going and June staying at home.

Next day, I'll never forget, it was Saturday afternoon, June 14, 1947, Nathan came home from Mr. Clifford's anxious to go. He got Mani so excited with his raving. "I know a place where a man has a bottom field we can drive to and walk just a ways and be where the water flows easy and the catfish are easy too. We'll take the Chevy and be back by midnight," he said.

It was an old '29 Chevy he'd bought and fixed up. June knew that when Nathan made up his mind, it was probably all over. He smiled and took her in his arms, and she laughed and giggled. But when he put her down, she asked, "With all that's happened, promise me you'll be safe over there."

He said, "Sweetheart, we'll be just fine."

He put poles and a shovel in the back of the Chevy. The little coupe had a trunk in place of a rumble seat. That car didn't look like much, but June thought it was a cute little thing. She liked to ride around in it with Nathan, proud they had saved up enough to buy it. The shovel was to dig worms when they got there. We jammed in the one seat, waved goodbye to June, and drove off toward some kind of midnight, only we didn't know it then.

It took us a little while to get over to Hatchie Bottom and down to the special catfish spot. The sun had set and it was getting dark fast when Nathan pulled off into a field and followed an old tractor road around the edge until it went deep into a copse of trees, where he parked so the car was out of sight.

Mani looked around wide-eyed and clung to his daddy.

There were tire tracks coming and going out of the field, and Mani said it didn't seem like a secret place to him. Nathan said it's probably just some other fishermen had found the spot. He hoped they hadn't taken all the catfish. I tagged behind with our old coal oil lantern as they set out across the field toward the woods on the other side where the dusky darkness was settling thickly. Nathan started teasing Mani. "You remember to bring the flashlight, Mani?"

Mani said he never thought about needing one.

Nathan ruffled his hair and laughed. "Now how're we going to see in the dark, Mani?" He took Mani's small hand in his and walked on.

In the woods, the ground too boggy and damp to be cleared by man and turned into a field, the trees stood heavily over everything like thick dark sentinels keeping watch. The air carried the sweet odor of rotting things. You ever been in a real swamp, Jesse? It can be like a live thing, one of the deepest, darkest places on earth, day or night, the way the ground sucks at your feet and night birds call—birds you never imagined before—and sounds carry and every tree root could be a snake and the streams come together and split again with no sound from the water, like the inside of a living creature, all moist and slick without a handhold anywhere. It was already getting dark, and soon would be dark as pitch, black as midnight.

In a little way, we came upon some tamped-down ground. There was an old wooden stool and a turned-up bucket where somebody had sat fishing. Nathan set off to dig worms, and Mani and I looked around. It was the blackest water I'd ever seen, not dirty, just black from all the leaves and wooden things falling into it, so that it seemed like a solid thing, like you could cut it with a knife. It didn't seem any catfish could live in something so dark.

In a minute, Nathan came back and said with a big grin, "All you have to do is lift a shovel full of dirt from this ground and the worms just tumble out. Here, take 'em and let's get started."

It wasn't two minutes before Mani had a catfish on the hook. Strong and a fighter, it bowed his rod and he squealed. Nathan whooped and got the bucket and scooped in some water. Together, they pulled the fish out, and Nathan declared it the biggest one yet, even though it was the only one. Mani loved his daddy for always being funny. He worked out the hook, and Nathan said, 'Drop that old booger in the bucket and let's catch another.' In no time at all, they had six big catfish between them. Then there was the groaning sound of a loaded truck coming down the road. Nathan cocked his head and listened. We could hear more cars coming our way.

I pulled the child up close. "Now what do you suppose that could be about?"

Nathan told us to pick up our stuff and move away from there. Mani wanted to know what was wrong. He said, "Nothing, son, but we'd better be scarce a little while till we see what's going on."

But the child wouldn't let it go. He wanted to know why we weren't supposed to be there? We trespassing? He looked at me because I had told him never to trespass on someone else's property, especially a white man's property. Get you in trouble, I'd say.

It went on like that, Mani asking questions and Nathan answering, all the while moving deeper into the swamp.

"I don't know what all those cars are coming down this way for, but it's not usual."

"What about the Chevy?"

"It'll be okay. It's hid pretty good back there."

"We going home?"

"No, we'd better just slip on down into the bottom a little more. Nobody will bother us. Won't even know we're here. Come on."

Nathan took him by the hand, and Mani asked what about the catfish? Nathan told him to leave them and come on. He led us deeper into the undergrowth, looking up now and then to find the openings in the trees and then down to feel with his feet where the solid ground lay.

Nathan said, "We're not going far in here. It'll be okay. Just stay low and be quiet till we see what the layout's going to be."

I blew out the lantern.

Some cars and trucks turned into the field, and headlights swung over the edge of the woods, and flicked off until it was dark again. Then another truck pulled in, and we could hear talk and the sound of wood being tossed. Thwack, clump, thwack, clump, it tumbled onto a pile. By the sound, it was growing, and then there was more talk and a loud shout like someone in command. There was low laughter too.

Mani wanted to know what they were doing. Nathan told him, "I don't know, son, but we'd better be quiet. We may be in a bad place for a little while, but if we stay quiet and still, we'll be all right. This may take a while."

It was as if Mani had no notion of what was happening, but deep down he knew. A child deals with bad things in ways an adult cannot. He can know a thing so bad his mind won't let him know it, but know it anyway. And Mani knew this thing without knowing it out there in the dark swamp, hiding like a criminal, like he'd done something wrong, but knowing he hadn't done anything except catch some of God's catfish after walking across a white man's field.

He held on to me tight, and I knew he understood this wasn't good. He closed his eyes and whispered, "Lord, I'll put those catfish back if you will just help us get back home."

The child was crying softly as we watched through the thick underbrush beneath the live oak trees. The pile of wood was now a bonfire, casting long shadows across the field that swayed and wavered as men moved back and forth before it. And that child knew what was coming when the huge cross started to burn. He'd seen that cross in front of Ellis's house that other night, but God almighty, this one was bigger and scarier than anything any of them had ever seen.

"Shit," whispered Nathan. There was nothing you could say about him cursing God's cross on account of this was something else, something else for sure.

Our neighbor, Mr. Gibbs, on his porch one night, told the children a story about such things, and the child thought it was just to scare them like a ghost story, but he knew it was a lesson being handed to them. It had to do with them being black-skinned. He asked me about it later. I hated to see his innocence being taken away. It was the first time the child had really felt different. It had to happen sooner or later anyhow.

But now here we were, him and his daddy and me, his bibi, squatted down in the Hatchie River Bottom watching the Ku Klux Klan live and in person as another truck pulled into the field. Two of the men in robes dragged a man out of the back. He wasn't standing up at all. He was limp as a rag, and we couldn't tell if the man was black or white or a Chinaman. There was no way to be sure anything was real in the awful darkness.

They dragged that poor man across the beaten-down grass and two of them took him up, one by the feet and the other under the arms, and began to swing him until they had a good arc on him, and then plain as day, they counted out loud. One, two, three, and let him go up onto the burning pile. Mani started to cry again, and I folded him up in my arms, and as quiet as the child's mother, began to hum a little song and whisper, "Don't, don't cry now, Mani, we're gonna be all right. I'll take care of you. Just be quiet and rest now. It will be all right." I saw his daddy turn hard like he changed all of a sudden into something else. It was like all that was good and innocent flowed out of him. He'd become someone else, and so had the child.

We stayed where we were until all the ruckus was over and the cars and trucks had pulled out. The Klan men scooped up the ashes from the bonfire into the back of one of the trucks. We could hear some talk about whose truck it would be. It seemed none of them wanted it to be his truck. Finally, one was chosen, and they picked through the ashes for a little bit and then scooped most all of the ash into the chosen truck, and it drove off. They didn't bother to clean up the burned-down cross. It was just a pile of ashes anyway.

Nathan reached over and took Mani and held him ever so close, and the child slept until it was almost daylight. Then we hustled over to the Chevy and headed for home as fast as it could go. Mani looked up at me. "What about those catfish that we left behind in the bucket, Bibi? They never hurt anybody. They were just living a happy life right where they were supposed to be, and they didn't deserve to die." I drew him close while Nathan drove.

June was up and waiting, and knew already that something awful had happened. She ran out in the yard when we drove up, and folded Nathan and Mani in her arms crying, "My sweet boys, my sweet family. God help us all."

Chapter 13

Jesse Wickham with Bibi Durber
April 7, 1975
Hatchie Landing, TN
Bibi's Version of Events of May 1946 to April 1948

I WORRIED ABOUT WHAT IT WOULD DO to little Mani. His daddy was good about helping him understand, and I did what I could, which was mainly to love him. The very next day, Mr. Clifford came through the quarter picking up men to help with the first hay cutting. Nathan told me later some of what happened that day so I would know and could help Mani deal with it. Nathan and Mani climbed into the back of the truck with the other men. When they got there, Clifford sent the others out on the wagon to start loading.

He kept Nathan at the barn to stack as the men brought up a wagon load at a time, while Mani mostly played in the hay loft. Nathan told me that when the other men had gone to the field, he and Mr. Clifford walked out to the garden lot and leaned on the gate. Mr. Clifford wanted to know if he had heard about what happened out in Parham's field. "Don't tell me you don't know. People know, and you folks down in the quarter know it better than anybody." "I know a little bit," Nathan told him.

He said Mr. Clifford got a little testy. "You know damn well all about it. What I'm getting at is, do you know too much? Cause if you do, and maybe I don't want to know too much about what you do know, but if you do, well, it could be bad for you. Just be careful, is all I'm saying. And tell everybody else too."

Mani was full of questions about what they had seen and kept asking to know how many men were in that field that night. Nathan told him to try and forget about it, but the child kept asking until Nathan gave in and said he thought there were maybe twenty or so. "But don't you go talking about it to anybody. You hear? I counted the trucks and cars. I wanted to know how many we'd be up against if they caught sight of us. Now don't talk about it anymore."

But he kept on asking things like "They didn't see us down there in the woods. Did they, Daddy?" and "It was bad, wasn't it, Daddy?"

Nathan would tell him, "Yes, it was. Don't need to ever see something like that again."

Mani told me that once, when they squatted in the shade against the hay barn to wait for the next wagon load, Nathan sharpened a stick with his pocket knife, and he tapped it on the ground between his legs. He scraped the dirt and made a circle. Then he scratched a second, smaller one that lapped over the first one. He poked the stick right where the two overlapped and told Mani, "We could be right there where these two circles come together. See. There's this big circle right here. That's those Klan men. And there's this little circle. That's everybody else." Then he scratched the dirt where the circles overlapped and stuck his stick in it. "Somehow they all come together," he told him. "What we don't know is where Bibi, Momma, you, and me are in the circles. We may be right in the center of things right here, where this stick is, or we may just be way out here at the edge. That'd be the best place, but we can't tell. If that scares you, well, maybe that's good, son. We'd all better be a little bit afraid, because if we aren't, we might slip up and say something we shouldn't, like who we saw out there. We've got to keep quiet. We don't want anybody to know we were even out there, and we didn't see anybody we know. You understand, Mani?"

After the work was done, Mr. Clifford dropped Nathan and Mani off at the top of the Quarter. I watched them coming down to our house. The street was quiet as they walked home. The flow of the ordinary things people do, like trimming their hedges or hanging out wash, kids playing, and such, was absent; the air itself was empty. The usual things don't happen when something goes wrong as it had then. The old woman you always see out on her porch won't be there, or the kids won't be playing cork-ball down in the open lot. The air feels different, and the light changes. I thought about my dream.

Nathan and Mani already knew what was wrong. They'd seen it with their own two eyes, but they didn't admit it was one of their own until they came down that quiet, empty street. Nathan put one arm around Mani, and they walked together down the middle of the Quarter to the house, and not one person was out on the street, just the two of them walking along home, and not a soul outside.

When they got home, I told them that Ellis was missing and everyone in the Quarter knew about it. Nathan didn't make a sound or move. He went out on the porch and sat for a long time. I hugged Mani to myself like a little mouse, cuddled up against me, and didn't say a word.

Next morning, June and Mani went to see Arlene and her kids. Reverend Holt came in while they were there, and the Sisters started arriving. They came with food and everything, like it was a wake, even though nobody knew for sure about Ellis. But it was like they knew deep down he wasn't just missing. They knew he was dead. Folks can know things like that without a shred to go on. Mani knew without knowing that it was Ellis they saw in the field last Saturday night.

Back home, Mani hid in his room and cried until I went up there and sat with him under the eave, and held on to him until he went to sleep. When he woke up in the night, he was in his bed, and I was there next to him with my arm over him. I hugged him a little, and he put his face against me, his hand over my smooth skin, and I guessed he could feel my face was wet too. He went to sleep then and slept until morning.

He's grown up to be a good man, Mr. Jesse, and I can tell you my Mani shouldn't be in that jail. He didn't kill that man, but that's another story. It's got something to do with this one that I just told you, but I don't know how exactly. I just know it is, and if you can find it, my Mani will walk free.

"Bibi, June, this has been hard for you. Thank you is all I can say. If you think of anything else that would be of help, call me."

"I can maybe tell you a little bit more, but Bibi has given you the whole thing. It was an awful time."

"I'd like to find out more about your Nathan and his time over in Paradise. There is so much more I want to know."

"We've gone this far. We might as well give you all of it. It was a lonesome time for us both," June replied. "I have some letters I'll let you read if you want. They're a bit personal in places, but they also tell something of what he did over there. I'll get them for you, but you must return them. They're all I have from him."

"That's very generous, June. I'll take good care of them and get them back to you right away."

"Then come back tomorrow, and I'll have the letters ready for you. Bibi can tell you her side of it and I'll tell you mine."

Chapter 14

———◆———

Bibi Durber
April 8, 1975
Hatchie Landing, TN
Relating the Events of the Evening of August 6, 1947

JESSE ARRIVED THE NEXT MORNING, and after small talk and settling at the kitchen table, he said, "Tell me about Nathan's exile."

It was August 6, 1947, close to midday, and the locusts were making such noise in the trees I couldn't hear myself think. They'd start to rasp in one tree and then another, and soon the air was full of sound. Like sinking down in deep water. But I love that kind of thing when the natural world comes in like that. It makes me think about something besides myself. But you didn't come to hear that.

Buster came by and told me to help put out a call for everyone to gather at the church.

I said I would, and it wasn't hard. The word went around like nobody's business, and on Wednesday night, everyone gathered. June, Nathan, and I left little Mani at home by himself while we went to the meeting. He was a good boy and said all right to that. I wasn't worried about him. I could always depend on him to do just what was right.

We walked over to the church in the twilight. Others were coming down off their porches and joining in. There wasn't much said while we all walked together. Just a little small talk here and there. Folks were worried about what was going to happen next. As people came in, the room filled with buzz and talk. Little knots of folks here and there around the room, not like on most church nights when the women went around and spoke to each other and hugged, and the men shook hands and slapped each other on the back and laughed.

I had been having my dream again for nights in a row. I knew two of those wild dogs for sure now. Their names were plain as day to me. In fact, they had been walking among us all the time. Nobody asked me about it, though. I wasn't afraid of them. I just didn't know to be scared. I didn't know they would come after them, come after Nathan and June, and try to eat up all the love between them, but they did finally.

You couldn't kill the love between those two, though. It was something permanent like stars in the night. No sir, you had to kill one of those two to kill their love for each other. I worried for them, but as long as I could see those lions and dogs from time to time, I wasn't afraid. I knew their names.

We went on up into the church when we got there. It was Wednesday night and prayer meeting, so everybody went right on up into the church house. Buster was greeting everybody as they came in, but there were so many and coming in so fast, not hanging back and visiting folks like usual, he couldn't get to all of them soon enough. It was all right, though. They were here and ready for some action.

Right at seven, Buster went up on the platform and stood beside the little pulpit. I never did like that thing. I thought it was too pitiful for a preacher to stand behind. Buster, though, liked using it to lean on. Even a preacher has got to lean on something from time to time. But tonight he didn't lean on anything. He commenced to say we had a big trouble on our hands and we needed God to help us.

Sanguine Moses spoke out and said amen to the trouble, but he didn't think God was gonna be any kind of savior. There were a whole lot of amens when Buster said he thought God could deliver us from our trouble just like he did the Children of Israel. Sanguine said he guessed that was true, but it didn't do Ellis Wiggins any good now, did it? That's what he said. Nobody said an amen to that, though. There was a rustle through the congregation, and some people bowed their heads and looked down. Others looked straight ahead. Nobody looked at Sanguine because what he said was the truth.

Buster called everybody to order, and we sang "Balm in Gilead." *Sometimes I feel discouraged and think my work's in vain, but then the Holy Spirit revives my soul again.* I always felt that way when I'd go sit out on the porch and close my eyes to think on things. And it's what Buster preached on. He said everyone feels discouraged sometimes. But don't stay down. No, you mustn't, he said. There is always a hope if you will just grab hold of it. He gave some good advice that evening, and afterward we talked about it in the pews. First one and then another spoke up. Sanguine spoke up every now and then and gave his opinion, and so did Jeremiah Hayes. Sweet Williams spoke up and said he wondered, just wondering now, he said, don't mean to say anything by it, just wondering, but maybe things will slow down if y'all lay low awhile, if you know what I mean. We all knew what he meant. And I didn't think much of it. What he meant was maybe Buster and Nathan should lay low, and lay low means get scarce, get out of town.

In the end, everyone agreed to hold on and pray. We would help each other and watch out for each other like we were all family. We sang again and went home. When we came out of the church, the High Sheriff's car was up at the corner, but he wasn't coming down into the Quarter. It was just up there, and we knew they were watching what all was going on down here.

That evening, I had the dream. Those two lions were walking back and forth with they heads down and looking. I didn't see the wild dogs. They were gone somewhere, and when I woke up the next morning, I hoped they weren't already prowling for us. That's what I hoped.

Chapter 15

———•◆•———

Bibi Durber
April 8, 1975
Hatchie Landing, TN
Relating Events of August 7, 1947

THE QUARTER WAS QUIET THE NEXT MORNING, like it was holding its breath, like something unknowable was coming. Even the air was humid and heavy with a dislocating breeze. Nathan picked at his breakfast, then pushed back from the table and announced he had written Galt and needed to go to the post office to mail the letter. I knew Buster had been talking to him, but Galt had got to know how bad things were over here besides us. He said he would get some gas in the Chevy at the E & A on the way back.

June told him to see how Arlene was doing, and gave him a list of a few things we could use that would give the excuse for stopping in. Arlene was so torn up, she was telling everybody that she didn't want any help or anybody's sympathy. We thought she'd leave before long, and I could hardly blame her. Nathan promised to talk to her.

What happened was that he parked the coupe in a space on Baltimore at the side of the post office. When he came out, Bennie Hoskins and Malcolm Oakes were in a patrol car across the street. He headed back toward the Quarter, and the patrol car followed him. He slowed down, hoping it would pass, but it slowed down also. At the turn into the Quarter, he pulled up to the E & A gas pump. The patrol car stopped across the street. He could see Arlene inside the store through the big plate glass window beyond the patrol car's reflection.

The two deputies got out of the patrol car as Nathan started up the steps. Nathan told us that Oakes put his hand on his gun, and I reckon Bennie did the same and hitched his pants like he always did as the two crossed the street toward the store. Nathan was at the counter while Arlene picked out the few items on his list. He asked her how she was getting along, and she told him as well as you might expect. She felt like she had to get her children out of Hatchie Landing. Said she was telling everyone.

Before Nathan could say anything, Malcolm came up beside him and leaned on the counter. Nathan kept his eyes straight ahead, waiting.

Oakes said, "Hanks, you ought to think about leaving yourself." Told him it was not a bad idea at all, especially for someone like him. He said plain as could be that it would be a shame for something to happen to a teacher over at the school.

The two men stood on either side of him. Arlene dropped something that clattered behind a rack of canned goods. She slammed one of Nathan's items beside the cash register and looked directly at Malcolm Oakes. "Y'all done killed my husband," she said. "He's dead, and y'all are not doing a thing about it. Won't any of us ever know what happened to him, so y'all might as well have been the ones to have done it." Arlene stood erect with her lips pursed, accusing the two men to their faces.

Nathan was fearful of what they would do to Arlene, but Oakes said, "Mrs. Wiggins, we will do our best to find out if anything happened to your husband in this county. So far as we know, he just took off. You know yourself, your menfolk do that sometimes."

Nathan told them Ellis would never leave. He *didn't* leave.

That's when Bennie shoved Nathan's shoulder and said, "Well, maybe you should rethink that statement, *mister high school teacher.* Maybe think about getting yourself out of here, too, like the missus here." He tilted his head toward Arlene.

Malcolm gave Bennie a look, but he said to Nathan, he should think about that. He said, "We'll keep your family safe while you're away."

"For everybody's good. So nobody else gets hurt," chimed Bennie.

That must have made Malcolm mad at Bennie, because he shut him up. He grabbed the deputy by the arm and marched him out of the store to the patrol car, and they drove away.

When they were gone, Arlene asked Nathan what in the world was he going to do? She didn't want him to get himself killed, not like Ellis. She told him to leave if he had to.

June ran to Nathan as soon as he pulled up in front of the house. She said Arlene had called. They walked hand in hand into the house. All afternoon, what had happened hung in the air between them. Nathan kept saying that he refused to leave his family and run away. He wouldn't talk about it anymore.

That night, just as soon as June and I had cleaned up after supper, I told Nathan that he had to decide what to do. I told him it was all right to be afraid. There's nothing wrong with that, but he couldn't leave his family wondering every day if something bad was going to happen to him or to them. I said if he left, June would still have a job, and he could come back now and then. Maybe it wouldn't last too long, but we all knew it would. I had seen those wild dogs and those two lions, especially that one named Trouble.

I went upstairs and lay down beside little Mani and held him till he was asleep. June and Nathan sat up and talked on into the night. June couldn't bear the thought of him getting hurt or killed. She spoke her fear out loud for the first time. She told him to go over to Paradise. It was in the back of everybody's mind, but none of them had said it.

I thought, hush, June. You'll call it down on us. Nathan kept saying he wasn't going to get killed. But June said, "They killed Ellis, and you're no more immune than Ellis was. You, him, and Buster were all in it together, and they won't stop until you are gone, and to them, dead is a good gone, good as any." That's what June said.

Nathan said he didn't think they would hurt Buster. He was a preacher, and they wouldn't bother a preacher. No, he didn't think they would go so far. And June snapped that they weren't talking about Buster. They were talking about him. She told him he didn't have the same kind of immunity. He had to go. Go over to Paradise for a while. Find some work over there. He could come back now and then quietly. Maybe they could meet somewhere else from time to time. And then one day, maybe not too long, this would all die down, and they could be together again. She would keep on teaching, and until he could get a job, we could send him some money. "Please, honey," she begged.

And that was it. She laid her hand on his face and kissed him, and that was it. But we all cried the day he had to leave.

I can tell you more, Mr. Jesse, but that's enough for now. You do with it what you can. Here are those letters that June promised you. You get them back, you hear? They're all she's got left of Nathan.

"Thank you. I promise," Jesse said.

Chapter 16

Nathan Hanks
May 3, 1948
Letter to His Wife, June Hanks

BACK IN HIS OFFICE, Jesse untied the string on the little bundle of letters Bibi had given him and began to read.

May 3, 1948
Dearest June,

I walked from my little house on Tanyard to the market on the corner of Royal Street. There were a few people on the street and in the yards I passed, and I spoke to them, but it only made me feel lonelier than ever. How is it, even in the midst of people, people who will do you no harm, you can feel so lost and alone? I bought a Blue Horse notebook and two No. 2 pencils, and some canned fruit and vegetables, two cans of pork and beans, a can of pears, and three cans of tomato soup. The notebook cost fifteen cents, and the pencils were a nickel each. The food cost a total of fifty cents. I am telling you this trivia so you can see I'm getting along just fine.

Insects buzz in the elm trees along the short block back to the little shotgun house I've rented. It reminds me of our street in Hatchie Landing. The few people I have become acquainted with always wave and speak, but I feel lost on a vast sea. I go around to the back door to go inside my house. You do that when you don't own your place, when it is rented like this one. I think of my family and our home in Hatchie Landing, where we can enter and leave through the front door.

I sawed me a piece of one-by-twelve planking to size to make a small lap desk for myself. I notched a groove to hold my pencils. Mani would like to use it the way he likes to print and draw. I'm sitting here in the late afternoon, with my knees together and my little desk across my lap.

I miss you today. This time in exile away from you is more than I could bear if I couldn't come to you now and then. Those times we've had since I had to leave you are what hold me together.

I need you. I always need you, ever since I first saw you sitting in your momma's porch swing with your feet straight out in front of you, just moving them a tiny bit to keep your swing. When I came up into the yard that day, you looked at me and I thought, she thinks I'm some kind of foreigner come into her yard. I remember I said Hey and you said Hello right back at me, and kept right on looking at me. I thought you were looking into my eyes, and still to this day, I like to think so. You might have been looking at my hat in my hands for all I could tell from that far away, but I felt like you were looking into my eyes, and I wanted you to see through them and down into my heart, which was beginning to melt away. I thought if you could see that far down, maybe you could do something to keep it from melting, save me from something I couldn't save myself from, and you did. You reached right down and picked up my heart when you said, "Come have a seat."

Strange, isn't it, how two people can all of a sudden know they're going to spend the rest of their lives together. I knew from that one minute what I'd be doing for the rest of my life, and I think you did too, only it took you a little while to admit it. Do you remember? I'd come up to your momma's house to tell her I'd be there the next morning to help her put in her garden. I'd promised her the week before, but Pickle, my old mule, threw a shoe and his foreleg was sore, so I had to let him heal a little bit. I shod him again, and his leg seemed all right to me, so I was ready to come on up with the plow. I was coming to tell her I'd be there. I'd seen you so many times before, but I had never felt like I did that day with you on the porch in the swing. I don't know to this day what it was that caused it in me, but it happened. Maybe there is a God after all who does things like that all of a sudden lest we poor human beings not recognize he is giving us a gift. Anyway, it happened and I've been glad ever since. Have you? I hope so, sweet thing. I love you. I'll come to you soon.

Your best friend in the entire world,
Nathan

Jesse leaned back in his chair and recalled the Nathan stories he and his little friend, Campo, used to beg for. They were only children then, playing in the dirt, flitting about the neighborhood like free birds. How could they have known the torture this man was enduring? We only know a few smatterings about the people around us, and even our closest friendships are mysteries. The only person we can really know in life is ourselves. Every house and street harbors its own secrets, even as hopes and dreams lift and swirl like leaves scurried by the wind. Perhaps men create towns to tether themselves on the journeys they make through life, not the geography with its snowfall and juniper, its languid days, but the long walks to now with their deviations and detours, hesitations and stay-overs, the inevitable journeys beginning and vanishing beyond distance, even silence. Perhaps it's more than that. Who can say? But a town like Paradise is conditional, something you can never possess, something you may acquire, but something you must lose like all the moments you witness, moments you can never return to, though shards of them lie buried in the middens of memory, though you sketch and color them in again and again.

Chapter 17

Jesse Wickham and Loyal Hall
April 9, 1975
Paradise, TN

THE NEXT DAY, JESSE CALLED LOYAL HALL. "Loyal, this story is fascinating. Bibi's account is riveting, and she isn't making this up. Someone died out there in 1947, and it had something to do with Nathan Hanks. I aim to find out the connection. Also, Bibi mentions her grandson, Mani, being in jail, and she connects all this together, but she doesn't seem to know how things fit or even if they fit. She just has this sense that they do."

"I think they are connected, and I'll be happy to tell you what I know about the disappearance of Ellis Wiggins back in 1947 and Mani Hanks's trial for killing a man named Bennie Hoskins."

"Hoskins," Jesse flipped through pages of notes. "Bibi mentioned him and a Malcolm Oakes."

"I can tell you what I know. Griffin Wynne is connected to all this, too. He drove to Hatchie Landing one night about that time and picked up a John Doe corpse. He called me for advice."

"I'd like to hear about that. When can you meet me? "

"Come on over to my house and we'll talk."

Jesse pulled up to the curb at Loyal's house on Highland. Loyal opened the door as he came up the steps. "Come in, Jesse, coffee's on the stove." When they were settled at the kitchen table, Loyal began.

You asked about the disappearance of Ellis Wiggins. That was in 1947, mid-June. It was much later, after 1960 when I was retired from the FBI and in private practice here in Paradise, that Mani Hanks went to jail.

I remember well the afternoon the Ellis affair first touched me in 1947. It was mid-June, June 16th to be exact. I was the Federal Bureau of Investigation Special Agent in Charge in those days. I could look out over the courthouse square from my office in the federal building. I could see the courthouse, the New Paradise Hotel, the newspaper office, and the Elks building. That was interesting work, and I was going through a stack of forms on my desk with their neat blocks, tiny typeface instructions. So tedious, but never boring. That afternoon, I was completing a report on my investigation of fifty gallons of gasoline stolen from a federal highway construction site. It wasn't the first theft, and it was a federal project; the FBI had to check it out.

I had driven the thirty miles to Hatchie Landing in the early morning, and as always, it was the people I talked to that made the work so interesting. What stood out to me was the poverty. Times were still not good for folks. The Depression was over, as was the war, but farming the soil just wasn't producing enough income. Winter had been cold, and the spring rainfall was well below normal. Sharecroppers could see they weren't going to get much out of the season's work, and the banks were hedging their bets on loans to the farmers. All of that was adding up to a bad year and more hunger. Folks will do what they must when they get hungry enough. This time, it was stealing gasoline from the government, probably to run a tractor or drive to work, though I thought it could be for purposes less noble.

Jack Schaad, the sheriff of Hatchie County, told me there had been an increase in general theft from grocery stores in the past six months. Mostly staples, he'd said. That part could go in the report.

You couldn't explain the why in those incident reports, but you could paint the picture with facts. Let them tell the story for you. I scribbled out my report in pencil on a legal pad. The pencil scratched across the paper like turning soil in the dry fields of Hatchie County.

I stacked the papers and stuck the reports in the top drawer of the safe beside my desk, shoved the safe drawer shut with a clunk, twirled the knob, and pulled the chain under the green-shaded desk lamp.

It was the same almost every night. I'd lock the door and step across the terrazzo to the elevator. The smell of disinfectant would be in the air, and you could hear the janitors working around the corner in the other wing. The lights on the big electric sign over the *Paradise Sun* offices were framed in the window at the end of the corridor. The sign was shaped like a huge sunrise and must have had two hundred bulbs that went out in unison and slowly lit up from the bottom-most arc of bulbs to the next, one after the other, until the whole sun was aglow, followed by rays angled out until it shone over the town as if to say *we are the light.* Then it would wink out and begin to say it all over again. No matter how many times you say it, though, it doesn't make it true.

"I remember that sign. I worked delivering papers, and later, I worked in the mail room. Did something happen when you left your office that day?"

Yes, I'll get around to it. I'm digressing. Just pull me back when I do.

I liked that old clanky elevator with its bronze doors that opened with a soft bong. I liked that sound, and I always closed my eyes to try and determine the exact instant of descent. Silly, isn't it? Just a little elevator game; like crime, the descent happens with the slightest indication and with no frame of reference. In one instant, you are in one place, and in the next, the doors open onto another world.

I spoke to one or two people and made my way toward my car, which was angle parked along the street in front of the building. Just as I started down the steps, Bob Joyner, the publisher of the *Sun*, came up the sidewalk from the direction of the newspaper and called out, wanting to talk to me.

I knew Bob, but we weren't friends, so I thought it a little odd. I waited. Information and sometimes confession come unexpectedly, almost a gift.

Bob Joyner was tall and big-boned, ruddy and going bald. We shook hands, and he told me he had gotten some disturbing information, something he couldn't evaluate very well. He glanced around as if afraid someone might overhear what he was about to say. He had taken a phone call a few minutes before. He kept repeating that it was very disturbing.

I waited. I may have prompted him, and he said it was from someone over in Hatchie County.

I told him I was in Hatchie County early that morning, and commented on the bad times over there. He allowed as how things weren't so good here in our county either. Soybean crops around here weren't going to be so good. Cotton should be a respectable crop, though, if it didn't decide to rain a monsoon just about picking time. But he said the phone call wasn't about that. He kept glancing over his shoulder like he was afraid someone would hear. Finally, he said a man had called to report a lynching.

I was surprised to say the least. Lynchings didn't occur anymore. Tennessee's anti-lynching law had been in place since before the turn of the century. Though it hadn't prevented them, I knew of no such events documented in recent times. He said the caller's name was Reverend Buster Holt, and Holt said a man who was his friend had been lynched. No one had reported it to the authorities yet.

I asked if the caller said lynching. Was lynching the word he used, or did he say murder? And Bob said he said lynching. That was the word he used.

I asked if he said when this occurred, and Bob said he got the impression it happened within the past few days, maybe over the weekend. It struck him as so out of the ordinary that he failed to ask. Can you imagine? He, a newspaperman, failing to get the facts, the basics, who, what, when, and where? He said he thought it occurred two days before. That would have been Saturday, June 14th.

I asked if this Reverend Holt gave him his number or an address so he could call him back? He had given him a number, but no address. Bob told me that Holt emphasized that he did *not* want any reporters around. Too dangerous. He would come to Paradise. He wasn't specific about when, just that he'd try to get there the next morning.

"Did Joyner keep any notes about the call?" Jesse asked.

He made notes, but he destroyed them afterward. That surprised me. What was I supposed to do after this revelation? A lynching may have occurred, a federal and a state crime, and a phone call directly addressing the fact, but all notes were destroyed? I was miffed. That sun sign on the newspaper building, winking out, and rays ascending wink on, wink on, wink on, wink on, the light of the world right here in Paradise, wink out.

I told him that I had to investigate now that he'd told me, and I'd need that telephone number. He handed me a slip of paper and turned to walk away. He seemed relieved as if he had given the problem to someone else. I asked him, "Will you be reporting it?" He seemed to ponder a moment and said no, he didn't think so. He said there really wasn't anything to report. If the man were to come and talk to him and something more developed, then perhaps. He headed toward the *Sun* without looking back.

———————————————

"Griffin Wynne called me later that night, concerned about a request to pick up a body in Hatchie Landing. I thought, what the heck is going on? I've had three issues in Hatchie Landing in one day. Prior to that, nothing for over a year."

"What did you tell him?"

"I told him to use caution, to make sure everything was in order, you know, paperwork and such."

"Were you concerned, too, at that point?"

"Concerned? No. Puzzled? Yes. After all, Hatchie Landing had already come up twice in one day, and here was a third time. Both of the last two concerned a potential death. I was concerned for Griffin, that's all."

"Did you ultimately investigate?"

"Cursorily. There was no body in connection with Bob's story. None ever turned up. So it was just a rumor at that point. A black man did go missing about that time, but no body ever turned up. Sheriff Schaad over there felt like the man had run away from home. At any rate, nothing ever came of it."

"So, did Griffin Wynne go to Hatchie Landing and pick up the body?"

"Yes. He did. He later told me that it turned out to be routine and his initial concerns were unfounded."

"Can you give me any details about that night? What did Griffin do? Who did he talk to?"

"I've told you all I know. Griffin Wynne could tell you, but he's dead."

Chapter 18

Griffin Wynne
Late Afternoon and Early Evening, Monday, June 16, 1947
Paradise, TN

GRIFFIN WYNNE RECALLED HIS FIRST JOB working on granite stones for grave markers at the Hatchie Stoneworks and later starting his own monument business. He recalled 1940, the Ku Klux Klan and Malcolm Oakes threats. He remembered the day he delivered a headstone to Thornton's Mortuary in Paradise. Ralph Thornton looked it over and told him he was a true artist, and invited him to come inside to watch him prepare a body. It was the beginning of their partnership and his journey from stonecutter to mortician, away from that world and into this world where he tended the grief of others.

He glanced around the room, noting whether a table needed dusting or how the fresh-cut hydrangeas were holding up. He grasped the pleated fold of a drape tenderly and carefully adjusted the fold from top to bottom. He was passionate about details, the details of anything, but in particular, he was passionate about appearances, a combination of natural tendency in himself and his training as a stonecutter.

He sat in one of the Queen Anne chairs in the corner and looked up at the picture of a white Jesus, smiling and beatific, and wondered at the paraphernalia of grief. What was it all for? At death, those still in the midst of the living require it. These things surely provide the handrails and catches to hold to when they come to honor their loved ones and peer beyond themselves into their own unknowable death.

He wondered at his choice of profession and the odd way we arrive at such choices, accidental it seems in hindsight.

A guest book lay open, blank pages like the great book of heaven, ready to receive the names of the holy and the good who come to knock at the gates of paradise. He smoothed the paper with his fingers delicately, a reverent motion, and looked up at the Jesus picture again. The eyes followed him as he moved about the room in the afternoon light. He sat down in the chair again, watching the shaft of light move up the wall toward the picture. The earth moves in the heavens, he thought. The earth moves and we move with it, small creatures in a vastness we don't even understand. The light crept up the wall to the hem of the garments and then on up to the face of Jesus. Wynne whispered, "What should I do?"

But no voice came to answer in the quiet. No kind word, no hand resting gently on the shoulder, no one to absolve. The eyes clouded again, the face went dark.

Vivian was shuffling papers in her corner office when Wynne stopped at the staircase. The second floor was his sanctuary, and under normal circumstances, she never followed him there unless invited. Vivian sensed when he wanted to be alone.

Here was his own small universe, a model train layout still under construction. He had begun building the town upstairs shortly after he took over the funeral home. It was phenomenal in its detail: the tiny wheelbarrow in front of the perfectly to-scale hardware store, the lettering on the miniature mortuary that read Griffin Wynne Funeral Home. The colors, the typeface, everything mirrored the larger world in which he lived as if he could vanish into this miniature universe and become one of the figures—immobile, fixed, and forever.

It reminded him of things he made as a child, such as a birdhouse made out of bark, and another out of dowels that had twelve separate rooms for bird nests, window openings, and a peaked roof painted red. For as long as he could remember, he had enjoyed detail. He was a small child growing up and self-conscious. He had been taunted by the bigger boys in the neighborhood. He remembered showing the birdhouse to a neighbor boy who made fun of it. Later, when he discovered it torn asunder, he confronted the boy, who confessed he had done it for no good reason. Wynne had carried the memory ever since with the question of *why* at its heart.

As he gazed over the layout, he thought back on the time and reason he had come to Paradise, his association with Malcolm Oakes and those other men in Hatchie Landing. He wondered at the weakness that had led him down that path. Was his need for association, to be accepted, that much? Had his childhood brought him to that pitiful point? He sighed and turned to his craft.

In this same way, he insisted on perfection as he prepared the bodies brought into his temporary care, assuming the role of boatman to the passage across whatever river they might have believed separated them from eternity. That he required no such eternity for himself, did not believe such a state exists, did not matter. What mattered was his passion for the details of the imagined journey, which he saw as not unlike his own journey from stonecutter to mortician. He believed these bodies in these final moments represented the impressions of a life for all its goodness and all its failures, and were thus ultimately important and worthy canvases for his art.

He stood looking over the whole panorama of miniature city, river, rail yards, cotton fields, cotton compress, and cotton oil mill. He wanted to duplicate the town completely and perfectly in as much detail as he could achieve. There was the federal building housing the post office and offices of other bureaucracies. His friend Loyal Hall with the FBI had an office there. Across the street was the courthouse square, and around it Woolworth's five-and-dime, the Black and White store, the newspaper, movie theaters, everything in proper place and perspective. Down Chester Street, all the houses he had completed so far were precise and in place.

The Iselin shops of the Gulf, Mobile and Ohio Railroad were there, as was the little company town of Cottonwood with its cotton mills and company houses just south of Paradise. The Forked Deer River ran between them and around the town to the south and off toward the Hatchie River bottom. This was the only compromise he had allowed in the current reality. The present course of the Forked Deer was as straight as an arrow from east to west south of town, redirected by the Army Corps of Engineers and the WPA. Wynne preferred the original wandering course that had meandered its way around the town's southern exposure.

All that was left of the old stream bed were a few oxbow lakes and slow-moving waters melting away in the swampy land. Wynne had found an aerial photograph clearly showing where it had once flowed.

Using a soft camel hair brush, he began dusting off the little house on Chester Street, which would soon be the representation of the house where Emily and Lula Bartlett lived. He thought about the intertwining of relationships as he worked. Wynne's sister, Lula, had married John Bartlett. Loyal Hall's sister, Emily, had married John Bartlett's brother, Art, so Loyal and Wynne became friends through their sisters. They solidified their friendship further after Wynne set up business in Paradise. John Bartlett died in 1929, and later, when Art passed away, Lula went to live with Emily. Now, the four of them had lunch together once each week in the "House on Chester" as they referred to it.

The house was a curiosity. It had a round tower at the front with an onion dome. The onion-domed roof was especially challenging to recreate. He had promised Emily and Lula that he would bring them up here to see their house when it was finished.

Wynne opened a pot of glue and began to attach tiny clapboards onto the house. He had whittled and sanded a perfect picket fence, which was already set in place in the front yard. There was just a little more work to be done on the house, and then he planned to place the roof tiles on the onion-domed tower. Those had been particularly hard to make. He tried out several techniques and discarded each, until one day Lula gave him an old paring knife they were about to discard. It had been sharpened so many times that it was a mere quarter inch of blade width and as thin as a razor. With it, he found he could shave off small shakes from a cedar stick, and the tiny shakes resembled almost exactly the real thing. These he had piled beside the railroad tracks near the shops. They looked like lumber waiting to be hauled off on the next freight out of town.

Wynne was so absorbed in his work that he didn't notice the time. He heard footsteps on the stairs and Vivian calling. "Mr. Wynne, I'm leaving now. It's five thirty."

"Fine, Vivian. Go on along. I'll lock up when I'm finished here. I may go home for supper and then come back for a little while."

"I'll see you tomorrow, then."

"Thank you for all you do, Vivian." He heard the front door close.

He looked over the layout and smiled. It's coming along nicely, he thought. He put on his coat and went down the steps. He turned on the vestibule and front lights as he left.

After supper, he returned. There was no funeral tonight, which gave him a rare opportunity to work uninterrupted on his model. He resumed his work on the House on Chester. He absorbed himself for over two hours. Carefully, he placed the last clapboard under the eave and set it in place, then sat back to look the house over for defects. He bent down and took it in from every angle, looking down, then up, and tilting his head sideways.

"Let all that sit until tomorrow, and then I'll tackle the tower," he said to himself softly.

A light blinked on behind him. He saw its reflection in the window across the room. He had installed the light system so that no matter where he was in the funeral home, there was a silent signal when the phone rang. Vivian could also trigger the lights from her tiny office downstairs. He stood quickly and reached for his suit coat.

At first, he expected Vivian to come up the stairs calling for him, but remembered the time and hurried to answer the phone himself.

"Hello, this is Griffin Wynne Funeral Home, Wynne speaking."

There was a moment's hesitation from the other end, and then a man's voice. "Wynne, this is Thornton's Mortuary in Hatchie Landing. We have a body here and need some help with it." The voice faltered. "Do you think you could take it for us?"

Wynne tensed. "Well, I suppose I could. This is not an emergency, then? Does the body need to be prepared?"

"This isn't an emergency to answer your first question, but there is some urgency. The body will be prepared here," the man said.

"Who is this speaking? Is Ralph Thornton there? May I speak to him?"

Again, there was some hesitation. "Mr. Thornton isn't here at the moment. I'm assisting him. Maybe this is too much trouble for you. I'd better try to find another place. Thank you just the same." The caller hung up.

Wynne replaced the receiver and sat for a moment with his hand resting on the cradle. He replayed the conversation in his mind. A man's voice calling him by his familiar last name, Wynne. Someone who knew him asked him to come to Hatchie Landing to Thornton's Mortuary and pick up a body. He wouldn't give his name and seemed unsettled.

Wynne found the listing for Thornton's Mortuary in his Tennessee Funeral Directors Association directory. He lifted the phone and waited. "Operator, I need to call long distance to Hatchie Landing. The number there is 6412."

The operator thanked him and placed the call. The ringtone rattled on the other end, but no one answered. He thought it must have rung more than ten times. He counted out five more rings and was about to hang up when someone picked up and said, "Yes, uh, Thornton's Mortuary." The voice was flat as though unaccustomed to answering calls.

"Hello, this is Griffin Wynne. With whom am I speaking?" He was formal.

"Wynne, um, Mr. Wynne, this is Malcolm Oakes." Then, almost as an afterthought, he added, "Deputy Sheriff. It's been a while since we met."

He remembered Malcolm Oakes clearly, pictured his face, recalled that other time, and the life he had left behind. It was the same voice he had heard on the first call. He remained formal. "Mr. Oakes, did we speak a moment ago?"

"Um, yes, we did. I called. We could use some help here."

"Well, I didn't mean to brush you off. I just felt I needed some facts and was frankly curious. How many bodies do you have, and what's the problem?"

"Just one, if you could, um, help us with just this one. We have a cooling problem and don't know when it will be repaired. We're trying to place all the"—he hesitated again—"customers, the remains, um, the bodies elsewhere until we can get it fixed."

"I see. There is another funeral home there in Hatchie Landing. Can you not place it temporarily there?"

"I don't know whether it would be right. It's"—a pause—"the colored funeral home." Another pause. "But we did try them. Can't get an answer over there. If it's too much trouble for you, we'll just make other arrangements."

Oakes seemed anxious to get off the line.

"No, if you really need help, I can come," Wynne said. "Especially since the body is already prepared. When will you have it ready for me to bring here?"

He felt himself being drawn back in time, down into things unpleasant, that unsavory business he had been happy to escape. Oakes was one of those hard-to-nail-down characters, always on the fringe of things, always using someone else to front for him. Wynne remembered the other man, Bennie Hoskins, always the sycophant basking in Oakes's light. When Oakes became a deputy sheriff, so did Bennie Hoskins.

"Well, it may be a little while yet. No, let's see, when would you be coming over?"

Wynne could hear someone talking in the background on the other end.

I'd rather not go there at all, he thought. "I suppose I could come now if necessary."

"Good. That'll be fine. We'll be waiting. Thank you very much, Mr. Wynne." Wynne thought he was about to hang up, but Oakes said, "Since you'll be taking the body to Paradise and since it's a John Doe, we'll have a check ready for you when you get here to cover your expenses of burial over there and so forth." Another pause. "So you won't have to come right back over here and all."

"I suppose so, but I'll need to be sure everything is in perfect order. You know, additional records are required when the deceased is unidentified."

Oakes told him everything was already in order and hung up. Wynne replaced the receiver in its cradle. He thought about what he'd agreed to do. He thought about the ramifications of there being some irregularity, some missing paperwork, for example. He wondered why Thornton hadn't been the one to call. He thought about Malcolm Oakes and Bennie Hoskins and others in that amorphous circle. It's all perfectly straightforward on the surface. Beneath it though, everything felt odd.

Chapter 19

Griffin Wynne
Early Evening, Monday, June 16, 1947
Paradise, TN

THROUGH THEIR SISTERS, Loyal Hall and Griffin Wynne had been friends ever since Loyal had moved back to Paradise from Philadelphia, where he was first assigned as one of Hoover's new Special Agents. Loyal had been excited by the idea of a lawyer being in law enforcement, and the federal post provided a sure income during the Depression, so he took the job and gladly moved to Philadelphia. When the opening came in Paradise, he jumped on it and requested the assignment. No one else wanted the backwater post. *Paradise, Tennessee? Where the hell is that?* was the typical response from his colleagues. He got the assignment and was surprised at the variety of work he encountered. There was the usual bit of background investigation of people being offered federal jobs. There was plenty of that as the country geared up for a war in Europe, and even now after the war. Also, there were cases involving theft of federal property, but none of the gangster crime Hoover had parlayed into fame for himself and the bureau. That sort of thing didn't touch Paradise.

Loyal's phone rang. "Loyal Hall speaking,"

"Loyal, Wynne here. I'm sorry to bother you this late."

"Griffin, you know it's never a bother, but with an entrée like that, I'm suspicious already." He chuckled. "What can I do for you?"

"I need a little sounding board and to alert someone before I do what I'm about to do."

Loyal sensed the unusual tenseness in Wynne's voice. "Whatever it is, I'm all ears, my friend. You're not about to do something drastic like retire to Florida, are you? If that's what you're thinking, then you need to come over here right now. We'll have a nice single malt out on the porch where we can listen to the summer night, and I'll talk you out of it." He chuckled again.

"No, nothing like that. I'm about to run over to Hatchie Landing. I've had a phone call requesting me to pick up a body, and there are some oddities about the whole thing."

Loyal waited for Wynne to elaborate. "I'd just like to review it with someone who can be objective," Wynne continued. "There's nothing illegal or even irregular about it, nothing unethical as far as I can see. It just seems to have some odd aspects to it."

"You've got my attention."

"Here's what I know and what I've agreed to do." He recounted the two phone calls, and there was a moment's silence as Loyal considered the possible connection of this call to the earlier conversation with Bob Joyner.

"Griffin, is there documentation to support this John Doe?"

"I don't know yet, Loyal. They claim everything is in order, but I'll have to wait until I get there."

"Well, be careful. Be skeptical is the way I'd approach it. Assume everything is not in order and insist it be in order before you even touch a casket. Ask to see the body. Paperwork is one thing. An actual body is another. I'll call Jack Schaad over in Hatchie and ask him a question or two if you want me to. The bureau works closely with county sheriffs anyway, so it won't be an issue."

"Oh yes, I know Schaad. Could you do that before I go over there? I'm supposed to be on my way right now."

"I'll place a call as soon as we hang up. I'll call you back in a few minutes. They have no choice but to wait for you."

"Thanks, I'll feel better about it." They hung up. He felt disquieted by what was happening. He had left Hatchie Landing to escape the circle of men Malcolm Oakes represented. He didn't like touching it again and hated involving his best friend.

He gathered up a black briefcase containing pens, paper, and legal forms to be completed. As with the model train and the bodies he took under his care, Wynne was particular about the formal details.

He answered the phone on the first ring.

"I called the Hatchie sheriff's office," Loyal said. "I implied I was following up on an anonymous tip about the theft of federal property. I was actually over there earlier this morning investigating the theft of gasoline from some highway construction equipment. Sheriff Schaad had no new information for me, but sometimes surprise is a good tactic, Griffin, so I came right out and told him about my investigation, hinting my informant had said there might be a John Doe body over in Hatchie Landing.

"He confirmed there is one at the Thornton Mortuary. He sounded surprised I would know about it, and said he had a deputy over there now. He told me there seemed to be some problem with the funeral home, but he didn't know what it was. He said his deputy had just called him about it a few minutes before."

"I see," Wynne said.

"Griffin, I know this man somewhat. I've worked with him on three or four occasions. I don't trust him to tell the whole truth. He won't outright lie to me, but he's one of those people who will tell you certain facts and leave out others. From what you tell me and his response, I'd say there is definitely a body there, but it may or may not be a John Doe. I'd be surprised if they manufactured the John Doe status, however. If they did, it would mean there is something terribly wrong in Hatchie County. If they are involved and ever found out, it will be the end for them. He'd most likely be ushered out of office and maybe go to jail. Nevertheless, you can't assume anything. Go ahead, my friend, but use care and record everything. Do nothing out of order. If they can't produce every single piece of paper you need, turn around and come home without the body. Let me know what you see and hear while there."

Loyal paused a moment and then said, "Griffin, you are my friend, so I'm going to mention something I normally would not. I received some information today that something unfortunate may have taken place over there. That's all I can say. If it's true, then it's possible that your John Doe could be connected. Just use caution and good judgment, my friend. Let me know what you find out and what you do."

"Okay, Loyal. Thanks. You're a good friend. We'll talk tomorrow."

Wynne picked up his briefcase and slipped a white smock off the hall tree beside the back door. He drove the hearse down the driveway to Chester Street, looked both ways, turned right, and drove west into the night.

Chapter 20

Griffin Wynne
Late Night, Monday, June 16, 1947

THE SHINY BLACK HEARSE bore through the night, down into the history Griffin Wynne had left in Hatchie Landing over six years before. Wynne thought about how a small town tethers its denizens to itself, even though they make their own choices. He knew he had let himself be drawn into a clique of men who were threatened by anyone not like themselves— men who were threatened by the changing times, and the attempts to build bridges over the slow waters separating black from white. He recalled his decision to leave Hatchie Landing and the moment Norman Parker gave him a way forward.

He remembered Malcolm Oakes suddenly appearing, telling him to come to another meeting; his angry response to Oakes that he was through with that business and leaving Hatchie Landing for good, that he hadn't done anything. His own guilt came flooding back as he remembered his own words and Oakes's chilling reply, "Well, that's more to the point, isn't it, Wynne. You didn't do anything at all, did you? Just like all the rest, nothing at all. You just let it happen. Leave if you want to, Wynne, but don't think you'll ever be out of it. You might as well have helped Bennie pull on the rope."

Wynne turned on the radio to relieve the tension. Swing music floated in the air. He talked to himself.

"After all, I broke with them. I even left Hatchie Landing and reestablished myself. I can come back here and touch them without catching the disease again."

The headlights punctured the darkness as he drove on until he could see the lights of the little town of Hatchie Landing looming out of the night.

He turned off the square and drove two blocks to Thornton Mortuary. There were no lights in the front of the low building, but one shone over the back apron, so he drove the hearse around and parked underneath. No one was about, but lights were on in the rear rooms. He thought he saw someone's shadow move across one of the curtained windows.

As he leaned into the front seat to retrieve his briefcase, he heard the rear door open and saw Malcolm Oakes walking toward him with his hand extended. He was a little heavier than when he had last seen him.

"Hello, Griffin," he said.

Wynne automatically took the hand. "Hello, Malcolm. It's been a long time."

"Thanks for coming all the way over here to help us out."

"Where is Ralph Thornton? I want to talk to him."

"He had to leave."

Wynne considered pushing for an explanation, but instead asked, "Where is the body?"

"Inside. Come on in, and I'll help you move it out here."

Wynne could hear others talking somewhere in the building and someone laughing, but no one came to the room where they stood. A gurney supported a casket in the middle of the room.

"Let's see the paperwork first, if you don't mind."

"Right here." Malcolm handed him an envelope.

Wynne opened it and examined the contents. "It looks in order. Any idea who this might be?"

"No. No one seems to know him. He showed up around town a few weeks ago and lived in a hobo camp down by the river. People saw him from time to time, but no one knows who he is. He never gave any trouble until now."

"Until now," repeated Wynne. "What kind of trouble did he cause just now?"

"Griffin, I don't know anything to tell you except what's in those papers. So let's just get him out of here and into your hearse out there. Don't ask so many questions. Come on, I'll help you."

"I do need to see the body first, Malcolm." He walked over to the casket.

"What for?" Malcolm moved toward the casket with him.

"Protocol, Malcolm. *My* protocol, if you don't mind. I won't move this casket until I see what's inside. Now open it for me, please."

"You're a little bossy, Griffin. I don't think you have any right to be that way here."

"No, I don't have any right whatsoever, but I do have the right to walk out that door without this casket, and it's what I'm beginning to think I should do."

"Griffin, don't get upset. You used to be one of us."

"One of us, Malcolm? What does that mean?"

"Just one of our town. That's all I was saying. You came all the way over here, and there's no need to get all uppity."

"Do you want to open the casket or shall I?"

"Go ahead and open it."

Wynne raised the lid and saw a filthy body in ragged clothes. The clothing was damp and smelled of vegetation. "My God, Malcolm. What is this? Where is Thornton? Why hasn't this body been properly prepared?"

"I told you Thornton had to leave. The cooling system is broken. He did all he could. Now let's get this thing out of here."

Wynne stood, gazing at the ragged remains. The body hadn't been embalmed. He closed the lid. He looked at Oakes, and Oakes glowered back at him. "This isn't a thing, Malcolm. This used to be a human being, a person. This is not like Thornton. What if I decide to leave without this body?"

"Don't do that to us, Griffin."

"Jesus Christ. What have you done, Malcolm?"

"I haven't done anything, so let's get this thing out of here."

"No, I don't think so. This all looks and sounds too unusual for my taste, Malcolm. I think I'll just go back to Paradise. Sorry." He turned toward the door and grabbed his briefcase.

"Griffin, you were with us once. You took an oath. You've got to help us now. You can't just leave us like that."

"Oaths are made to be broken. Sometimes for good reason."

"You don't have a reason. If you don't help us out, there'll be consequences."

"It's your problem, Malcolm, not mine."

"No, you're wrong there. You were with us. If something happens now, you get pulled in, too. I'll see to it. You took an oath once. Plenty of people know about it. You went with us before on nights just like this one."

Wynne's shoulders sagged as he looked at Oakes. "You're dirt, Malcolm. Pure dirt. I'll take care of this. You get out of my sight."

"I'll help you roll it outside."

"No. I'll do it myself. You get out of my sight. If I ever see you again, it will be the last time. Now hand me those papers."

He took the envelope, opened it, and shuffled the pages. "Sign this. Here and here."

Oakes glared as he signed and shoved the papers back to Wynne. Wynne put them in his briefcase, placed it on top of the casket, and rolled the gurney to the hearse. After the casket was latched down inside, he shoved the gurney toward the building. It crashed into the back door, and he immediately regretted doing it.

He settled into the driver's seat and began talking to himself again. "Poor Thornton is in the same fix I'm in. Life's a huge regret." He put the hearse in gear and drove his burden toward Paradise.

Chapter 21

Rev. Joe Galt, Nathan Hanks and Rev. Buster Holt
Tuesday Morning, June 17, 1947
Paradise, TN

THE NEXT MORNING, Joe Galt turned into the narrow drive beside the Paradise A.M.E. Zion Church, where he was pastor. Sections of stucco had peeled away from the small sanctuary and were painted white to keep it from looking too unsightly. It gave a patchwork appearance that Joe felt was unseemly. He wished they had enough money to redo the stucco properly.

On the other side of the drive were hedges. He eased his car, careful not to scrape against the church or damage the hedge. Wilma Lane, from her porch, saw across the hedges everything that passed into and out of the church. Joe cautiously maneuvered his old black Ford to the rear, switched off the engine, and got out. He stood up slowly and stretched. Sweet Lord, he felt old.

He saw Mrs. Lane watching from her window and waved, climbed the back steps, and stepped into the coolness of the kitchen. Small but adequate, it held the smells of years of coffee and meals prepared for all sorts of occasions—births, deaths, baptisms. No matter what the occasion, you can depend on the women to come and do the thing they do better than anyone. It was demonstration he was thinking about, not cooking. They can put more *how* into a moment than any man can ever hope. A little food put out on a table and some quiet talk will show how life goes on.

The kitchen opened into the front of the sanctuary off to the side of the pulpit and choir loft. The windows along each side were frosted and painted with New Testament scenes. There was a huge wooden cross painted gold hanging on the wall behind the pulpit. Joe walked to the back. He turned to look up the aisle at the pulpit and the cross behind it.

He sat in a pew and closed his eyes. The word was out already about the events in Hatchie Landing. Nathan Hanks had called early that morning to tell him Ellis was missing. "We think he's dead, a lynching. It's bad over here, Joe."

"Is there any proof?"

"No, not yet. We don't even have Ellis's body, but he's been gone for two nights now." Nathan had paused. "And, Joe, my boy, and I saw something awful. Bibi saw it too. Mani's scared to death, and I'm concerned. I think we may have seen what happened to Ellis. I don't know what to do."

"Just be normal for now, Nathan. Don't run. Don't go out of your way to ask questions. Don't do anything yet. Does Buster know?"

"Yes, he knows. Maybe you ought to call him."

"You need to talk to him. He's your pastor after all. I'll call him too. Tell me more."

Nathan had recounted what he knew, including the scene he, Bibi, and Mani had witnessed in the swamp.

"Was this because of the voter registration? Was it because of what I did?"

"You didn't do anything, Joe. Don't feel bad about it. It's still the right thing to do. We tried. You, me, Buster, and Ellis. All the others, we all went over and fought in the war, and they still won't let us be citizens. We shouldn't be ashamed, and we shouldn't have to be afraid, and we shouldn't give up."

"True, but be careful for now."

As Joe replayed the conversation, wondering what he should do, he looked around the little sanctuary. The decorations in the room were sparse and simple, things arranged with an air of immediacy, the platform low, only a step above the pews, the pulpit itself without decoration. The cross with its gold paint was the only ornamented object.

"Funny how we use symbols," he said out loud to himself.

"Yes indeed," replied another voice. Joe turned to see Buster Holt standing in the vestibule doors. "I was about to call you," Joe said. "I'm glad you came. I heard from Nathan this morning. We talked about you."

"Then you know about the trouble over in Hatchie Landing. I'm dealing with it. I spent the morning working on it. Phone calls from people. Bad stuff over there, and I don't know whether I'm up to it. So, I left for a while. Got out."

"Arlene Wiggins's cousin is in my congregation," Joe said. "She heard from Arlene last night and called me with the news. Then Nathan called this morning and told me all he knew. It sounds bad, Buster."

"Well, folks are afraid, sort of unhinged. They want their pastor around. But how do you tell them God is in this somewhere when they've lost a good man, a husband and father, to a killing?"

"Tell me what all you know, so maybe I can help too."

Buster sat down in the pew beside Joe and told him what he knew, including what Nathan told him about seeing the burning.

"Nathan told me about the burning. Awful, awful."

"Folks are doing their best to keep that part secret in case somebody comes asking. That's making it harder on Arlene, and it isn't helping Ellis if he's still alive."

They talked on for an hour before Buster said he needed to leave.

Joe saw his old friend to his car. They spoke for a few minutes, then Buster turned the key and stepped on the starter. He put both hands on the steering wheel and gave out a long, slow sigh. He sat that way for a second before pulling away and heading toward

Institute Street. He waved once in the rear window without looking back.

Joe turned back toward the church. Mrs. Lane was watching from her front porch. He put his head down as if in deep thought. He didn't want to banter with her now, but she caught him anyway.

"You want some iced tea, Joe Galt?" She always called him by his two names.

"No, thank you, Sister. I've got some business to take care of. I can't stay."

"You going to be in your study? I'll bring it over to you in a minute."

He wanted to be alone to absorb and process Buster's tale, but he couldn't see a way around Mrs. Lane's offer. He recognized she was fishing to find out what was going on, so he said directly, "I need to be alone for a while, Sister. Trying to work something out in my head, but I would enjoy a glass of tea. I'll come sit with you on the porch for a few minutes."

She seemed delighted at winning. "I'll go bring out the glasses."

They sat in rocking chairs. Joe sipped the tea. It was sweet and cold with a crushed mint leaf floating among the ice cubes.

"That your friend Buster Holt over there with you?" she asked.

"Yes, Buster came over from Hatchie Landing to see me."

"He looked awfully serious for a friendly visit."

Joe thought, Sister, you can cut to the chase. He smiled at her. "Sister Lane, I'll level with you. He was serious about something, and I don't want to talk about it."

"I knew it. He was here about that business over in Hatchie County."

Christ almighty, how word travels. "What business?"

"Don't know about it, actually, but something's going on over there. We all hear things, you know, even though this town's newspaper won't print anything at all about it. Silent as dark, it is, in spite of that big sun."

"Well, there are some things that don't need stirring up."

"Some things get stirred up anyway, Joe Galt, no matter what anybody does or doesn't do, you ask me. You don't pay attention, and something happens anyway."

They sat without speaking for a couple of minutes, then she added, "Like boiling purple hull peas. You set the stove on simmer and walk off, and the lid pretty soon be jiggling away up there, and them peas pretty soon be spilling out all over your clean stove."

Joe finished his tea and stood. "Sister, I need to go."

"I'm right, Joe Galt. I am right and you know it."

"Yes, Sister, you are right. Too much right this time."

Mrs. Lane kept right on rocking as Joe walked across her front yard and up the steps into the church.

Chapter 22

Rev. Buster Holt and Griffin Wynne
Late Morning, Tuesday, June 17, 1947
Paradise, TN

AFTER LEAVING JOE, Buster stopped at the intersection at Chester to wait for a mule-drawn wagon with rubber tires to pass. Such sights wouldn't be around much longer. Times were changing in some ways, but not in others.

He glanced over at the Griffin Wynne Funeral Home and pulled across the intersection, making a sharp U-turn into the curb. He climbed the steps and knocked on the front door. A neatly dressed gentleman with a kindly face opened the door.

"Good morning," the man said. "May I help you?"

Buster removed his hat. "I'd like to speak to Mr. Wynne. Is he in?"

"I'm Griffin Wynne. Come inside." He gestured toward an open door to a small office. "Let's go in here. How can I help you?"

Buster hesitated, then stepped inside. The room was cool compared to the early summer heat outside.

"Please, have a seat." Wynne indicated the sofa against the wall and pulled a chair closer to the sofa.

Buster settled onto the couch. He put his hands on his knees and looked down at them for a long moment. When he finally raised his head, he looked directly at Mr. Wynne.

"I need some information if you can give it," he said, suddenly realizing he had launched directly into his mission without even introducing himself. "I'm sorry. My name is Lincoln Holt, Reverend Lincoln Holt. I'm from Hatchie Landing. Most people call me Buster. It'll be fine with me if you call me that."

"I'll try," Wynne smiled and reached out his hand.

"I don't know quite where to begin, Mr. Wynne."

"Reverend Holt, I'd prefer you drop the Mister. You can call me Griffin, but most people just call me by my last name, Wynne."

"I'll try to make myself comfortable with that, but under the circumstances, you see, I have some trouble with it.

"I hadn't planned on coming here until just now, as I was driving by, I saw your sign and realized this is the place."

"And what place is that?"

"Yesterday, last night actually, there was a phone call made by someone who may have been from the Hatchie sheriff's office to here."

"I see. And how do you know about this?" Wynne sat back in his chair and folded his arms across his chest.

"Well, a terrible thing has happened in Hatchie Landing. A man is missing, been murdered, to be truthful about it. A lynching is what it was."

Buster didn't want to reveal there were witnesses, much less that one of them was a young boy. "I know about this because when the man's wife realized something must have happened to him, she called me. I called the hospital in Hatchie, but they knew of no killing and no one had been admitted with injuries. I called the sheriff's office in Hatchie, but they knew nothing of the sort. The man I talked to was a man named Bennie Hoskins. He's a deputy. I've run into him before—had an altercation, is a better way to put it. When I told him what I was calling about, he hesitated and asked me the name. I told him Ellis Wiggins. There was a long silence, and then he said no, they had no report of any accident involving that name. I told him it would not have been an accident.

"After I hung up, I called the two mortuaries in town. Parchman's is for the black people, and Thornton's is for the whites. There wasn't a body at Parchman's, but Mr. Ralph Thornton told me right out that a body was sent over his funeral home last night."

Buster paused, keeping his eyes on Wynne. "Mr. Wynne, that deputy as much as told me by the hesitations in his voice, and the way he answered my questions, that I'm right about what has happened. Mr. Thornton simply confirmed the lie."

"What did Bennie Hoskins say?"

"He told me there's been no report of a murder in this county in a long time. There's been no accident involving an injury reported today, last night, or the day before, but if he's missing, there must be a good reason for it. People who mind their own business don't go missing."

"Well, it's not exactly an admission, but he obviously has an opinion about it from his last remark."

"Mr. Wynne, there may be some big trouble ahead, and I'm in the midst of it like it or not. I think you may be thrust into it also. We are, you might say, compatriots in a game, but not one of our choosing."

"Tell me everything you know and I'll do likewise, Reverend. Lincoln. Sorry, Buster. Let's start there and see where we go and what we must do."

Buster sensed that here was a man without guile and proceeded to tell him all he knew. He explained the voter registration attempts in Hatchie Landing and the resistance to them. He said there were certain people in the sheriff's office in Hatchie who may be active participants in the resistance. He recounted the Saturday attempt by himself, Nathan, and Ellis to register and the registrar, Mr. Henderson's reaction, the attack by Deputy Hoskins and Deputy Oakes. Finally, he talked about the burning of the cross.

Griffin Wynne had been sitting forw ard in his chair with his elbows on his knees and his fingers knit together. When Buster had finished, he sat back.

"I see," Wynne said. He got up and walked behind his desk, and stood with his fingertips on the desktop.

"Reverend,"—he paused—"I'm sorry, but I'm more comfortable calling you Reverend."

"Whichever," replied Buster.

"Reverend, last night about nine o'clock, I received a phone call. It was a man, said he was calling from the Thornton's Mortuary in Hatchie Landing. But he was not the man who owns the funeral home. I know Ralph Thornton. This man didn't give his name at first nor say by what authority he called. When I insisted, he identified himself as a deputy with the sheriff's office. He asked me if I could handle a body, and of course, I said yes. It is my profession after all, and there is nothing remarkable in such a request in and of itself.

"I asked him where the body was and if the coroner had been called. He told me the coroner had pronounced the body earlier in the evening, and the caller wanted to know if I could handle it. I thought that last was a bit strange, and I asked him why.

"He must've realized it was unusual, because he then said, 'Well, maybe you could come and pick him up for us.'"

"Him? Us? Did he say those words, him and us?" asked Buster.

"Yes, he said him, and he said us. When I arrived to pick up the body later last night, a man came out to meet me. There may have been two or maybe three others there. I didn't see them."

"Go on," Buster urged.

"I asked him for the papers and who the dead person was, and he told me the body was a John Doe, unknown to anyone. That corresponded to the information on the papers."

"Did he give you any indication how the man died?" asked Buster.

"No, and I didn't ask. That's the coroner's responsibility, so normally I don't need to inquire at that juncture. Usually, I'm dealing with grief at that point, though I'll admit, there was no grief expressed last evening."

"You say this was at the Thornton Mortuary?"

"Yes, at Thornton's Mortuary around midnight. As I said, the call came around nine, and the caller seemed anxious and hoped I could come immediately. I asked why it couldn't wait until morning, and he told me the funeral home had a coolant problem and needed to move the body.

"It only takes forty minutes to drive to Hatchie Landing, so I relented and drove the hearse over. I know where the funeral home is."

"And you got there about midnight?" Buster asked.

"I got there about eleven thirty, and the lights were on. I drove to the rear, and someone came out to meet me."

"Do you know who?"

Wynne looked away.

Buster leaned forward. "Mr. Wynne, do you know or won't you say?

"Was there anyone there you recognized?" Buster prompted.

"Reverend, I'm sorry. I want to help you, and I promise I will, so please don't assume I'm withholding from you. A sheriff's deputy was there, and he was the man who came out to meet me, but I saw no one else last night. I'll tell you, it's my impression, my sense, there were others there. But no one else in sight or whose voice I recognized other than this sheriff's deputy."

"I apologize. I believe you, sir."

"Thank you, Reverend. I need you to believe me. I'm disturbed by what happened last night, especially now you've come to me. I'm disturbed to the extent that last night I called a friend of mine who's in law enforcement. Someone you probably don't know."

"Tell me if you don't mind."

"A man by the name of Hall, Loyal Hall. He's a good friend and happens to be the Special Agent in Charge of the Paradise office of the FBI."

"Is he interested in all this?"

"Yes, I'd say very interested. But as far as I know, I'm the only person to contact him about it."

"Will he investigate?"

"Maybe. I don't know. It would have to be something within his jurisdiction. I'm not familiar with their protocols. Besides, is there anything really to investigate with regard to last night?"

"But a man died under suspicious circumstances."

"A man died, yes, but were the circumstances suspicious? Is the body I picked up last night connected to the person you refer to? It isn't the same person because it is the body of a white man. So if not, then what's to investigate? All you have is a missing person and an allegation of murder."

Buster didn't reply right away. "Would you ask him to check with the coroner to try to find out how the man died? I'd appreciate knowing."

"I already know what the coroner's report says. I called this morning. I have to record these things, even though the death did not occur in this county."

"What did it say?" Buster leaned forward again.

"Unknown causes. Possible drowning."

"Then there were no signs of injury?"

"I didn't make a close examination. It wasn't my purpose at the time. They told me the body was already prepared, but it wasn't. I'll do that shortly. I'll look closely then."

Wynne shrugged his shoulders, and the two men were quiet. Then Buster stood, stuffed his hands in his pockets, and stared at the big oil painting of Jesus hanging on Wynne's office wall. He shook his head.

"Thank you for telling me all this." Buster reached for his hat.

"You're welcome. I'd like to know what's happening, and I'll help if I can," Wynne reassured.

"I'll tell you if I can, but I'm afraid there may not be a damn thing anybody can do."

Wynne walked Buster to the door and shook his hand.

"You haven't told me how you think this man died," Wynne said.

"I know this: my friend's body won't be found."

"How do you know?"

"I can tell you that, but I won't, sir."

"Very well, I understand. Who was he?"

"A close friend and member of my congregation. His name is Ellis, Ellis Wiggins. We flew together in Italy during the war. He has a son, a daughter, and a wife. He tried to do what he thought was right, and it cost him his life." For an instant, Buster let his grief spill over.

"What did he do?"

"He believed in something because somebody he admired made a speech. A man by the name of James Weldon Johnson."

"Oh, yes, 'blacker than a hundred midnights in a cypress swamp,'" Wynne quoted.

"Yes, there's that and more. It seems Ellis either heard or read a speech by Mr. Johnson in which he addressed the disfranchisement of Negro citizens. Ellis and I have a mutual friend here in Paradise, Reverend Joe Galt, who came to Hatchie Landing and preached a sermon on this same topic. My friend believed those words and took it upon himself to do something about it. He tried to get Negroes to go to the courthouse and register to vote. I went with him on more than one occasion. So did another friend."

"And this is what did him in?" Wynne asked.

"I'm afraid it did, although I don't have any proof. It's my belief it did, yes indeed."

"Even though it can't be your friend, would you like to view the body? It's here. I'm waiting for the funeral home in Hatchie to call and tell me what to do next. Since this is a John Doe and the cause of death is unknown, I'm required to wait until the sheriff in Hatchie County tells me it's all right to proceed with the burial. I assume there's an investigation underway."

"I think maybe I would like to see the body," Buster replied.

Wynne escorted him down the hallway to the preparation room. The room was cold. Off to the side, there was a wheeled table with a casket on it.

"This is it." Wynne opened the lid. Inside was the body of a white male. He was dressed in soiled and ragged clothes, a derelict for sure: hair matted, face unshaven, fingers dirty, and mud on his face.

Buster looked away. Wynne closed the lid.

At the door, they shook hands again.

"Thank you, sir, for listening."

"Not at all. Not at all. The man back there obviously isn't your friend."

Looking at Wynne with great pain in his eyes, Buster said, "Mr. Wynne, I didn't expect to see my friend in there. There isn't going to be a body to lay to rest for him and his family. The man I knew was burned. He is gone up in smoke, perhaps the possibility of charred bones, but there won't ever be a body. That's all I'll say."

Wynne watched Buster pull away from the curb and saw him look back once and lift his hand. It was more like a salute than a wave. Wynne closed the door and headed back toward the preparation room. Vivian looked up from her work, but didn't speak.

Wynne opened the casket and looked at the body. Disgraceful, he thought. Once he had the man on the embalming table, he went to close the casket and noticed two smudges along the satin bed cover, and the fabric pulled loose from the sides. Underneath was a burlap bag.

He lifted the bag onto a gurney, untied the string, and looked inside. He folded the burlap down and rolled the table under the brighter lights in the center of the room. In the bag were only ashes and bits of bone. "My God," Wynne whispered in the empty room.

He closed his eyes and moaned. "Oh, God, what now? What now? What have those men done?" He sat that way for a long time until Vivian knocked at the door.

"Mr. Wynne, I'm out to lunch now. I'll be back in an hour."

"Go ahead, Vivian. I'll handle things. Lock the front door, will you? I'm not expecting anyone else for a while. Put the sign out."

"All right, Mr. Wynne."

"Thanks." He heard her heels click down the hall and the front door open and close. He listened for the lock. Wynne went over to the poor man on the table. With tablet in hand, he inventoried the man's clothes, his only belongings. Then he removed the clothes. They were filthy and ragged. He checked the pockets and found only an ancient pocketknife. There was no identification. He placed the clothes in a bag and dropped them in the trash can. He placed the knife in another bag and marked it.

He couldn't tell how long the man had been dead. The papers given him at Thornton's said the man died of natural causes the day before yesterday. In light of what he had discovered and Buster's comments, he wondered if that was correct. He looked over the body carefully. There were no marks of violence. Bastards!

Tenderly, he began to bathe the body. He lifted each arm and leg, bathing the hands and the feet. He held each hand gently in his palm. He bathed the man's face and shaved him, then washed his hair, toweled it dry, and combed it. He noticed bruises on the man's neck. So this is how he died, Wynne thought, another death to cover the first. Would there then be another and another?

When it was all finished and he had properly dressed the man, he sat again in the corner chair and closed his eyes. He thought about the men he had known and what they must now have done. He remembered 1940 and how he had given in and joined them the one night they called for him to go. Teach a lesson, they had told him. Stand together. He had known he wanted to be free from them, and only that once did he participate. Coming to Paradise was his escape, and now he was pulled in again.

He mounted the stairs leading to the second floor and the model train layout. He gazed at the town before him, the replicas of Loyal Hall's house on Highland, the house on Chester where his sister lived with her sister-in-law, the courthouse, and the federal building. Where to turn? What to do? He sat there until he heard Vivian unlock the front door. He listened to her movements as she opened the door, removed the 'Out to Lunch' sign, and went to her office. He heard her chair scrape and thought of telling her, but decided against it and went down the stairway.

In the embalming room, he took a canister from a shelf and gathered as much of the contents as possible from the burlap bag and retied the nape. He put the canister on the shelf and carefully stowed the empty bag beneath the satin cushion in the casket. He gently lifted the derelict body and arranged it on the satin. He touched the man's cheek and brushed a lock of hair from the man's forehead. Standing beside the casket, hands resting on the side, his eyes closed as if in prayer, and then he closed the lid.

That evening, he walked the short block down to the House on Chester, where he and Loyal met their sisters for dinner. They passed a pleasant evening. Afterward, when they were leaving, Loyal asked about the trip to Hatchie. "What happened?"

"It turned out to be routine," answered Wynne. "There was a body, a John Doe, a derelict. No identification. We'll bury him tomorrow morning at Riverside Cemetery in the Potter's Field corner.

PART II

1948

"I know how men in exile feed on dreams of hope."

— *Aeschylus*

Chapter 23

Jesse Wickham, Campo, and Nathan Hanks
May 3, 1948
Paradise, TN

JESSE AND HIS FRIEND CAMPO were playing in Jesse's backyard when the two ten-year-old boys saw Nathan for the first time ever as he came walking up the street with a mattock and hoe on his shoulder.

He was a tall man, and his dark skin glowed in the sunlight. He turned at the house next door and went around to the back and stood at the kitchen door. Mrs. Kelly came out and told him where she wanted him to dig her garden and what she wanted planted in it. Jesse looked at Nathan's tools and thought it was going to be hard for him to do all that with just those two tools. Nathan asked her if she had a shovel, and she said she did, but it was in the shed with Mr. Kelly's tools, and she didn't think she could let him in there to get it without Mr. Kelly at home. Nathan said he could manage all right without it. He spoke with a deep voice that was smooth and formed his words artfully.

Campo and Jesse played for a while, then got a drink from the garden hose out back. Nathan was digging next to Mrs. Kelly's fenced-in chicken yard. He wielded the mattock without stopping until long after noontime and had a big plot dug up in rough clumps, then he began chopping those with his hoe, never hurrying. He chopped the clods until they were little bits and moved on to the next one.

Campo was always into something or other, and he wanted to go watch, but Jesse was afraid he'd do something that would get them into trouble. Jesse asked Nathan his name.

"Nathan," he said without stopping.

"Mine's Jesse, and this here is Campo."

"Pleased to meet you, Mr. Jesse and Mr. Campo." He kept right on chopping the clods. Jesse watched his muscles bulge and slide underneath his skin, skin as black as midnight shining slick in the sunlight. He wanted to sweat and have muscles like that, all ropey and bulged. He thought Nathan must be thirsty from all his chopping for so long without a single break, and said so.

"Well, I'm a little dry, but I'll be finished before too long, and then I can get me a drink."

"You want me to get you one?" Campo asked.

"No, you don't have to, Mr. Campo. I'm all right, but in a little while I'll stop and get me one."

About then, Mrs. Kelly came out the door and yelled at them to leave him alone and let him get his work done. "He needs to finish that plot before Mr. Kelly comes home," she said.

"He's thirsty!" yelled Campo.

"Well, come up here and get him some water out of the hose. I'll give you a jar. Then you two leave him alone to work."

Campo hurried off and came back with a fruit jar of cold water from the hose. Nathan took the jar and gulped it all down in three or four big swallows. Everything about him was huge, it seemed to the boys.

"You two boys are mighty kind angels," he said after he'd drunk the water. "I'll tell you a story sometime when I'm not too busy."

"How about when you get done here?" Jesse asked.

"Maybe so and maybe not. Depends on how soon I get finished. Now you two had better run along and let me finish before Mrs. Kelly gets mad at all of us. Go on now. Shoo!" They ran off to play Cowboys and Indians around the house, but late in the afternoon, after Campo had gone off home, Jesse watched Nathan smooth out the dirt in the plot he'd made. The dirt was as fine as if he had sifted it, and the plot was perfect, about twenty feet long and ten feet wide. Nathan grinned a huge smile. "You like what I've done for Mrs. Kelly?"

"That's some garden you made, Nathan. She'll be proud of it. I'll bet my momma is gonna want one just like it when she sees this one."

"Well, I can make her one if she wants it." He lifted up his two tools and started for Mrs. Kelly's doorway. She met him there.

"Lord, Nathan, it's the prettiest garden plot I believe I've ever seen. It's a work of art. I'm sorry you had to work so hard on it."

"Next year it won't be so hard. We've already got it broken up now. Do you want me to plant it for you?"

"No, I don't think so. I can do it with Mr. Kelly's help, but thank you anyway." She reached into her apron and took out four one-dollar bills. She handed them to Nathan. He thanked her and put them into his pocket.

Jesse followed him to the street. "Four dollars doesn't seem like much for a whole day's work."

"Oh, it'll get me by. And I didn't work all day, just about six hours, so it's not bad pay for me. You want me to tell you a story now?"

"I can't pay you anything for it."

"Child stories are free. You don't pay for them. They're part of God's world. They're what people and animals are all about. They belong to them, so they don't cost anything. He smiled with a huge toothy grin and rumbled out a laugh like thunder.

They walked over to the chinaberry tree in Mrs. Kelly's front yard. Nathan squatted on the ground, and Jesse climbed into Mrs. Kelly's yard swing. "Tell me one, then." And Nathan began a delicious story about the animals in the jungle all getting together to learn each other's languages.

His voice went soft, its depth capturing and pulling Jesse into him.

"This story goes like this," he said. "Each animal claimed his language was the best one. The lion roared and said they should all learn to talk like him; the baboon whooped and hollered and said they should all learn to talk like him; the elephant trumpeted through his long nose and stomped his feet and said they should all learn to talk like him; and on it went way into the nighttime. But they couldn't understand one another for trying to out-talk each other, until at last, the whydah bird with its long, long tail spoke up in its little squeaky voice and said, 'Listen to yourselves. You ain't animals who want to talk to each other. You're like the jungle at night, all sound and confusion. Then the whydah bird said, 'We will learn only one language today, and it will be the language of the butterfly because it is simple and beautiful. When we have learned to speak like the butterfly, we will learn another one tomorrow and another one the next day, until at last someday we will all know each other's languages. Then we can talk to each other and reason and be at peace.' So that is what they did. They set out to learn each other's languages. But there are so many of them, my little friend, they're still working at it, and until they're finished, they'll only partly understand each other. But the most important thing is they're working on it, and someday they will succeed." After Nathan finished the story, he walked off down Institute Street with his hoe and mattock on his shoulder. Jesse stood in front of his house, waving goodbye to him, wishing Nathan could come and live with them. It went on like that most of the summer.

Chapter 24

Nathan Hanks
Letter to His Wife, June Hanks
May 4, 1948

DEAREST JUNE,

I dreamed of you this morning as I was waking up. You know how dreams come in that twilight between sleep and wakefulness? That's the way it was. I could almost feel the early morning seeping into the bedroom. The only noises were the sounds of small insects in the locust trees outside and the tick of the clock on the table. An image of you standing on our porch steps in Hatchie Landing rose up in my mind. A light shone in the window behind you, and fireflies winked on and off by the thousands over the yard and in the shrubs and thickets, almost synchronized. Your face was in shadow, but I knew the details of it, the soft hair on your neck, and your eyes like deep pools. A longing swept over me, baby, and when I looked again, you had turned and stepped back onto the porch toward the doorway. He heard you call something to someone inside—Mani or Bibi, I guess—then you were gone, and the light in the window switched off, and there was only this loneliness there in the dark.

It was nearly five o'clock when I woke up and put my feet flat on the floor. I prayed. God, if you are a god at all, take care of June, Mani, and Bibi. Keep the devil of harm from them and help me move my feet on the right path. I don't know why you have done this to us. I truly do not, but I'll trust for a little while longer. I will keep on going the way I'm headed now and hope. That's all I can do is hope that someday, someway, we'll be together *again with our arms around each other. I would like to go to sleep every night with my sweet wife beside me and my son asleep in the next room. I would like to wake every morning with my arm across her warmth. Please give that back to me again if you can. I hope you are the kind of god who will.*

Then I dressed in my work clothes and put grounds in the percolator. Isn't that first sip of coffee wonderful, sweetheart? I miss our mornings there in the kitchen when all else is still and quiet, just the two of us. I sat at the table with my coffee and thought about the job I had to do for Loyal Hall today. I cut open a cantaloupe I'd bought at the little market down the street. It was so sweet and juicy! The seeds tumbled out into the sink when I cut it open, and I spooned a huge mouthful. Somehow it made me feel better to eat like that, standing over the sink, looking out the window into the back alley behind the house.

Babe, I don't want to scare you, but I think I saw somebody in the back of the house. Anyway, something moved. I kept eating, but watching. Nothing. Then, more movement to the left. I shifted my eyes back and forth like Daddy taught me to hunt in the Hatchie River Bottom. You sometimes can't see a thing directly, Daddy always said. So move your eyes back and forth and pay attention to what you see off to the side. You have to look askance to see it; the same thing for the mind. If you can't figure something out, think sideways, Daddy told me. Move into it from the side, walk around it. Soon enough, it will show itself. Just be patient. Suddenly, I knew I was seeing a person moving low across the alley. Why would a person act like that? Someone up to no good? Afraid of being seen? Did the person out there in the dark pertain to me?

Finally, the shadows quit moving and daylight began to slant between the houses, and I wasn't sure there had really been someone out there. Who would have been stalking out there in the dark, here in Paradise, and for what reason? Is someone watching where I live? I need to go back to Hatchie Landing soon, to you and Mani. I'm no good here. You need me there.

I will come.

Nathan

Chapter 25

Nathan Hanks, Jesse Wickham, and Campo
Mid-Morning, May 4, 1948
Paradise, TN

JESSE AND CAMPO made little rumbling noises that sounded like engines for the tiny cars and trucks they were playing with in the dirt beneath one of the huge elm trees in Jesse's front yard. They saw Nathan come walking up the center of Institute Street and ran to meet him, shouting his name. "Naaathaaan! Naaathaaan!"

Nathan grumbled a sound Jesse could feel in his chest. "I don't have time to tell you two children any tales today. Now go on. I don't have time today."

They begged him to tell just one. His stories came all the way from Africa about things deep and mysterious to them. It was like touching something in the dark that they had never felt before, and their imaginations would run away. They ran around his legs like buzzing insects as he strode, around and around, in and out, begging and trying to find an opening, but he wouldn't give in. He shooed them away again and again, but they continued swirling around.

He stopped all of a sudden and gave them a look they'd not seen before. Gently, his deep voice commanded, "I don't have time to tell you two children any tales today. Now go on, I don't have time today."

But neither of them caught the edge in his voice. He always gave in and told them some wild tale, so they persisted, circling in the street as he tried to move on, but his eyes were far away as he walked, and he wouldn't look at them anymore. They circled and feinted, and Jesse asked him again if he reckoned he could tell them a tale today. He just kept walking down the middle of the street. They looked like the children of Hamelin dancing around the piper, except Nathan wasn't piping, and he wasn't speaking, and his eyes were dark and staring at something far off in his mind.

"You two children, please leave me alone today, you hear?"

They finally stopped begging, and Jesse asked him what was wrong, but he didn't say anything, just kept walking with that long stare. Jesse watched his dark eyes, hoping they would suddenly smile to show he was kidding, but he already knew it wasn't going to happen. He sensed something had changed.

"Come on. Let's go." Jesse turned to go home, but Campo kept begging, almost taunting Nathan. Finally, Nathan turned and looked right at him.

His voice rumbled. "I said, leave me alone. Now you two children go on, get away."

Campo started to cry, then he turned and spat at Nathan. "Damn nigger," he said.

Jesse hit Campo. "Shut up!"

"You gonna do something about it?" Campo turned on him.

"He's my friend. Just leave him alone." The two boys glared at each other. "Something's the matter with him today." Jesse watched Nathan walking away. Unsure what, but certain that something had permanently changed.

On the long walk through town out to Loyal Hall's house on Highland, Nathan thought about the shadowy figure. It could have been a paperboy, someone leaving for work in the darkness, or coming home after a shift. None of the notions was convincing. At Loyal Hall's house, he knocked at the back door. Loyal had asked Nathan to run hot-and-cold water pipes beneath the house and up through the floor into a little closet off the downstairs dining room so he could add a small bathroom.

"Morning, Nathan. Coffee?"

"No, Mr. Hall. I've had my coffee for today. I'd better get started on that plumbing."

"Well, coffee's right here on the stove. If you decide you want some later, just turn on the gas and heat it up. I'm going to the courthouse today and then probably over to Emily's."

"All right, Mr. Hall. I'll be fine here, I suspect. I'd better get started."

"Everything's out back in the tool shed, Nathan. I'll show you." The two men crossed the back yard to what had once been a small garage, but was now filled with tools and an assortment of junk collected over the years. The exterior paint was peeling away. The interior was accessed by way of the double garage door. Nathan swung the doors back to let in daylight. The floor was packed earth, and odds and ends were stacked everywhere, with only a narrow opening left to access a workbench. There were tools over it on a pegboard and shelves at the back. The place smelled musty from disuse. "There's a pipe threader back there against the bench. If you have to trim any of those pipes, you'll need it and some pipe oil. You know how to use that?"

"Yes, sir. I'll have this all done for you when you get back home today. I may be gone by then." He began setting up the pipe threader outside.

"Oh, I almost forgot, your money is in the kitchen on the table. When you're finished, if it's not enough, just tell me how much more I owe you."

"I'll do that, Mr. Hall, but I don't think you'll owe me any more."

"How's everything with June and Mani?"

Nathan began gathering up the tools he'd need without turning to look back at Loyal. "They're all right. June sends me letters. She says Mani is doing just fine, but I've been thinking I might head on back there for a while," he said.

"Really? Are you sure it's safe?"

"I don't think it's much safer around here anymore, so I might as well."

"Why do you say that?"

Nathan told him about the figure he had seen early that morning behind his house.

"Are you sure he was watching your house?"

"It was somebody bent down, running along behind my house. I'm sure it was a man."

"Because of you and not something or somebody else?"

"I felt like it was somebody watching my house. When I looked out the window, the guy went running away down behind the houses into the ditch back there."

Loyal tried picturing the houses where Nathan lived, but couldn't bring them up. He realized he'd never even been in that part of town and felt a pang of guilt. "Nathan, you tell me if anything like this happens again. If you're threatened by anyone, you tell me."

"I don't think it'll do any good. If somebody wants to get me, they'll get me, Mr. Hall."

"You won't do anything rash, will you, Nathan?"

"I'll be careful. I won't do anything to anybody, but I think I have to go back home to June and Mani and Bibi for a while. I wrote to June and told her."

Nathan pointed to a stack of black iron pipe near the front of the shed.

"Are those the ones to use?"

Loyal nodded but said, "Are you sure, Nathan? Is it safe for them? If it's what you feel you have to do, be careful. You know you can bring your whole family over here to Paradise if you want to. Surely, we can find some kind of job for June."

Nathan began moving the pipe outside to the threader. "I know you want to help us, Mr. Hall, but June has a good job teaching school over in Hatchie Landing. She'll never be able to get something like that here." He hefted one of the pipes in his hand, then let it clang down on top of the others.

Chapter 26

Nathan Hanks
Letter to His Wife, June Hanks
May 4, 1948
Paradise, TN

THAT EVENING, NATHAN SAT ON HIS PORCH with his lap desk and wrote again to June. This time, he didn't mention the figure skulking in the dark.

Darling June,

I'm tired and uneasy. Some boys taunted me in the street today. They were little boys, about ten years old, I guess. White boys. One of them kept telling the other one to quit saying those things to me, but the other one kept on. They're just children, but it hurt some, especially since both those little boys like to come to where I'm working and hear me tell them stories. I think of Mani when I tell them. It makes me homesick for you all.

I was thinking about Tuskegee yesterday. Ellis, Buster, Galt, and I did pretty well there. We all learned a lot, and I think we are all pretty smart. We had some good times, too. I just wish it could have kept on after we graduated. I met a lot of smart people there, but not many of us get to use what we learned. Buster and Galt made pretty well as preachers. They do some good. You'd think people would take an educated man for what he is, but it doesn't happen. People see what they need to see, like looking through a colored glass to make the world seem like what they believe it to be. Maybe that makes it easier to get along. I don't know, but it's hard for people to take you on new terms. Everything wants to stay like it was.

The news on the radio sounds pretty good these days, but I think maybe there's going to be another war before too long. Once a country gets geared up to fight, it can't seem to stop. Maybe I'll have to go to it. There's talk they may call up some who were in the last one if it happens. I don't know if they will want any Negro men this time or not. When they called us up before and we went down to Tuskegee to learn to fly, I thought we'd surely come back home to some respect. Why couldn't it happen? When men go off to war, can't the people back home know what they went through and take them back on new terms when it's over? Maybe not. Maybe everything has to settle back to the way it was before. Maybe everything bad in the world is like that. Awfulness happens, and the world doesn't recognize it. It just keeps on being the world while the people come and go, and the awfulness comes and goes, and makes it nearly impossible to be human and be sane at the same time.

It's all that and this little bit of trouble I've got here that keeps my mind on you, sweet darling. I'm looking forward to Friday night when I can see you again. I'm sorry we have to live apart like this so much of the time. Maybe, soon, the times will change, and we can be together all the time like I dreamed of that day on your momma's front porch. I hope so. You're the only one I dream of, the only one who truly matters to me in spite of my penchant for getting involved in all the action. Maybe I shouldn't have helped Ellis register the voters there in Hatchie Landing. It led us into all our troubles. I don't mean to leave you out, sweet one. I would never ever leave you out if I could do anything to make our life better. You know that. I know you do, but I wish you were here with me now so I could say it to you and I could hear your soft voice in my ear and hold you close to my chest. Just know I love you.

I have to go now and eat something and get some rest. Yesterday I worked for Miss Emily and Miss Lula. When Mr. Loyal came to have lunch with them, he said he needed me today. Mr. Wynne came over, too. He wants me to come up to the funeral home and do some carpentry for him. It's nice to be needed and to have some work to do, though I wish I could be doing something more worthwhile. What good was Tuskegee if day labor is all I can find to do? I love you and I'm looking forward to Friday. I'm thinking this time I'll come home for good. We can talk about it when I get there.

Your best friend in the whole world,

Nathan

Chapter 27

Bibi Durber
May 6, 1948
Hatchie Landing, TN

JUNE PUT NATHAN'S LETTER ON THE TABLE, smoothed it with her hands, and waited for Bibi to notice. "You might as well read it to me," Bibi said. So she read the part where he said he wasn't just coming for a visit this time.

"Will it be all right?" June asked.

Bibi could tell she was scared. "Honey, don't worry, he's going to be all right till he gets here, and then we're gonna have us a celebration right here in this kitchen." But she didn't tell her that she'd had her dream again in the night. Those two lions and that pack of dogs were walking back and forth over there, and they were looking across at something coming. "June, everything is going to be all right. Nathan will come home and be safe."

The day Nathan was supposed to come home from Paradise, Bibi rocked on the porch at noontime like always and hoped for a cool breeze to blow on her face. She said her prayers to Jesus, and dreamed a little bit more, and then she saw those dogs with their names written on their faces right above their eyes, and they were still looking out toward something beyond her, but this time when she opened her eyes, she knew who they all were.

Mani came out the screen door and broke her reverie, but she didn't mind. That boy was her favorite, and she didn't mind saying so. She had been partial to that child ever since he was first born. It was like he was sitting right beside her all the time, even when he wasn't there at all. Bibi was the one who gave him his real name, Mani. June had wanted to call him Markus after Mark in the New Testament, but Bibi knew the child came from some other place than the New Testament. In her mind, he came down, down from some high place, and so she called him Mani, which means from a high place, and that's what almost everybody called him now.

While they were talking there on the porch, Nathan turned into the Quarter and came down the street. The street where they lived didn't have a name, so they just called it "the street." It was the main one in the Quarter. There were some little ones off it, but no big ones. Bibi called out to June and told her he was coming, and she let out a whoop and came out the door smiling like the sun. Mani jumped up too, and both started running to see him. Those three carried on like they had just found each other. Of course, in a way, they had. Nearly three months is a long time for people in love to be away from each other.

June was hanging on Nathan like a tick on a hound, happy and giggly like she was just a girl. Mani was, too, and they hugged and laughed and cried all at the same time.

"It's gonna be good now that Nathan is home for a while," Bibi said.

June looked at her, the happy expression melting from her face. She knew, like Bibi knew, that this wasn't going to last, that Nathan would have to get out of there again, where it was safe. But today they were together in Bibi's kitchen at her table with her good food on it, and they were happy like a family should be.

Mani was just home from over at Mr. Clifford's, where he'd been helping out with the cotton picking. He was growing up, that child. He liked to have some spending money, and Mr. Clifford let him help out on the water wagon. He told June he wouldn't let him in the fields to pick because he was too young for it.

Bibi turned toward her stove, thinking: there are lots of lions like Trouble out there looking in on folks. Another one is Death. He's old and mangy, and he doesn't care about himself because he only wants to get to us. Thing is, he always does sooner or later. He'll come across the line and tag us out, and when he does, we have to go with him back over. But, Bibi thought, that's all right in this family because just as soon as one of us gets over to that side, there's a new job. And that's to look out for our family, that's still over here. That old mangy lion will creep off then and go look for somebody else.

Chapter 28

— ◆ —

Horace Clifford
May 7, 1948
Hachie Landing, TN

THE NEXT MORNING, MR. CLIFFORD came into the street. Eyes were on him from behind screen doors and curtained windows and the recesses of rooms because not often did any white people come into the Quarter, and when they did, it often meant trouble. He drove slowly past the church and pulled up in front of the Hanks's house. June got a panicky feeling, and she told Nathan to go hide somewhere and stay out of sight, but he said it's only Mr. Clifford, he's come to ask for help on something; but they went on inside anyway.

Horace Clifford seldom drove his pale green Hudson coupe, preferring his red pickup for the farm work. By the time he had driven down the street into the Quarter, it had dust all over it. He stood there for what seemed like a whole minute, and the wind didn't stir a leaf, as if everything went on hold while he was standing there beside his car. He put his whole palm against the door and pushed solidly until it chunked shut. His handprint was in the dust on the door, and he looked at it a long time. Then he lifted up his straw hat and wiped his head with a red bandana. He looked around to see who was watching, and then he looked back down the street from where he had come, and June thought she was right, that there was some kind of trouble coming. Then he started up the walk.

When he got close to the steps, he took off his hat again and stood out in the sun and called out toward the house. "Miss June, Bibi, y'all in there?" Bibi heard him clear as day and went to the screen door and stepped out onto the porch.

"How can I help you, Mr. Clifford?"

"Miss Bibi, I need to talk to Miss June. Can I come up on the porch a minute?"

"Sure, you can, Mr. Clifford. You're always welcome at our house."

"June, it's Mr. Clifford here to see you," she hollered inside, and June came to the door. Bibi asked, "Y'all want some cold sweet tea?"

Mr. Clifford held his hat like he was about to ask permission or something. "Yes, ma'am, that'd be nice. I'd like that a whole lot." He bobbed his head as he said it.

She brought out the tea and went back inside, where there were nothing but ears in the house in the shadowy dark. Those inside could hear every word. "Please have a seat, Mr. Clifford," June said. "What can we do for you this morning?"

"Thank you, Miss June." He sat in the glider instead of the swing, waving his hat like a funeral fan, and June waited for him to speak first. She thought maybe Nathan would come on out, but he didn't.

"Mani's here, Mr. Clifford. Do you need him to come to work?"

"No, Miss June, I don't need Mani today, maybe tomorrow though. The boy's a good worker, he is. I love having him around. I do indeed." He stopped talking, but kept on fanning himself.

"Miss June, I sure appreciate what all y'all have been through here lately. And I want to say, want you to know, I don't think it's right at all. Not right at all." He shook his head back and forth two or three times while he looked down at the floor instead of looking at June. It was like he felt he was to blame for what was happening.

"Mr. Clifford, you are not responsible for any of this, you know that, and we know it, so don't go apologizing for something you didn't do. Now tell me what's really on your mind."

About then, a car turned into the street up at the corner, the same way Horace Clifford had come. They could see it was a sheriff's car coming down, driving slowly. June stiffened and glanced back into the darkness of the house, and Horace watched the car, and saw Bennie Hoskins driving, and then he looked over at June.

"That's the deputy that came here the other night and told Nathan to leave town," she said.

Clifford went kind of pale all of a sudden, but he kept on fanning and holding his sweet tea out over the porch so the sweat off the glass wouldn't drip on his nice pants. He watched Bennie Hoskins drive on down the street, then turn around and come back past the house. He didn't stop, but he made sure they saw him looking when he went on by. He didn't wave or say anything, just drove on out of the Quarter and out of sight.

Finally, Clifford spoke again. "Miss June, that is just a sample of what's in store around here, and it's why I'm here right now. I appreciate your hospitality, but I'd better get to the point. You know how I feel about all this and how I feel about what has happened to your family. It isn't right, but I can't do a thing about it. Those people know by now that Nathan is back at home. They ain't going to like it one bit. I debated about coming here to tell you this because I don't want you to think I think like they do. I do not. I do not."

He shook his head in the same way again, and his eyes were the eyes of hopelessness. "I cannot make this go away, and I'm afraid for you and your family. I'm not trying to make peace with all this. I'm not trying to keep a lid on things, as they sometimes say, Miss June. I'm just saying to you, I'm afraid there is danger. I won't tell you and Nathan what to do. I'll just say what I think: Nathan should go away again, at least for a while longer. Maybe it won't last forever. Hell, there's another war coming over in Korea as sure as we are sitting here, and it may change everything. For now, though, Nathan should leave again is my advice."

"If he won't go, will you stand by us?"

He looked at June a long time with those hopeless eyes, and then he said something none of them would ever forget. "We didn't fight a war to come to this. If it costs me my life, I'll stand beside you and your family, Miss June, because it is that much wrong—but I may be the only man in this county who feels like that."

He handed June his glass, and looked into the darkness of the house and breathed a deep sigh. June wanted to touch him, put her hand on his arm or something, but she only let herself watch him put his hat on his head and go down the steps to his car and drive up the street and out of the Quarter.

Chapter 29

Nathan and June Hanks
May 8, 1948
Hatchie Landing, TN

INSECTS WERE BEGINNING TO MAKE THEIR NOISES in the grass and bushes outside the window. Nathan opened his eyes and could see blue sky. The attic fan pulled cool air over the bed where he lay beside June. Her eyes were closed, and her lips were parted, turned ever so slightly into her pillow as if about to give a kiss. He raised himself up on one elbow to look at her while she slept. Her skin was smooth and dark, and the hair on her face just in front of her ears was as soft as down. He touched it with one finger, and she stirred. He stroked her cheek, and she opened her eyes and smiled at him. He kissed her face, and she closed her eyes, turning her mouth toward him. They kissed slowly for a long time and then embraced each other. Slowly and softly, they made love. Afterward, they held each other without speaking until they heard Bibi stirring in the kitchen.

"It's Saturday, but it's time to rise and shine," said June quietly, and kissed him again. "I'm so glad you're home. I missed you. Mani needs you. Can it possibly last?"

"I hope it can last," Nathan said.

"But Mr. Clifford thinks we're in danger. He made a special trip down here to tell us. No white man's going to do that for us without the danger being real. He thinks you need to go away again, at least for a little while. I don't like it, sweetheart."

"We'll just have to see."

They dressed and went into the kitchen. Bibi had coffee made, and Mani was making shuffling noises up in his room. "That boy dancing up there. He's growing up, and he's going to be the death of me yet." Bibi smiled.

Mani came into the kitchen, and June started dancing with him. "Now, you two, calm down and sit. Behave yourselves," Bibi commanded. They stopped their swinging and sat down.

"What does everybody want for breakfast? Now, don't go thinking I'm going to cook to order for y'all. Make up your minds and tell what you want. I've already fixed the biscuits, so you can count on them, but what else you want?"

June began helping Bibi while Nathan played and talked with Mani. "Want to go fishing today?" Mani yelped at the idea. Then quieted.

"Where are we going fishing, Daddy?" Mani asked.

"Oh, we'll just go down to the powerhouse pond. How about that? No need to go over to the river or the bottom." Nathan thought he should heed Mr. Clifford's troubling warning and stay close to home. Besides, Mani had seen horror that no child should ever see. No need to dredge all that up again.

"I need to go into town first, though. I need to talk to Buster. I'll get some bait, some minnows up at Ellis's station on the way back home." Then he realized what he had said. Ellis wasn't there anymore, wasn't even alive anymore, and Arlene was barely able to keep the station going since Ellis disappeared.

Bibi said, "Arlene said she gonna go live in Chicago with her brother." Everyone was quiet.

"It doesn't seem natural for Ellis to be gone," Nathan said.

"No, but he is." Bibi went on stirring the gravy. "Let's eat. Y'all get you a plate and come over here to the stove and fill it up. Then go sit at the table and wait for the rest of us." They did as she told them.

Nathan prayed they'd be safe and able to stay together like a family should. When he said amen, June leaned toward him. "You don't have to remind Mani," she whispered. "He's frightened enough."

"I'm sorry. You're right. I hope it didn't scare him."

"You can't tell by looking."

After breakfast, Nathan got his hat, told them he'd be back as soon as he could, and went down the steps. He backed the Chevy coupe into the street and headed out of the Quarter. He steered the old car down Harding toward town and pulled in at the E & A Service Station and Store.

Arlene was on the porch wiping down the window glass, the E & A painted in black-and-gold letters. They stood for Ellis and Arlene.

"Morning, Arlene. How are you today? Anything I can do?"

Arlene didn't turn around. She looked at herself in the window reflection. "The *E* is missing, Nathan. What's a woman supposed to do when her partner's gone?"

Nathan thought about it. In a way, he and June had each lost a partner too, but not like this, not like Arlene. At least there was still hope for them if he could just hold on and somehow get them living together again, either here or in Paradise. He thought about what Loyal Hall had said to him about helping them move to Paradise.

"Arlene. I just came to check on you and see how you're getting along."

"Well, I'm all right in some ways and dead in some others."

"Some nights over there in Paradise, I feel like I'm dead to my family, too. June and Bibi said to tell you they can come up to help almost anytime you say you need them. And Mani's a good worker too. Mr. Clifford likes to have him work for him."

"Thank them for me, Nathan. I don't rightly know where I'm going yet. I'll probably go live in Chicago with Bert. He's my oldest brother. You remember Bert?"

"I remember him, but I hope you can find a way to stay here and live. I understand if you can't. We'll all miss you if you go."

"You got enough on your plate to be missing me and my kids, Nathan. You've got to worry about June and Bibi and your boy."

"We talked about maybe we'll have to go to Paradise if I can't stay here. You going to be open for a while? I'm going into town and thought I could stop back by here on the way home and get some minnows and take Mani fishing down at the powerhouse pond."

"What else am I gonna do? Until I get something fixed up for Chicago, I don't have a choice, do I? I suppose I'll be here awhile, Nathan."

"I'll drop by on my way back in a little."

He drove away toward town and parked just off the square. In Biddle's Hardware, he selected a Belknap toolbox and a small level, and stood to the side while a white man purchased some nails and talked about football to the man behind the counter. When they finished, Nathan paid for his items and went out.

He drove around the square and turned back toward the Quarter and Buster's church. He parked at the curb in front. The church was small and made of clapboard with a little steeple at the roof peak that needed paint. The front lawn was sparse and dry. Some of the Sisters had put impatiens in pots on the steps leading up to the front door, and someone was taking good care of them, for they bloomed profusely, red and white.

A sheriff's patrol car turned in at the corner as Nathan started walking over the lawn toward the front door of the church. The patrol car slowed, and he heard his name called. "Nathan. Nathan Hanks. That you?"

He turned to look at who was calling him from the car. Bennie Hoskins leaned across the front seat toward the window so Nathan could see him. "Yes, sir. I'm Nathan," he answered.

"Goddammit, I know who you are. I'm calling your name. Do you understand?"

"Yes, sir, I understand."

"Then, by God, come over here like I told you."

"I didn't hear you tell me to do that, come over there."

"Look, boy, I'm telling you something and you better listen. Listen good, you hear?"

"I can hear. What are you telling me?"

"I'm telling you to get your ass back out of this town before something bad happens."

"I live here. My family lives here. My wife works here. She teaches school."

"I know all that, you sonofabitch. You think we don't know all about you and your family? Well, we do. So you better listen good. I'm telling you to get your black ass out of Hatchie Landing and do it quick or you'll be dead just like that other uppity sonofabitch."

"Dead? You say Ellis's dead?"

Bennie skipped a beat. "I didn't say nothing. Except you better get out of town or there'll be trouble."

"More trouble. I can see."

"I hope you see or there'll be more than crosses burning in somebody's front yard." Bennie pulled back behind the steering wheel and moved off down the street, around the corner, and out of sight.

Nathan turned to go inside the church and saw Buster standing at the door, shaking his head. Nathan looked at him, bewildered. Sweat stung his eyes.

"What are we going to do, Buster?" They were seated now in the little kitchen at the back of the church.

"I don't know. I honestly don't know. There is more trouble coming."

"I'd better leave town again, I think."

"Well, maybe that'd be a good thing to do for a while. Can you go back to Paradise?"

"Yes, there's a man, Mr. Loyal Hall, his sister helps me and gets me work. He works for the FBI. He knows what's going on, and he's trying to help. He told me to bring June and Mani over there, and he and some others will help us. But June has a good job here. She shouldn't have to leave it. I don't have anything much anymore, so it doesn't matter about me, but June can still keep on teaching. I don't think even Mr. Hall can get her a teaching job over in Paradise. Those kinds of jobs are too precious."

"Still, you've got to think about safety, yours and June's and Bibi and Mani. Think about it, Nathan. What good are you to them if you're dead or crippled up?" Nathan stood and looked at his friend. Buster reached out and covered Nathan's hand with his own.

As Nathan pulled away from the curb, the patrol car came around the corner and followed him. He drove on toward the Quarter. At the E & A, he decided not to stop. Arlene watched from the porch as he turned into the Quarter and saw the patrol car behind him.

Nathan pulled into the yard beside the house and stood next to his car as Bennie drove past and turned around. He drove slowly and leered at Nathan, motioning with his thumb back over his shoulder. He mouthed the words "Get out," then continued out of the Quarter.

Chapter 30

Nathan Hanks
May 9, 1948
Hatchie Landing, TN

EARLY ON SUNDAY MORNING, they all went together to the bus station. Mani stood close beside Bibi in the gray light as Nathan and June walked to the corner of the platform and stopped. Nathan pulled her to him and held her for a long few minutes. Bibi and Mani watched silently. The three white men inside watched them. The ticket lady watched them. The fry cook in the café watched them. Across the street at Joe's Pool Hall, the paperboys who had stopped for doughnuts before heading out on their routes watched through the dirty windows.

The bus driver came out of the terminal and climbed into the bus. He started the engine and then stepped back onto the sidewalk to wait for passengers. A young woman came out and set her suitcase on the sidewalk. She smoothed the front of her shirtwaist dress and then rummaged in her handbag for a brush. She leaned her head to the side and brushed her long hair a few strokes, then returned the brush to her bag. She looked at the driver, and he smiled and lifted her suitcase into the underneath stowage. He looked at Nathan and said it was time to go, but didn't offer to handle his luggage.

Nathan lifted his one suitcase into the stowage. The driver pointed to the aft compartment. "Hey, don't put that there. Put it in the back." Nathan looked at him and obeyed. Then he went over to June and Mani. "I'm sorry you had to see that."

"It's the way things are." June pulled Mani to her, and Nathan dropped down to give him a hug before stepping onto the bus. He made his way to the rear.

The driver closed the stowage compartments, then climbed into the driver's seat and pulled the door shut. There was no traffic this early in the morning as the bus swung into the street.

Nathan stood looking out the back window.

The driver yelled at him. "Mister! You'll have to sit down now."

Nathan obeyed again. He swiveled around in the seat to look at his family standing on the dock as the bus pulled away. Their hands were lifted as if to wave, but motionless, palms out, fingertips curled slightly in the air around them.

Nathan watched them diminish as the bus slid away into the early morning. When he could no longer see their faces, he turned in his seat to face the eastward journey toward Paradise. As the bus crossed the Forked Deer River and pulled into Paradise, he thought about what other rivers he would have to cross, and how he would survive all the tomorrows to come and their mornings and their evenings. At the station, he checked the strap around his small suitcase, and the weight of the world seemed to settle on him as he began the walk toward his house on Tanyard.

On Monday, Nathan wrote in his Blue Horse notebook, and he wrote a letter to June, then walked to the House on Chester to let Emily and Lula know he was back and ready to work. Emily remarked how burdened he looked. Then he walked to Griffin Wynne Funeral Home and told the same to Vivian. At the post office, he mailed his letter and continued on to Highland to tell Loyal Hall. He returned home in the afternoon feeling tired and helpless, trapped in a place that was both his salvation and his prison. He stretched out on his bed and closed his eyes. He made a fist and rapped his forehead, thinking he wasn't even able to provide for his family.

Chapter 31

Griffin Wynne
May 10, 1948
Paradise, TN

VIVIAN TOOK THE CALL and pressed the button on her desk. The doorbell rang in the embalming room and out back under the portico, and the red light bulb blinked on and off in Griffin Wynne's office and upstairs in the model train room.

With a thin little brush, Wynne lifted a tiny dab of glue from the glue pot. He carefully smeared it over the backside of a tiny cedar shake, and with tweezers was attempting to place it delicately onto the onion dome on the round tower of the House on Chester Street, and as he bent close to look at it, to see it as if he were one of the occupants, Emily or Lula, he heard the bells ringing and saw the light winking on and off. He quickly covered the glue pot and, shedding the apron over his suit, rushed to the top of the stairs.

Vivian waited below. "Close by, down on Tanyard Street, it's a house fire, and the fire station called. You are up next on their board." There were three funeral homes in town, and the city and county rotated their services and paid a small fee. "Slip off your coat. I'll hang it. Here's your smock and the keys." Wynne took the keys, slipped his arms into the smock Vivian held, and hurried out to the ambulance.

Guiding the big white vehicle down the drive, he flipped on the cherry light and siren. Be careful, he thought. Watch for children. When he reached the intersection with Tanyard, he saw the fire trucks, hoses, and people. Always the people. "Lord! It's where Nathan lives," he breathed to himself. The crowd parted as he pulled the ambulance as close as possible without interfering with the fire equipment.

Jesse and Campo looked up from the dirt where they played with their cast metal cars. The sounds of fire engines rumbled and sirens wailed through the summer air. The engines came closer and closer, then passed down the street in front of them. Another siren began way up the street. They heard this come swiftly too, with its high pitch—an ambulance!—and they jumped up and ran down the sidewalk, pumping their legs faster and faster. Campo was fastest and passed Jesse, but Jesse cut across old man Mallory's yard and through Creasey's backyard, past the billy goat and through the Johnson grass in the fallow garden behind Campo's house. Campo cut in behind him, and they both ran toward the sound of sirens winding down just ahead on Tanyard Street.

They burst onto Tanyard above Nathan's house and saw a wisp of smoke curling up from beneath the eave. Firemen were uncoiling hose, and someone yelled, "Where's the damn hydrant?" They were hooking the hose to the pumper, and people were out in the street, wide-eyed and wondering like Jesse and Campo. Nobody knew what had happened. Someone said it was only smoke they saw. Somebody else called the firehouse. *Where is Nathan?* Somebody else wanted to know. *Where is Nathan? He working? He up at Mr. Loyal's today? I saw him come home. I saw him down at the store. I saw him up on Institute.* Nobody knew for sure.

The two little boys sat on the curb and watched the firemen, the fire trucks, the people milling about, and wondered where Nathan was.

Chapter 32

Nathan Hanks
May 10, 1948
Paradise, TN

NATHAN OPENED HIS EYES and saw a band of sunlight streaming through a pinhole in the window shade. It broadened into a beam of yellow light with dust motes drifting through it. The motes seemed to be alive, circling, lifting, then diving out of the beam down into the dim space between the table and the bed. He could hear a mockingbird singing outside in the chinaberry tree and beyond that, somewhere, someone was calling his name.

He watched one bright mote lift quickly up into the sunbeam, sparkling like a piece of glass. He remembered his mother's one little piece of jewelry, a necklace with beads of glass, all identical, all symmetrical. He had played with it one afternoon on the floor of their little house in the Quarter in Hatchie Landing until he got tired and lay his head down on the cool linoleum floor and went to sleep.

He remembered his mother lifting him off the floor, and with him in her arms, she stepped on the necklace. She had sighed softly as she had laid him on the bed, and he had watched her go back and pick up the necklace and hold it up. The light caught the chipped edge of a single broken bead.

He heard his name being called again and again and thought, Momma, I'm sorry, I didn't mean to break it, I didn't mean to. I just wanted to feel it in my hands. I'm sorry, Momma, I'm sorry. Then he smelled smoke coming from the old Warm Morning stove in the corner of the room and wondered why his momma had lit a fire in the summertime. He saw the light beam had moved up the wall, but was dimmer now. He drifted back to sleep.

He woke again to the sound of his name, Nathan, Nathan, someone was calling him. The mockingbird was still singing in the chinaberry tree. He could see the berries hanging ripe on the limbs, or was he remembering that? How the robins come to the chinaberry tree to eat the overripe berries, get drunk on them, and can't fly. He, Ellis, Buster, and Galt got drunk in Italy. How brave and alive they felt when they returned after escorting the British bombers over the Alps. He remembered shooting down a Messerschmitt, and the sadness he felt when the plane diminished toward the ground and ended with only the smallest puff of smoke, and how his heart hurt for the pilot, but also how happy he had been.

His pillow was hot, but he couldn't wake enough to turn it to the cool side. He wanted to go back to sleep, but the person kept calling him. He dreamed again about flying in formation with Ellis and Buster and Galt, and the Messerschmitt streaking across and above them. Then he watched poor Ellis turn in the sunlight and gracefully arc his plane toward the ground, the bright red tail of his airplane flashing in the sunlight as it began a slow twirl and a thin trail of smoke hanging behind it. Ellis was such a good friend to lose, he thought, but then he saw the plane stop its spiral and hold for a second in its straight down dive and begin to nose up a fraction, then a fraction more and slowly like a child's crayon drawing an arc on paper, it trailed its thin smoke back up into the sky and turned toward home. Ellis wasn't going to die today. Nobody else would die today. They were all going to live to go home to Hatchie Landing someday and do all the things they dreamed. The world would be different, and they would walk in it and be a part of it. They would dance and sing and make love and, most of all, they would walk through the world and be proud and the world would be proud of them for what they had done.

He smiled as he remembered the bomber pilots calling them angels because they were always hovering at their wingtips, their red painted tails flashing, protecting them. He remembered the British pilot who came to him in the hangar one afternoon and clasped him close and even put his hand on his face and thanked him and said, "You are truly an angel. You saved us out there."

And he watched the light beam move on up the wall and heard the voice outside in the chinaberry tree mocking him, and it wasn't his name anymore being called, and he felt sleepy and tired, and the stove was too hot and the smoke burned his nose. He wished his momma would put it out. It was summertime, and they didn't need a fire. Why would she light a fire on a hot summer day? Then he heard something crash and felt a whoosh of cool air on his face, so he smiled again and drifted off to dream he was an angel in the blue skies outside, but there was nothing except what was down below him on the ground where two small boys sat on the curb watching firemen roll a gurney outside and there was a body underneath a black rubber blanket and then he was just light and shadow drifting in the trees.

Chapter 33

Griffin Wynne
May 10, 1948
Paradise, TN

WYNNE TOOK IN THE SCENE BEFORE HIM, the urgency of the firemen, the agitation and concern of the onlookers. Someone darted behind houses. Two little boys sat wide-eyed on the curb across the street.

One of the firemen raised his hand, signaling Wynne to stand by. As he waited beside the ambulance, he heard people asking one another whether Nathan was inside the house or not.

A white man, roughly dressed and unshaven, came from between houses beyond where the ambulance was parked. He stopped and looked furtively at the scene. Wynne expected the man to join the crowd in the street, but instead, he turned and walked to a battered old pickup truck parked at the corner. Wynne stared at the truck. The man looked back toward the activity again. He started the engine, turned up Institute Street, and drove out of sight. Wynne thought he looked vaguely familiar.

A fireman came to the pumper truck, closed the valve to the hose, and shut down the pumper engine. Another fireman retrieved a stretcher, then trotted off between houses. The fire captain signaled Wynne with one finger to be ready. Wynne opened the rear door of the ambulance.

In a few minutes, two firemen came back carrying the stretcher. A rubber sheet covered a body. Wynne unlocked the gurney and pulled it out of the ambulance. The gurney legs clattered downward, and he readied to transfer the body to it. Two firemen took the body, one by the shoulders and the other by the feet. "Ready?" They shifted the body onto the gurney. Wynne quickly strapped it down and shoved the gurney with the clanking of metal on metal back into the ambulance. He locked it down and closed the door. The fire captain came over and told him to hold on; the coroner was on his way. Within minutes, the county's elected coroner came striding over. Wynne opened the back door of the ambulance. The man lifted the cover from the body and checked the pulse at the neck. He looked at his watch and wrote on a notepad. Wynne saw that it was Nathan. He looked like he was sleeping with almost a smile on his face.

"Does anyone know what happened?" he asked the fire captain.

"Just another fire. No one seems to know how it started. There wasn't much actual flame, mostly smoke. The smoke killed him. He must have been asleep inside. We thought maybe he was smoking in bed, but there was no flame in the bedroom where we found him."

"I know who he is," replied Wynne. "His name is Nathan Hanks." The coroner wrote down the name. "He did some work for me once in a while, a good man. As far as I know, he didn't smoke at all."

"Too bad. I'm sorry about it. I wish we could have gotten here in time, but by the time we did, it was probably all finished for him. He was on the floor at the door to the hallway outside the bedroom. He must have tried to get out, but the smoke was too much for him. It's not the density of it, you know. It's the toxic stuff that kills you, the poison gases in it. Sometimes, one breath is all it takes to put a man under."

The firemen headed back to their trucks and stowed the remaining equipment. They started up their engines and trundled off toward Royal Street. At the corner, they turned left and lumbered away, the sound of their big engines rumbling behind them. A knot of people walked past the ambulance as Wynne opened the driver's side door. They all seemed to be talking at once. He heard Nathan's name and someone say "a man back there," and they walked off down the street, heads almost leaning together as they conferred on what they had witnessed.

Wynne sat behind the wheel and started his engine. He looked toward the corner of Tanyard and Institute, where the man coming from between the houses had gotten in his truck and driven away. He thought about what people in the crowd were saying and the mention of a man back there. Back where? he wondered. Same man? He pulled away from the curb and watched the two little boys cutting through a backyard, heading toward Institute Street.

"It was Nathan," Campo said. "I know it. He's dead. They don't turn on the sirens when the person is already dead."

"I know it," Jesse agreed.

They went back the way they had come, only this time they didn't run through the Johnson grass, not feeling the cuts from the blades swishing past their bare arms and legs. They walked slowly toward home and parted at Campo's house.

Before Jesse got to his own house, he began to cry. His mother asked him what the matter was, but he was silent and went to his bed. He dreamed he saw a beam of light shifting about in the sycamore tree in his backyard. It seemed to smile at him when he looked up at it. He watched it grow and diminish as it moved back and forth in the leaves, and he thought he heard it say something to him before it finally went out. He thought it said it had a story to tell him someday.

Chapter 34

Lula Bartlett
May 11, 1948
Paradise, TN

THE FIRST THING LULA BARTLETT HEARD every morning in summer was a bird call. It felt luxurious to be so comfortable at this hour in her room in The House on Chester, as she and Emily called it. It was as if she were the sole inhabitant of the world. Outside, other than birdsong, there was only the occasional car or truck on the street, the sounds of the first commerce of the day.

Lula kept her room in a state of neat disarray at ground level in the tower. She could see out its windows, beneath the huge elm tree, onto the street or into the small, peaceful garden beside the porch on her side of the house. It was a bookish place Art had called the library. A pretentious notion, Emily always claimed, but Lula liked the idea and the mahogany shelves. She loved the concavity of the walls in her room. They made her feel safe and protected, even though the convex walls they created in the parlor made corner nooks that were difficult to deal with.

Emily's room was on the left side of the house at the back, across the hall from the kitchen. Thus, they could be together or be separate as needed, each having access to the whole house and to each other, but not so much as to smother. The rest of the house was a sort of common ground for them. The rooms on the upper floors were no longer visited except to tidy and dust them.

Lula straightened her bed, slipped on her robe and slippers, and went directly through the parlor and out onto the little side porch she loved so much. She settled in a rocking chair to watch the day begin. At this hour, everything is in progress, she thought. Nothing is static. Even I am rising up as if I'm coming to life all over again each morning like this. She smiled to herself.

Death must be the reversal of this, not like running a movie backward with the characters making silly sounds instead of words, and their motions unexpected and with time going forward in reverse. Instead, death must be like stepping into anticipation. She wondered if anyone else held that notion, as she went back inside to dress for breakfast.

When she felt presentable, she went out the front door and down the steps to retrieve the morning paper. She tucked it under her arm and made her way toward the sun room to where Emily sat in the white wicker chair in her favorite corner, holding her saucer and sipping her first coffee of the day. She smiled as Lula entered the room and said, "Good morning, dear." Their day was underway.

Lula sat in the other wicker chair across from Emily, and as on almost every morning, Emily watched her delicate fingers carefully unfold the paper onto her lap, then turn it to the bottom fold. Lula always read the bottom fold first. Odd how we each approach life differently, Emily thought. She noticed Lula pause for a moment on an item, then look away, then back to the item. She saw one small crease beneath the curl of hair that always declared its independence over Lula's forehead and detected a small question in Lula's eyes.

"What is it?" she asked.

Lula removed the first section of paper and handed it across to Emily. "The item on the left, below the fold, the one about the house fire. I think we know who it is."

Emily took up the gold-rimmed glasses that hung about her neck and scanned the item quickly. "Nathan?" she questioned. "This is poor Nathan! He was just here the day before yesterday until just after noon. I heard the fire trucks go out yesterday, but no; it couldn't be, could it?"

"I'll call Griffin. He will know for sure. It's too early to call yet. Let's eat and then I'll phone." They barely spoke as they ate their breakfast.

After an hour, Lula went into the hallway where the phone sat on a white doily on a round table beside the staircase. She lifted the receiver and spoke, "One oh oh seven, please."

On the second ring, she heard, "Griffin Wynne. This is Vivian speaking." In her mind's eye, Lula could see Vivian's glasses pushed down on her nose, her hair mostly an uncontrolled abandon. The large and friendly woman, who in a way was beautiful, would have a cup of coffee on her desk corner and a stack of papers in the middle.

"Lula, I was about to call you or Emily. You've read the paper, I suppose. It was poor Nathan. Griffin was called to the house fire late yesterday to pick up the body. The firemen brought him out, and the coroner declared him dead."

"What will his family do? What'll happen now?"

"Griffin says he called Reverend Galt, who's calling the family over in Hatchie Landing. That's about all I know. The reverend told Griffin he expects the family will want him to prepare the body. He wasn't burned. It was smoke that killed him."

"He was a good man and a good worker for so many of us. I suppose we could have done more for him and his family, you know, but we didn't, did we?"

Vivian didn't respond. Instead, she said, "I'll call you with the next news I get."

Lula told Emily what she had learned. They both sat silently in the kitchen for a long time. "We should've done more," Emily finally said. "Now the chance is lost."

"What did Dr. Hailey say the other day when we took food up there? The Lord visits in strange ways and times. He presents his opportunities in unexpected ways, and it's up to us to see them and recognize Him. That's what I remember."

"But we didn't do much, did we?"

"No, we did a little bit, but not the whole thing."

Chapter 35

Loyal Hall
May 11, 1948
Paradise, TN

LOYAL SHOVED HIS FEET into his calfskin slippers and was about to slip on his old white terrycloth robe when he noticed stains on the right sleeve. I'm getting old, he thought. Then, out loud to himself, "They say you know you're getting old when you begin to spill food on yourself. When you get to the point where you do it and don't care, that's when you are really over the hill." Loyal was a tall man, still lean but slightly stooped because of a bad back from sitting long hours at a desk. He brushed his long, almost white hair back above his ears. He was farsighted, but needed glasses for close work. He wore his glasses pulled down on his nose so that he seemed to be constantly peering out from behind them. It gave him a friendly look.

He went into the kitchen with one hand, rubbing the small of his back, and reached for the aluminum percolator resting on the drain board. Only way to make coffee, he smiled to himself, and reached for the brown can of CDM coffee on the second shelf of the cupboard. He carefully measured out one heaping soup spoonful for each cup. "Six plus one for the pot," he said to no one. Then he added water to the six-cup line and scratched a match beneath the cabinet. It spurted into flame, and as he did every morning, he quoted out loud the wonderful line in the Browning poem, "the quick blue spurt of a lighted match," and for a moment missed his wife deeply. After ten years, he still carried his torch for her. He watched the flame for a moment, then held it to the burner and turned on the gas.

He buttered a slice of bread, lit the oven on low, and shoved the bread in on a cookie sheet. By the time he returned with the morning paper, the coffee and toast were ready. He turned off the stove and poured his first cup of coffee. The aroma was thick and the color dark, implying exotic places. He sat down at the little white enamel-topped table he had used exclusively since Susan died, and took the first sip. The lovely liquid slipped over his tongue, and he thought there was more to this than caffeine. Coffee correctly brewed and savored brings the whole day alive, and you with it.

He unfolded the paper, lifted the buttered toast toward his mouth, and stopped midway as he read a small headline partway down the left column: FIRE ON TANYARD STREET. The article described the fire department's response and the death of a Negro male named Nathan Hanks. It went on to say Hanks lived alone, and death was by asphyxiation.

Loyal sat for a long time, very still and quiet. When he finally brought his coffee cup to his lips and sipped again, the liquid was cool, and he set the cup down. He wondered if Emily and Lula had seen this yet. He looked at the clock over the stove. Only six thirty, "I'll wait a bit before I call." He rinsed his cup in the sink, poured himself fresh coffee, and sat back down with the paper to read the item again. "My God. What now?"

He let his eyes roam around the kitchen. The few items left in the drain board from last night's supper, the mop standing in the corner of the open closet, the cans lined up on shelves in the pantry. Almost all was in order. The only thing missing was Susan, and all he had of her in this room was memory and her photograph on a narrow glass shelf in the window amid her African violets, which continued to thrive. Their velvet leaves and blue and purple flowers seemed to reach out and around her photograph like arms, and he believed she would have liked that.

Interesting, he thought. "I think this is the first time I've thought of you in the perfect tense." A little more final, this thing that came between us when nothing else could. Death is a marvelous thing, not in the sense of something to be desired, though that's the case often enough, but marvelous because it does such incredible things to lives. The living and the left behind are reborn after such a loss. They must be, or they too will perish.

His rebirth had come slowly, like the dawning of a realization, an understanding reached at last, that the world was not ended, not devoid of joy after all. A light was gone, but where it had shone there was now a different light, a faint glow, a memory. Strange, he thought, that the face you held close to yours in both hands so many times, the lips you kissed, the tiny hairs on the neck are harder and harder to recall. Instead, there is in their place this sensation of presence, dim and glowing warmly.

He went to the window, picked up the picture frame, and looked at her face. Beautiful. He set it down and walked toward the door, but stopped to look one more time at Susan. It seemed she smiled at him, and he smiled back and turned to face the day.

He lifted the telephone receiver. "Two oh four one," he told the operator, and listened to it ring.

"Good morning, Emily," he said when she answered. She immediately asked if he had heard the news. "Yes, I read it just now. It says Wynne picked up the body. Why didn't he tell us?"

They talked for a few minutes, and when they hung up, Loyal called Wynne. "Why didn't you call us about Nathan?"

"I couldn't bring myself to tell you. I'm sorry."

They agreed that the four of them would meet for lunch at Emily and Lula's as usual, then hung up.

Chapter 36

——◆——

THAT MORNING, BIBI KNEW something bad had happened, for she had dreamed her dream of the lion named Trouble, but she didn't know it was about Nathan. June was away at school teaching, and Bibi was rocking on the porch, her chair creaking in time to her rhythms and wondering what was coming when Reverend Buster Holt got out of his car right in front of their house. As he came up the walk, she was certain it was something bad he was coming to tell them. He stopped before the steps, and she kept on rocking with her head against the chair back and her eyes closed. She touched her handkerchief to her face, but she didn't open her eyes again until Reverend Holt spoke.

"Sister Bibi, can I come up and sit with you for a while?" Buster's voice was resonant and soft.

She told him to come on up and sit. Tell her what the trouble is about. He came onto the porch and sat down in the glider and said right out it was bad news he was bringing. It was about Nathan, he said, and Bibi opened her eyes.

"Somebody needs to go tell June. She's going to be all torn up when she hears this." The reverend hadn't even told her what it was about yet, just that it was Nathan, but she knew then, even before he told her.

"Bibi, Nathan . . ." he stopped. He had sat with many of his congregation sharing their grief, but now he had no words to tell about the loss of his friend. They had been a part of something great in the world and shared the dangers and had come home men of a different sort, proud but humbled. "Bibi, Nathan is dead. He died in a fire at his house in Paradise. He was sleeping, so I don't think he felt any pain, but he is now departed from us." He hung his head and wept. She knew they had been good friends, but until that moment, she didn't know how good.

"Buster, y'all got to go over to the school and get June. Y'all got to tell her about this before Mani hears about it. This is a bad, bad thing that's walked into our lives. I knew about it, though. Last night when I dreamed, I knew something awful was walking over to us." She didn't tell him about the lion she saw and the wild dogs, and she didn't tell him she could see the names on those dogs. There was that lion named Trouble and those dogs with their names on their faces, and she could see them. One of those dogs looked right at her in her dream, and she read his name was Bennie Hoskins. But she didn't tell Buster about it.

After a bit, Buster stood up and wiped his eyes, and she wiped hers just a little. "I'd better go on over and tell Sister June," he said.

"And I'd better go on in here and get to cooking some food for the people that're going to come." It took her a little more effort to get up out of the chair, and Buster reached out to help her. And she told him to get away and leave her alone. She wished she hadn't done that. He wasn't that old lion. He was just trying to help out, and he did for a long time. He was a big help to them, especially to June and Mani.

Buster went to the schoolhouse and brought June and Mani home. Bibi had a stove full of pots going, and she went to the door and could tell June didn't need her, but Mani did, so she wiped her face and knelt down at the door and waited for them to come up the steps.

Mani stayed outside on the porch at first and waited like he didn't know what to do. He put his hand in his pocket and fumbled a marble around. He looked at his momma and at Bibi. She held out her hand to him, and he touched it, but he didn't come to her. He clung to his momma, and Bibi touched him, and the tears flowed then. Buster too.

Buster thought they ought to pray, but Bibi said, "Sometimes a prayer ain't going to do a damn bit of good. Later on, it will help you out to pray, but sometimes a prayer only gets in the way of grief, and at a time like this, you've got to grieve. After all, it's Nathan that we've got to pay the honor to. Plenty of time to ask God to help fill up the hole left in your soul. God just needs to step aside for a while until it's time."

So they all wept right there at the front door until the smell of purple hull peas scorching on the stove wafted out of the kitchen. Bibi tried to stand up, but her knees gave out, and Mani had to help her stand. "Child, you are the sweetest thing," she said. She turned off the peas and poured off the good ones in a bowl and scraped the scorched ones out of the pot. "Scorched peas mean more trouble is coming," she said, but she couldn't imagine any more right now.

News travels fast in a place like the Quarter, where houses are nestled close to one another, and people were coming to the door already, and Buster went to answer their questions. He told one of the Sisters to take charge and get things organized. "People can't be bringing the same kind of cake or the same kind of casserole, and they can't all be bringing them to the house. Plan on who takes what to the church after the funeral, too. If God would put you Sisters in charge of this world, there wouldn't be any trouble in the first place." He wished that would lighten the atmosphere, but he knew nothing can do that in the beginning moments of grief.

Chapter 37

Nathan's Funeral
May 14, 1948
Hatchie Landing, TN

THE FUNERAL WAS THREE DAYS LATER, and everybody said it was the most beautiful funeral ever. It wasn't only because it was Nathan's funeral. It was just a beautiful thing. There was no way to explain it. Oh, they were all still feeling sad, but by the time they got to the funeral day, they were ready for God, whoever he might be to them, to come on into the room. It was like Bibi always said, "God just needs to move over at first when a sadness like this comes and not get his feelings hurt because folks can't pray to Him right away. He doesn't mind a bit. Really, He doesn't, because He has got to be pretty big or else He ain't God."

Griffin Wynne brought Nathan back home in the hearse all the way from Paradise. Loyal Hall rode with him, and they came right to the Quarter and turned down the street like it was Main Street USA, and the people all lined up outside of their houses, and stood on the curb to watch the hearse pass by. Wynne saw what was happening and drove slowly, and looked straight ahead all the time as Nathan's body passed by each and every house. And each and every family honored Nathan when the hearse came to them. Mr. Wynne slowed at each one, and they bowed their heads. At the end, he turned around and came back to the Hanks's house and stopped.

He and Loyal Hall got out and came up the walk to ask if they were ready for the body. June told them, "Yes, we are." Wynne said they needed some men to help, and they went back to the hearse, which was shiny and clean. They had driven so slowly passing by the houses, even the dust had not risen up to get on it. June didn't have to say anything or nod. The men just came down and lined up along the walk. Everyone thought it was beautiful to see all those men standing there from the front door out to the street and on down the sidewalk. Wynne and Loyal eased the casket out to the back edge of the hearse, and some of the men lined up along the sides to carry it as if they had planned all this out ahead of time, but they hadn't. It just happened. They carried their burden slowly and in step, every one of the men taking a little step and then pausing, and then up the steps they came and into the parlor. Mani held the door for them, and June stood right there beside Mani without making a sound, only tears.

Some of the men followed right behind with a stand for the casket and flowers. They set it up in the parlor and put the flowers all around. It was lovely and the smell of flowers was wonderful. Wynne said he always liked to have fresh flowers around at a wake and at a funeral, so that is what he did. Bibi asked him how much this was going to cost, and he said it was all taken care of. She wanted to know by whom? But he wouldn't say. He just said somebody had taken care of it, and she shouldn't worry about it anymore. He took her up in his arms. No white man had ever held her before. She didn't know what to do there in front of all the people, but he held her just a moment and told her he was sorry about what had happened. He said he knew Nathan and knew he was a good man.

The next day, Wynne came back from Paradise and took Nathan to the church. Reverend Galt came over, but it was Buster who preached such a good sermon. He reminded them of what Nathan and Ellis had tried to do, and he reminded everybody that God didn't plan for them to die. Sometimes, God lets us work things out by ourselves, he said, and this was one of those times. Buster believed it, and Bibi guessed she did too, but she wasn't as sure of it as Buster. He told them Nathan was working by himself on something God wanted him to work on. He preached that Nathan and Ellis and himself had tried to do what God wanted done for his people, show them how to go over into the Promised Land of this great nation. He said someday they would do it, but right now God wanted them to grieve for Nathan, to remember what he had done for them, and they needed to thank God for Nathan and Ellis trying to show them the way into the Promised Land. It was a beautiful sermon.

Nathan was buried in the Hallowed Ground Cemetery next to the grave that was still waiting for Ellis. Somebody had already put up a stone for Ellis. It wasn't a grand one, just a little one that said "Out of the depths I have cried unto Thee, O Lord." Ellis, Nathan, and Buster all cried out, but their voices weren't heard. There was no answer. Buster was the only one still alive, and he never gave up on God for leaving them to do it all by themselves.

Chapter 38

Griffin Wynne
May15, 1948
Paradise, TN

WYNNE STOPPED CONSTRUCTION on the model of the House on Chester with its tower roof, and instead began building all the houses on Tanyard Street. He replicated Nathan's house perfectly. He made trips down Institute to Tanyard and walked all around the house. He took pictures and studied them. He looked at the smoke-darkened boards on the side of the house and beneath the roof eaves. He noted the blistered paint, the loose plank at the top of the back porch steps, and the screen door left propped open. Someone had replaced the back door where the firemen axed their way inside and had found Nathan's body, but the new door didn't fit the frame and stood ajar. He stepped up onto the porch and looked in the window. One pane was broken, and everything in the kitchen had soot on it. An empty lard can was tipped over on the floor. The label read Old Azalea Lard, Orangeburg, SC.

He pushed open the door. The smell of smoke and char was still strong. No attempt had been made to clean or disturb anything. He took the lard can outside into the light. He thought it smelled of coal oil, but maybe that was just the soot. He set the can on the porch floor and pulled the door shut. He looked behind the row of houses in the direction of Institute Street and imagined the man he had seen walking suspiciously between the houses toward the truck.

He could hear children playing somewhere nearby, but there was no one out in the street. He wondered if the two little boys who had watched everything were all right. He liked little Jesse, who came up now and then to watch him operate the trains. He would speak to his mother to be sure he was all right. He got into his car and drove back to the funeral home.

Over the next month, he concentrated on "the Tanyard section," as he called it. He reconstructed all the houses and placed the fire truck and ambulance precisely. He carved a replica of the battered old truck he had seen and painted it carefully. He loved the details of modeling. He even painted numbers on the truck's tag and placed the little boys sitting on the curb. He talked to their mothers about what they must have witnessed to be sure they were all right. He asked Jesse if he would like to help him work on the layout, and Jesse said he would. After that, Jesse came often to help him with the work. One afternoon, as Wynne detailed the burnt house in the Tanyard scene, Jesse said, "I saw a man coming from between the houses on Tanyard. The firemen made him get out of there."

"What did the man do?" Griffin asked.

"He went out to the street and walked down to the corner. Why are we spending so much time on this little part?"

"The man who died there was a good man," Wynne explained. "I knew him, and he didn't deserve to die. His family didn't deserve that."

"I knew him, too," Jesse said. "He told me and Campo stories."

PART III
1960

"What broke in a man when he could bring himself to kill another?"

– Alan Paton in Cry the Beloved Country

Chapter 39

Jesse Wickham
June 30, 1960
Paradise, TN

JESSE PAID FOR A COFFEE and poured a paper cup of regular, no cream, and sat at an empty table, oblivious to the few students visiting and talking between summer term classes, milling about the big room of the Student Union. He had just come from his mailbox, where the only piece of mail was a notice from the bursar's office stating he was past due on his tuition payment. He was able to attend the college only by virtue of their generosity in allowing him to pay his tuition month by month, the only stipulation being that he pay each semester's tuition in full before enrolling in the next.

He already held two small part-time jobs, three if he counted the stipend he got as the campus news writer for the *Paradise Sun*. The other two consisted of a job bussing tables at the Downtowner Inn, and a now-and-then job working nights for Paradise Frozen Foods that processed produce from local farms during the summer months. During the winter, he worked as needed, moving pallets of frozen produce about the huge quick-freeze facility. It was cold work and only available in an on-call capacity, so the income was unpredictable.

He opened his used copy of *English Poetry of the Nineteenth Century* and tried to concentrate, but put it down. Someone had left a copy of yesterday's *Sun* on the table. He scanned past the ads for the flotsam and jetsam people wanted to acquire or get rid of to a help-wanted ad: "Driver Needed – Occasional funeral service, night and weekend ambulance duty. Apartment furnished. Contact Griffin Wynne at Griffin Wynne Funeral Home." It gave the number to call. He thought about it for only a moment.

He remembered the afternoons when he was young that he and Wynne had spent working on the fabulous model train layout upstairs in the funeral home, the model trains running along the tracks, the little clicks as they moved over a crossing, the intricate detail of the miniature city upstairs. He hadn't seen it since he was a small boy and wondered if it was still there. He tore out the ad and stuffed it in his pocket as he hurried toward his English class. As soon as the assignment was pronounced, he bolted for his rented room on College Street just off campus. He changed into a pair of khaki sport pants and a dress shirt. He knotted his tie, grabbed his blue blazer, and headed out the door, hoping he'd be one of the first to apply.

He cut across campus to Main Street and then across the railroad tracks to Royal, and turned up Chester toward the funeral home. As he started up the steps, he saw Griffin Wynne standing on the porch near the front door, staring off into the distance.

"Lord, who is this coming up the walk?" Wynne said. "Is this Jesse Wickham? You were barely a teenager last time we saw you. What brings you here this morning? Is everything all right?"

"Yes, sir, everything is just fine. I saw the driver job you advertised. I need a job. Is it still open?"

"In fact, it is. It's so good to see you, son. It really is. We lost touch after your mother passed away."

"I've lived with my brother and his family over in Gibson after Mom died. Now I'm at the college."

"Well, come on in and let's talk. If you really are interested, I'm certainly willing to give it a go with you behind the wheel, so to speak." He chuckled at his own bit of humor.

Jesse followed him through the parlor and into his office. It was as cluttered as the first time he ever saw it as a child, come to watch

Wynne work his train layout on the second floor. From the looks of it, he guessed it was some of the same clutter.

Vivian saw him following Mr. Wynne and yelled from her little cubby office. "Hey, Jesse. Don't you look spiffy this morning?" She was always quick with a smile.

Jesse smiled and waved at her, waiting for Mr. Wynne to speak next.

"Have a seat, Jesse." He beckoned to a chair and launched into a more detailed job description than was in the paper. "The salary will be fifty dollars a week plus the apartment. The phone in the apartment is not for personal use, but for ambulance calls instead. You may have a phone installed, but you will be responsible for the bill. In return for the apartment and salary, you will be on call nights and weekends to drive the hearse after a funeral or to transport bodies, which may also occur occasionally, though not often. You'll also be required to respond with the ambulance in emergencies if the police or someone calls."

"That will be okay."

"There's a phone downstairs here in the common room you can use for personal calls—unless there's a viewing or a funeral in progress, or if families of the deceased are present—but keep them to a minimum. The ambulance work can be a little off-putting, Jesse," Wynne said. "There are the occasional accidents, there are the natural deaths, and then there are just crank calls from time to time.

"You can live upstairs in the second-floor apartment, which isn't much, but it's furnished and has its own bath. You'll have one night a week off, and I'll let you choose which one, so long as it's not Saturday. Emily, Lula, and I have a standing date with Lawrence Welk on Saturday nights." He smiled.

Jesse agreed, and the job was his. He would begin on Friday evening and could move in as soon as he wished. He thanked Wynne profusely and chatted a moment with Vivian, then walked back toward campus. At the railroad tracks, he waited for a passing switch engine.

The switchman standing outside the cab, talking to the engineer, was a young black man. Jesse hurried on when the track was clear.

Chapter 40

Mani Hanks
Encounter with Bennie Hoskins
June 30, 1960
Paradise, TN

LATER THAT NIGHT, as Mani Hanks and Maze Wantland worked their evening shift, Mani coupled a boxcar and signaled it was safe to pull out. When Maze headed the switch engine out of the siding, Mani threw the switch and hopped back on. Summer night noises filled the air as they rode back toward Frogmoor yard. The chorus of frogs from the wetlands around the yard was louder than the engine's noise, and Mani wondered if that's where the yard got its name. Images of that other night in a swampy land rose up, and he wiped the palm of his hand over his eyes. Maze asked if he was all right, and he answered that he had been thinking of a fishing trip.

Their orders were to make up a freight bound for Tams and Saint Louis. Maze pulled to the siding they were using, and Mani hopped down and threw the switch. He swung his lantern to signal it was safe, and Maze backed onto the siding and stopped. Mani uncoupled the car and signaled to bump it. Maze revved the engine and gave the car a little shove. It rolled down the siding and bumped the others, coupling itself. Another brakeman would couple the air hoses when the train was ready to be moved out. They headed back into Paradise for two more cars up at the Polar Ice and Coal Company.

They passed the Paradise Cotton Seed Oil Mill and eased up the tracks beside the icehouse and frozen food plant to repeat their coupling procedure for the fourth time that night. Just when Mani was about to signal that it was safe to move into the siding, he saw a man lying beside the tracks up ahead. He raised his lantern directly above his head and waved it back and forth to signal an emergency stop. The engine's brakes hissed and screeched as Mani ran to the man.

The man was lying face down, and Mani rolled him over. He saw no injuries and felt for a pulse. It beat steadily. Drunk. He lifted the man by his shoulders and dragged him to the loading dock at the icehouse, then lifted the man onto his shoulders, fireman style, and rolled him onto the dock. Mani climbed onto the dock, dragged the man over to the wall, and propped him up. A light shone from the end of the dock onto the man's face. Mani felt he had seen him before, but couldn't place him.

Back at the engine, he told Maze what he had done.

"You're a good man, Mani Hanks, a good man. I've seen him hanging around the yards. Probably gets drunk every Saturday night and passes out somewhere. This time, it's his good fortune that you saw him. Let's get moving or we ain't gonna finish this train tonight."

Maze brought the engine to the next set of cars with the gentlest of touches, then Mani locked the coupling and went back to throw the switch when Maze had cleared it. As he waited, the images of that long-ago night in the Hatchie Bottom loomed again. He thought about the man on the dock and was certain he knew him from Hatchie Landing, and it suddenly came to him: the sheriff's deputy in Hatchie Landing, by the name of what? What was his name? He couldn't recall it. The vague outlines of the memory, hesitant and uncertain, formed like the shadows across the rail yard, a memory of a nighttime, a memory he had put away, voices in his house, his father, his mother, and strangers. This was the man who had come to talk with his daddy one night. He remembered the unpleasant conversation and the aftermath, his daddy leaving Hatchie Landing and living away from him, Momma, and Bibi. This was the deputy who made all the trouble for them.

Sonofabitch, maybe I should have left him on the tracks, he thought, but quickly reprimanded himself. It's awful to think of killing someone, but who hasn't had such a thought deep down inside them? Who hasn't imagined a quick stab of a knife or the flame of a gun and a bullet punching into someone he hates? Who hasn't thought the world would be better if a certain person were not in it?

Maze slowed the engine as the last car cleared. Mani threw the switch and ran to hop on the train. All the way to Frogmoor, he pondered the man's face. What was his name? Why was he so fixed in his mind, yet he couldn't recall the name?

Back at Frogmoor, Mani signaled Maze to bump the two cars into the siding. Maze pushed them, then reversed the engine. The cars rolled silently down the tracks and bumped into the others with a loud noise echoing down the line of cars. Barump, buroom, barump, settling down to bum, bum, bump. Mani listened to the sound and thought about the man again, and his name came to him suddenly. Bennie, that's his name. Bennie Hoskins. He remembered Bibi and his momma calling the name. How had Bennie Hoskins come to be a drunk beside the railroad tracks in Paradise?

Mani looked at his pocket watch. Ten forty, the shift was ending. They'd be back at Iselin by ten fifty and close out the shift.

He rode the rest of the way listening to the diesel's rumbling and the big steel wheels clacking over the tracks. The image of Bennie Hoskins hung before him, Bennie lying beside the tracks, Bennie propped against the concrete block wall of the icehouse, Bennie moaning in his stupor, Bennie in his momma and daddy's house in Hatchie Landing with those other men, Bennie grinning when the men told his daddy to leave town and keep his mouth shut. How did he himself end up with Bennie in his own arms in the dark?

Bibi would have told him a story to explain it in her way. She would have some mystical explanation, but it was just a coincidence to Mani, a strange, improbable coincidence that their paths should cross once again. He wondered if he could ever find Bennie sober and ask him questions about what happened. He thought of the night in Hatchie Bottom in his daddy's arms. He remembered the man being tossed onto the fire. Was that poor soul already dead when they threw him up onto the burning pile? Who caused it to happen? Why? Was Bennie involved in it, too? Was it why he was at their house that night, ordering his daddy to leave town? Had Bennie ever been sorry? Was he, Mani, sorry Bennie had ended up like this? He felt pity, but was he sorry? Bibi would say questions are what make you go searching. She'd say something like, if a question comes to you and you can't find an answer, it will cause all kinds of grief in you until you are satisfied you have an answer. That's what she would say.

Chapter 41

Mani Hanks
July 22, 1960
Paradise, TN

THREE WEEKS LATER, on the same Friday three-to-eleven shift, Maze and Mani were making up a train for Fulton. Their orders took them to the siding at the Paradise Frozen Foods plant next to the Polar Ice and Coal Company. It was August, and beans and okra were being trucked in for blanching and freezing. There were three refrigerator cars to be picked up and attached to the train. As they pulled onto the siding below the icehouse, A figure stumbled along the tracks and fell across the rails. Maze blew his whistle and applied the brakes. The man looked up into the engine's blinding light and raised up on one elbow. He laughed and rolled over onto his back.

Mani jumped down and ran toward him. My God, what now, he thought when he saw it was Bennie Hoskins.

"Mr. Hoskins, you need help here?"

"Don't need help. Got help. Just get me back on my feet. Be all right soon as I get on my feet. Be going along." Bennie raised up on the elbow again and looked at the figure standing before him in the glare of the engine's light. All Bennie could see was a tall, dark silhouette. Terror came suddenly into his eyes. He began to crab away from Mani and the light.

"Don't touch me!" He held his palm out.

"Come on, Mr. Hoskins, let me get you up off the tracks here so you won't get hurt."

"No, don't come close."

"You can't just lie here on the tracks. Train's going to cut you in two if you do that."

Bennie seemed to cry out to someone or something other than Mani. He waved his arm over his head and behind him. "Please, help me, please."

Mani looked around, but saw no one. "I know who you are, and if anybody had a wish to hurt you, it could be me, but I don't want to hurt you. I truly don't. I just need to get you off this track here so the train won't cut you in two. Now come on." He reached down and took hold of Bennie's outstretched arm, grabbed him under the armpit, and pulled his arm over his own shoulder.

Bennie continued to mumble. "Sumbitch nigger, take me off tracks. Goddamsumbitch. I ain't do nothing to no sumbitch he don't deserve. Not going to hurt me. Kill sumbitch he try." Bennie slumped onto Mani and passed out.

Mani wrestled him over to the icehouse loading dock, not far from the place he had left him last time. He shoved his body onto the dock, making sure he was far enough from the edge and not likely to roll off onto the ground. He looked for a moment at the broken deputy who had once stood in his momma and daddy's house, threatening his daddy, telling his daddy to leave Hatchie Landing and not make trouble.

"Did you kill Ellis? Did my daddy die because of you?" The questions tumbled out of him. Bennie lay still. Spit dribbled from the side of his mouth. His breathing was slow and regular.

"Burnt on the pile. Didn't kill nobody. Burnt on the pile," Bennie raved into the night. Mani turned to look at him, but he was out cold again on the concrete. His mouth and eyes were open. Mani went back and felt his pulse. It beat against his finger. He hurried back to the engine. "Let's go."

Maze said, "That poor bastard makes you wonder how he got like this."

"He's what's left of somebody I maybe knew one time."

Maze looked over at Mani, then back to the track ahead. He slowed the engine at the switch. "Ain't no maybe about it," he said, glancing at Mani. "Either you know him or you don't."

Mani climbed down and threw the switch. When he returned to the engine, he looked up at Maze from the ground. He couldn't bring himself to tell the whole truth, even to this white man he worked with every day and was almost friends with. When he climbed into the cab, he looked out the window into the darkness and said, "I think he lived over in Hatchie Landing one time. He may have been a deputy over there. I think he may have done some bad things once. Don't know, though."

They worked out their orders and headed the engine back to Iselin for the shift change. Their week of three-to-eleven shifts was over. The incessant tang, tang, tang of the engine's bell as it moved down the track seemed like a knell instead of a warning.

Mani enjoyed the walk down Magnolia to Royal, then up to Short and over to Institute, where he lived. In summer like this, the frogs and peepers were in full chorus in the lowland, and cicadas and locusts in the trees made a deafening racket. It reminded him of Hatchie Landing, and he felt homesick. The days were better than the nights. He lived on South Institute, not far from where his daddy had lived in Paradise. He could walk from the Iselin shops to his house in less than twenty minutes, and he did on most nights. He didn't own a car. The city bus came down to Iselin and Magnolia, so he could ride the bus when the weather was too bad, but on evening shifts like this, the last bus was always gone by the time he got off. Maze offered him a ride, but he declined. He said he wanted to walk and enjoy the night. "I'll see you on Sunday at midnight." He waved goodbye. Maze drove out of the parking area onto Iselin and over to Magnolia.

He wondered if Bennie Hoskins was still passed out up on the loading dock or if he had woken up enough to get home. He wondered where home was for him. How long had Bennie lived here in Paradise?

These questions rolled through his mind like train cars humped on a siding. Unanswerable questions clunked into each other, but nothing coupled. They didn't make up a coherent train of thought. They were just questions without answers. Perhaps if he could find Bennie when he wasn't drunk, he could get some answers. Would he talk? Mani thought about the question. If he could ever find Bennie sober, he might find the answers. He decided to try to find him one day soon.

He turned on Royal Street, but instead of turning onto South toward home, he continued walking on Royal, wondering about Bennie Hoskins. He wondered what kind of man Bennie started out being and what brought him to the kind of man he was now. Everybody begins as an innocent little baby and then turns into something else. Little babies aren't evil. People make them evil. Had Bennie Hoskins become an evil person, or was he just caught up with evil people? He pondered as he walked for almost an hour until one o'clock in the morning. It could be unfortunate for a black man on the street at this hour, but he was a railroad man dressed in his work clothes, and this was the tracks again and the depot across from the icehouse.

At the depot, Mani crossed the tracks toward the icehouse. Bennie was nowhere on the loading dock. He crossed the two sets of tracks and the sidings and scanned up and down the tracks, but didn't see him anywhere. He hoped the man had gotten home safely, wherever home was. He turned toward his own home, wondering how he might find Bennie sober to ask him his questions.

Chapter 42

Mani Hanks
July 23, 1960
Paradise, TN

MANI ALWAYS WOKE BEFORE THE WHISTLE at Iselin Shops sounded, even on days off. The big whistle was the community clock and marked shift changes. It blew at quarter to seven every morning and again at seven to mark the shift's beginning. He turned over in bed and closed his eyes again. His week of shifts was over. He had walked the tracks and streets into the early morning looking for Bennie, and he wanted to sleep.

He heard someone yell at a child to calm down, and it made him think of the night Bennie came to the door with those other men and told his daddy to come outside, the fear in his momma's eyes when his daddy went out on the porch with them. His daddy looked them in the eye and smiled like they were old friends. Bibi was holding on to his momma's arm like she was afraid June would go out there with his daddy. He remembered Bibi's little bony arm wrapping him up close to her. He had wanted to be just like his daddy, not afraid to go out on the porch with those men.

Bibi had grabbed at him, but he pulled away from her to open the screen door. His daddy was standing between him and the men who were talking. Their talk sounded quiet and solid, almost like the men down at the cotton gin. He thought Mr. Clifford might be with those men out there on the porch, so he pulled away and went out to stand beside his daddy.

He could still hear the sound of the door banging shut behind him and his momma calling out to him. His daddy turned and put his hand on his shoulder and told him to go on back inside, but he hadn't wanted to. He wasn't afraid of those men, not after what he had seen out in the swamp. He wasn't afraid of anything anymore. His daddy told him again to go back inside, but he didn't want to leave him out there with those men. Mr. Clifford wasn't with them, and he had known with the certainty that only a child's mind can have that they were among the men he and his daddy saw that night. They might be there to take his daddy away and hurt him, and he had wanted to be beside him to help him out, but his daddy told him to go on back inside with Momma and Bibi. It hurt him. He wanted his daddy to know how much he loved him and how much he would do for him, but his daddy hadn't wanted him to.

He rolled over and looked at the little slits of light coming in underneath and around the window shade. The shade had two spots on it and a pinhole, so when the sun was just right, a tiny bit of light crept across the linoleum beside his bed. He watched the little pinpoint of light slip across the floor and thought about time and how it crept along just like that. He wondered what time would be like if there wasn't any sun to measure it by, no slits, no pinpoints. He guessed that if you didn't have time, people couldn't change, because if they could, that would be something fixed, and then you could measure from one change until the next change. He thought time passing was just people in different places doing different things. He wondered, if they hadn't been in the swamp that night, would none of this have happened?

His teacher back in Hatchie Landing had taught them the names of rivers, like the Tennessee and the Mississippi and the Congo, and countries and mountains, but she didn't teach them about the Hatchie River. It was just something out there, not far away, and he had guessed they were supposed to already know about it.

He sat up on the side of the bed and rubbed his face with both hands, then ran them over his head, feeling the little soft curls of hair.

In the bathroom off the hall next to the kitchen, he washed his face, brushed his hair again with his wet hands, dried his face and hands, and went to the kitchen. He took two cold biscuits from the refrigerator, broke them open, and slathered butter over the insides, poured sorghum over them, and wolfed them quickly with huge swallows of milk, and then wiped his mouth with the back of his hand. His momma would fuss at him for doing that.

The thought of her and Bibi made him smile, and he decided to catch the bus over to Hatchie Landing and surprise them. He could go over on the Memphis bus tomorrow morning and come back on the Nashville bus late tomorrow afternoon in plenty of time for the eleven-to-seven shift tomorrow night.

He went back to the bedroom and took clean coveralls and a shirt from the closet. Mrs. Lane, next door to the church, did his washing and ironing and kept his clothes neat. He dressed and put on the good high-top shoes that he kept polished beside the bed.

Up Institute to Chester, and through the alley beside the Griffin Wynne Funeral Home, he strode to Baltimore, then up Spencer to East Main, to the Greyhound bus station. He paid for a seat on the Sunday morning Memphis bus stopping in Hatchie Landing. He asked the woman whether there would definitely be a bus from Memphis to Paradise late on Sunday. She told him there was one scheduled to stop in Hatchie Landing at six o'clock and would be in Paradise by seven thirty. He bought the return ticket and put both tickets in his shirt pocket. He thanked the woman and went down Main Street to the Black and White Store and bought a new white shirt to wear tomorrow.

He left the Black and White Store with his new shirt and thought about going over to Mrs. Lane to see if she could wash and iron it for him, but decided it wouldn't be right to ask her to do it so late on a Saturday. He could hang it up and press out the wrinkles himself at home, so he turned back the way he had come and went into Woolworth's for a Coke and a sandwich. At the counter that until recently had been labeled "Coloreds Only," Julia Bell came over to wait on him, and he ordered a Coke and an egg salad sandwich. He loved those egg salad sandwiches on toasted white bread. He watched her drop two slices of bread into a toaster. In a minute, she served him his drink and sandwich. He smiled at her. She smiled back.

"You doin' okay, Mani?"

"I'm doing just fine, Julia. I'm going to Hatchie Landing tomorrow morning. Want to come with me?"

"Shoo, I'm going to church tomorrow. I don't have time to go to Hatchie Landing. I ain't lost a thing over there." They laughed. He liked Julia. She wasn't married, and several times he had thought about asking her to go out with him on some Saturday. Maybe they could be friends, or maybe more. He didn't have many friends and didn't make friends very easily. Bibi always said he was a private man. Ever since the night in the swamp, he hadn't made many new friends. Family was what he stuck to mostly, and they were all in Hatchie Landing.

He put sixty cents on the counter and thanked Julia. "I'll see you later, maybe next week."

She smiled hugely at him and told him not to be so long. "Maybe one of these times I'll go to Hatchie Landing with you, if you give me a little notice," she said. He grinned at her, and she told him to go on.

Outside, Mani stopped at the curb. He thought about catching a ride on the city bus for a while. Sometimes he did this, just got on the little city bus line and rode around town, sitting in the back looking out the window at the passing scene. Sometimes he rode over to the Lane College campus and walked around. It was pleasant over there. There were trees and nice buildings and colored boys and girls who attended school there. He thought maybe he would enroll someday, even if only part-time. Then maybe he could learn about time and what it meant and other things.

When he rode the bus, he never had to talk to anyone much. He could just ride and see the houses and think about his family, his bibi, his momma. He worried about them. Right after Daddy died in the fire, Momma said she didn't think she could hold on, but she was better now. They all were. He hoped so. It was still hard for him.

He moved a few steps away from a group of white women waiting for the bus. They held packages and talked among themselves about children and dresses and things they had bought in Penney's or Woolworth's. One of them wanted the others to go with her to lunch at the S&T down the street.

Across the street, a man was curled on a bench on the courthouse lawn with his back turned to Mani. Pigeons walked among the legs of the benches and pecked at crumbs among the feet of the old men who sat whittling and swapping knives and stories. Mani saw the man stir and sit up, and realized it was Bennie Hoskins. One pigeon came pecking beneath the bench, and Bennie kicked at the bird. It flew up and settled back. Mani wondered if Bennie would make a scene if he confronted him with all the questions he wanted to ask. Would people gather around?

A man came out of the courthouse and stood briefly on the steps, then walked down one of the sidewalks leading away from the entrance. To Mani, this was just another person in the bustle of a Saturday at the county seat. He approached the bench where Bennie sat just as Bennie looked across at Mani, but the bus pulled up, blocking his view. The women got on the bus, and it pulled away.

Bennie was still staring across the street at Mani. Suddenly, he called out, "Hey, you. Black sumbitch. No room on the bus for y'all? Serves you right, black sumbitch."

The man Mani had seen was now coming toward Bennie, telling him to shut up. Maybe this man was somebody who could help him ask Bennie his questions, but he thought he could never ask such a thing of a white man he did not know, and he couldn't talk to Bennie here, not with him this way.

Bennie said something to the white man, and the man said something back. The white man's jaw was clenched. Bennie stood up and shuffled off along Church Street toward Chester.

Mani followed at a distance as Bennie turned west and stumbled along until he came to the old Riverside Cemetery. He didn't seem to notice that someone was following along behind him. At the cemetery, he struggled over the low brick wall. Mani peered over the wall and saw Bennie stretched out on the ground in the shade of a big catalpa tree. Thunder rumbled in the distance.

Mani made his way along the wall to the entrance. Crumbled bricks and broken pieces of headstones lay about on the ground nearby. The old cemetery was in disrepair. How sad, he thought. He saw Bennie stretched out on the ground near the back wall. Other than the questions pressing down on him, he didn't know why he had followed this man to this place. He had given the incident at the bus stop too much attention and was now put out with himself. Why would a man like this hold so much hate? Is it just me he hates, or is it everybody, or just black people? What makes one man hate another? He couldn't answer his own questions among the stones. Thunder rumbled again. Closer. Wind stirred the catalpa leaves.

Mani worked his way among the stones toward where Bennie lay sleeping, not making a direct path toward him, but as if walking through a pencil maze, moving in first one direction and then another, between graves and headstones. He stopped twenty feet away and leaned against a tall monument, watching Bennie's chest rise and fall slowly.

"Hello," he said. The man slept on.

"Hello," he said louder, and then moved until he stood over Bennie. He could see he was filthy and ragged. Spit drooled from the side of his mouth. His face was covered in fine hair that grew in ragged patches. Mani touched him with his foot. His breathing kept on, up and down, in and out, the same air Mani breathed. Again, Mani reached out with his toe and jostled Bennie's shoulder. When he opened his eyes, Mani said, "Hello."

Bennie sat upright. His eyes went wide. "Git away from me, you black sumbitch. Git away." He scooted back in the grass until he came against a monument.

"I'm not going to hurt you, Mr. Hoskins. I just need to know something."

"Don't know nothing about nothing. Ain't talkin' to you."

"Please. Here's what I want to know."

"Don't know it. Don't know it. I ain't seen nothing and I don't know nothing." Bennie seemed out of his head.

Mani repeated, "All I want to know is, why do you hate me?"

At first, Bennie said nothing, as if he was contemplating the question, but his eyes were glazing over. Then he muttered, "Black sumbitch. Leave me alone." Bennie began to pull himself up against the stone. He looked at Mani, and then he opened his mouth. His teeth were brown, and some were missing. His sneer was full of scorn. "Leave me alone. I don't truck with no nigger."

"Why do you hate me?" Mani asked him again.

"They made me do it. Made me because I'm white."

It made no sense. Mani turned to leave, then said again, "I only want to know why you hate me. There has to be a reason. You can't hate somebody without a reason. Explain it to me and I'll leave you."

"Hate," Bennie mumbled. "Ain't hate. Defense. Pure white."

"What?"

"They told me. Pure white. The only color. Pure white. Clean, sent from Jesus. They told me."

"Who told you?"

"Them in Hatchie. My daddy and my brothers. My friends. They told me that."

Mani felt his scalp crawl. The awful night in the Hatchie Swamp came to him again. "You know about Hatchie Bottom?"

"Lots. Been there lots. Pure white and clean, and fire purifies," he said.

What made Mani ask the next question, he could never say. "You ever see anything bad in Hatchie Bottom?"

"Bad? Bad? Make everything pure in the fire. The fire makes you pure and white."

Mani turned to leave and tripped over a low gravestone. He stepped between stones and picked up his pace as he went. Bennie called out behind him.

"Killed one sumbitch in Hatchie Bottom. Shoulda killed all of 'em. Pure then. Pure in the fire."

Mani stopped still. He turned and went back to Bennie. He couldn't believe that by a strange accident and his own unbelievable behavior, he had found one of those men from the awful night in the swamp. He'd never guessed Bennie was actually one of those men. He'd always assumed Bennie was just a deputy who looked the other way.

"What did you see? Tell me what you saw."

"Black sumbitch. Brought him down in the truck. Black sumbitch. They told me to do it."

"Who told you to do what?"

"Get pure by the fire."

"Made you do what, goddamn it?"

"Wasn't only me. Made two of us."

Holy Jesus, thought Mani. It's true. This is the same awful thing.

"How many times did you get pure?"

"Only takes one time to get pure. Pure and holy forever. Pure and white. They told me. God loves me. My pure whiteness."

This poor man has lost his mind over it, thought Mani. "Tell me about it. Please."

Bennie looked at him and sneered again. "Ain't telling nothing. No black sumbitch gits anything from me."

"I don't want it, I just want to hear it. It will still be yours even after you tell it. Tell it to me."

"Took him up. Feet and arms. Onto the fire, pure white fire. Leave me alone. You ain't God. God is pure white."

"Who took him up? What fire? Where?"

"Me. I took him up. Onto the fire, and Jesus saved me. I'm pure." Bennie started to cry.

"I know about it. I know what you did. I saw you do it. I watched you from the swamp. I saw you put that man on the fire, and I prayed to the same God you prayed to."

"No. No. Not same. God don't hold with you."

"God loves me too."

"No, no God don't love you. Only the pure and the white like Jesus."

"But Jesus wasn't white." Mani could no more tell what made him say this than he could say why he was having this bizarre conversation with a derelict in a cemetery.

"Jesus made me white. I'm pure." Bennie's eyes grew wilder. Spit came out of his mouth as he talked. He waved his arms about and looked around as if to find something he had laid down.

"God help your soul. I saw what you did, but God help your soul." Mani turned again to leave. He took a step and heard a sound coming toward him. He turned to see Bennie lunging with a piece of broken monument in his hand. Crazed Bennie held it high, his eyes off in the distance. He screamed as he came.

Mani ducked. Bennie fell across him, hitting him on the shoulder with the stone and on his face. Mani felt blood on his skin, and Bennie hesitated. "Blood," he said.

Mani got to his feet. "Red, just like yours." He started once more to walk away, but Bennie leaped up with the stone and hit Mani on the head. More blood came, and Mani couldn't see. It was in his eyes. He struggled with Bennie. He could smell Bennie's awful odor and taste it in his mouth. He clenched his teeth and pursed his lips. Bennie hit him again, and Mani grabbed his arm and wrestled the stone from him, but he clawed, and Mani hit him with the stone, and he fell to the ground and lay still.

"Oh, God. Now what have I done? I've killed him. I've killed a man."

He dropped the stone and looked around. A car stopped out on the street, and a door slammed. He ran to the back wall, climbed over it, and dropped down into the bushes on the bank of the river that flowed so slowly beside the cemetery. He slid down the bank and lay in the shadows of button bushes and willows, settling into the weeds, listening to the sounds of katydids and cicadas, wondering how they made their sound, which sounded like grief to him, a low moan that came and went and came again louder. He heard something like the same sound coming from his own throat, and he thought he heard something on the other side of the wall, like that same kind of moaning, and something like footfalls and the sound of someone stumbling on gravel. He thought maybe he didn't hear anything at all from where he lay. A low thunder rumbled further off to the north. He wished he could hear Bennie walking, but he was sure he would never hear him again.

Tears streaked Mani's face, and the sound of grief came out of his throat. Cicadas and katydids sang, and the dark water moved almost not at all out in the lowland, and a turtle was the only thing with life out there next to all this death. He thought about his own life, how it had come to this, how it was now wasted, how it was so improbable that he had saved Bennie's life not once, but twice, and then he had killed him. He put his hand to his own forehead and saw blood on his hand and couldn't be sure whether it was his own or Bennie's blood. It was dark like the water. He lay in the shadows and wept and waited for darkness.

When night fell, the water was still and black like the water in the Hatchie Bottom. He remembered the night so long ago when the two men swung Ellis up onto the burning pile. Now he knew one of them was Bennie. Anger flared in him, and he thought he had done a good thing to kill Bennie, even though he hadn't meant to do it, had only wanted to know the answer to his questions. Why? Why did they do it? Did they kill his daddy, too? Why does any man kill another, and what happens in them that lets them do it? He knew what had happened to himself. He could tell that story firsthand now.

He looked around in the shadows and heard katydids in the trees and listened for other sounds, but there weren't any. He kicked off his shoes and slid down the bank into the river and let the slow-moving water wash away the blood. He cried. He sang. He sang "Jesus Loves Me." He sang "All my sins have been washed away." He sang "Washed in the Blood," but he didn't think this blood on his hands and face was the same.

He slipped when he tried to climb out of the water, and his knee went into mud. He waded out deeper into the dark water. His feet felt mud and old stumps and roots like snakes. He rubbed his pants leg until he thought the mud was gone. Then he waded back through the water and roots to the bank. He grabbed the trunk of a willow and pulled himself up and felt around for his shoes, but they weren't there. Where am I, what have I done? He took a step and felt a shoe under his foot. He bent down and found both shoes, then made his way along the stone wall of the cemetery until he could see street lights on Riverside through the trees and bushes.

Nothing moved on the road as he put on his shoes, so he started walking back toward town. If I can get home, maybe I can clean up and change. Maybe I can forget about Bennie, pretend I didn't kill him, let someone else find him, and wonder who he is and how he died. He walked along thinking these thoughts until he was on Chester Street.

Chapter 43

Bennie Hoskins
July 23, 1960
Paradise, TN

BENNIE OPENED HIS EYES and saw the twilight shadows of tree limbs and gravestones, grass and weeds, a faded plastic flower, and a small, ragged flag that was lying on the ground. Bennie thought it was a shame. People shouldn't do that to the flag of the United States of America. He would never let it happen. His daddy and the Klan had taught him to honor the flag and God. They were respectful of the flag.

He knew someone had hit him, but couldn't remember who it was. He had talked to someone, maybe in a dream, maybe not, maybe for real, while he was drunk. He licked his lips and wished he had some whiskey. Anything right now would be all right. He rolled his head and saw only another gravestone. He moved his legs a little and listened to the katydids and the cicadas in the trees and far-off thunder. Nighthawks circled slowly overhead in twilight that was almost gone into darkness. He groaned as he tried to stand, at first not quite making it, and then he pulled himself up by a gravestone and leaned there awhile, breathing hard and heavy.

He didn't feel drunk anymore, but his head hurt. He wanted to feel something on his tongue, something to wipe out the awful taste and thirst. Beer, whiskey, even some mouthwash would help. He needed to talk to somebody, get some whiskey, and tell about the colored man at the bus stop. He wondered if Malcolm Oakes would be at the Supper Club tonight. Malcolm would help him, would give him something. He needed to go on down to the Supper Club and tell Malcolm about it. He would know what to do. He's making money down at the Supper Club, gives me whiskey when I come, go down and tell him about it, and get some whiskey.

Bennie struggled toward the stone wall separating the cemetery from Riverside Drive. He leaned against the wall for a long time and moaned again. His head hurt so badly. He held his head in his hands and saw the blood on his hands in the dim light. He tried to climb over the wall, but didn't have the strength. He slid down to the ground and sat for a long time in the fading light. When it was dark, he made his way along the wall to the gate, then out onto the street and down to Riverside. He struggled along the graveled road toward the Supper Club. Darkness was falling on him, thick and moonless. Katydid and cicada song in the cypress trees around the cemetery obliterated all other sound, and a bullfrog roared in the low water, and Bennie struggled along until he could hear music and see a dim, blue light and cars parked in front of the club. Malcolm will want to hear about this. Malcolm will give me something to drink. He trudged down the sloping pavement into the parking lot and leaned against a gleaming '55 Chevy, blue and white four-door. He could open one of the doors and climb into the backseat and sleep awhile, but he wouldn't get anything to drink if he did.

The door to the Supper Club opened, and a wide swath of bluish and yellow light washed over the little wooden porch and across the lot, casting long purple shadows over the cherty stones. The sound of music and people having a good time flowed out with it. There were young voices in the sound, young people dancing and having a good time. Bennie remembered his own youth and wondered why he had not had good times like these. Why had he been such a loner, though he didn't think that word. Separate, was what he thought. He stuck to his guns and his hunting and fishing, mostly by himself and sometimes with one of his brothers. His daddy had never said much to him, and he didn't know who his mother was. Bennie sometimes hated his daddy for not telling him about his mother.

The pale glare from the doorway narrowed, and he heard a soft sound as the door closed again, the music fading away to a soft thump and murmur. He heard a clink and saw a small flame go to a cigarette and another clink as a lighter closed. Bennie watched the place where the light had shone. Like a beacon, a small glow swelled up, then faded in the darkness, then swelled again and faded.

He wondered who was smoking out there on the porch. He thought it might be Malcolm, so he called out in a whisper. When no one answered, Bennie began moving through the darkness. The intermittent cigarette glow beckoned him. A neon Pabst sign shown in a side window, but Bennie kept on course toward the man smoking. Malcolm, is that you? He thought he said it out loud, but he wasn't sure if he did or not. He wasn't certain of anything anymore except that somebody had to do something about the nigger boy who had hurt him. The nigger boy shouldn't have. Somebody had to do something about that. His daddy would do something if he were still alive. He hated his daddy, but he missed him as he crunched over the dark gravel.

The man on the porch called out, "Who's there?" The cigarette arced like a meteor out into the dark and fell to the ground. Bennie watched it and thought how beautiful some things are. The fire was beautiful to see as the sparks trailed behind.

"Malcolm? That you?" Bennie whispered into the darkness.

"Who is it?" the voice asked.

"Malcolm, it's me, it's Bennie. I'm hurt. Some boy hurt me." He heard steps coming toward him. The gravel crunched under heavy shoes, and suddenly his old friend Malcolm was in front of him. "Malcolm, I sure could use something to drink."

"Bennie, old buddy, you've got to get hold of yourself one of these days. You know that? You've got to get hold of yourself, or something bad is gonna happen to you. You're practically dead already.

You just don't know it yet. Drinking yourself into the grave, Bennie. What the hell's the matter with you anyway?"

Malcolm didn't like Bennie much. He had a whole big room full of potential trouble inside there, and now he had to deal with this poor, drunken sonofabitch who wanted Malcolm to call him a friend. Bennie, our friendship died a long time ago, buddy. That's what he wanted to say, but he didn't say it. Instead, he asked Bennie what he needed.

"I'm hurt, Malcolm. Some nigger tried to kill me."

"Aw, Bennie, what you want to go making up something like that for? Grow up for once. Ain't nobody, even a Black, going to try anything on you. Nobody would want to. You're already so broken down, nobody cares, Bennie."

It didn't hurt Bennie's feelings to hear this kind of talk. Malcolm could tell him the truth, and he wouldn't care at all. He needed someone to be honest with him. He thought maybe he could love Malcolm like a brother if Malcolm would let him. He reached out a hand toward him. Malcolm brushed it away.

"Bennie, I'll get you something, but you've got to go away from here or the cops will come for you. Now, stay put for a minute. When I get back, though, you've got to leave." He turned to go inside. "Malcolm," Bennie said, "it was somebody saw what we did that hurt me, tried to kill me."

Malcolm stopped and turned around. "You better shut up, Bennie, about all that. It's over and done with, what we all did. It was a long time ago, and now it's done. Don't go talking about it. Do you hear me?"

"But he did, Malcolm, he did. He hunted me down and came after me. He tried to kill me. I did the best I could, Malcolm. I wished I had a gun like when we was with the sheriff in Hatchie. He wouldn't come at me like that then. No."

Malcolm was silent for a moment, the contempt on his face shrouded in the palpable darkness. He opened the door and went inside, spilling music and bathing Bennie in the yellow-blue light before the door narrowed and the light was shut out, and the music was only a thump in the air, and the darkness was once again palpable. He leaned against the porch rail and waited for the light to wash over him again. If he could stand in it, he thought it would cleanse him, the yellow-blue light. It did come again, and so did Malcolm with a bottle. "Here, Bennie, take this and go around back. You can sit and tell me what all happened back there, wherever you came from just now."

Bennie shuffled around to the side of the building and squatted down on one of the crossties outlining the parking lot and facing a pile of stones that remained from the grading. He unscrewed the cap on the bottle and took a long swig. His lips smacked. He screwed the cap back on and closed his eyes.

Malcolm watched him. "Tell me, Bennie. Who was it and what did he say?"

"I don't know who it was, but he knows what we did, and I told him to shut up, and I tried to shut him up, Malcolm, I tried to, but he took the rock out of my hand and he hit me with it. I fought him, Malcolm."

"Bennie, you dumb shit, if he didn't know you had something to hide before, he does now. What else did you tell him?"

"I didn't tell him anything, Malcolm. I just told him the fire was what saved me, what purified me. It's true, too, Malcolm. It's true. We did it together, you and me, and we was purified." He took another swig of the whiskey and then another. He tried to screw the cap back on and said nothing else.

Malcolm looked down at him and listened to the wind blow through the willows in the lowland behind the club and wished Bennie hadn't come here. He wished Bennie hadn't told him about the fight with the colored man, whoever he was. He watched Bennie for a while.

Bennie drank more from the bottle, closed his eyes, and tried to stretch out along the crosstie, but it was too narrow. He rolled face down.

Malcolm looked at him and then at the stones on the ground. He knelt down and picked up a stone and hefted it in his hand.

The front porch of the Supper Club was bathed in a splash of blue light. The music spilled out. Then the light narrowed, the music softening to its quiet murmur as the door shut behind Malcolm.

Bennie lay on the grass and stones, the same grass that took up his blood. He thought he might be having another dream. This one was soft and full of light, and he wasn't drunk anymore, and he had no pain, and he was clean and pure and walking toward a bright light in the distance, but the light dimmed and got dimmer and then faded away.

Later, a couple came out back laughing and teasing each other until suddenly the woman stopped and pointed toward Bennie's battered body. She screamed and both ran around to the front porch. The man yanked open the door, and everyone inside heard the girl screaming and her boyfriend telling her to shut up for God's sake, and everyone stopped dancing and the band stopped playing and High Boy Bailey stopped singing his version of "Long Tall Sally." Everyone looked toward the door where the screaming wouldn't stop. Someone else told the voice to shut up, shut up. Then another voice said to call the police, someone's dead out back.

Malcolm poured the rest of Bennie's whiskey down the men's room drain and washed off the bottle. He dropped the bottle into a stained cardboard box with the words "Mrs. Sullivan's Pies" on the side. He came out onto the dance floor and commanded everyone to stay put. "Don't anybody move or try to leave," he said. He went outside. Faces and bodies crowded the door, trying to see what would happen next. The blue light behind them, mixed with the blinking beer sign, shone so dimly they couldn't see anything beyond the porch.

Malcolm walked around the side of the building. He gazed down at Bennie one more time. "Damn, Bennie, how come you had to tell me about all that?" There was no sound from Bennie. Malcolm noticed how much blood was on the ground, then went back to the front and waited for the police.

Chapter 44

Mani Hanks
Evening, July 23, 1960
Paradise, TN

MANI HEARD SIRENS WAILING past the cemetery and then on beyond. He kept on walking until he got to Chester Street. passing the big house with the round tower, without knowing his own father had worked there sometimes. He walked head down and hunched over, mulling the mess he was in, even though he had saved Bennie's life two times. A car crept up behind him. He walked on as the car came alongside and drove slowly for a moment before a voice asked him to stop walking.

He saw it was a police car, and he stopped where he was and stood very still with his hands at his side like Bibi had taught him. His face was in shadows, and he heard the motor stop and the door open and close. The policeman came around behind the car toward him.

"Where're you going, boy?"

"Home."

"How come you're so wet and muddy?"

"I fell down back at the river."

"Have you been drinking, boy?"

"No, sir, I don't usually drink hard liquor."

"What were you doing back at the river, and where're you headed?"

"I was just having my day off, and I slipped and fell. That's the truth. I'm going home."

A crackling noise came from inside the car, and the man called him boy again and told him to stay put. He said all this without malice but firmly as he shone his flashlight in Mani's eyes. The policeman went to the car, reached inside for the radio as it crackled again. Mani couldn't make it all out, but he thought he heard him say he had someone who might be involved. There was something inaudible, then he turned to Mani. Mani didn't move.

The policeman asked him once more where he was going. "Home," Mani said. "I live down below Tanyard Street on Institute."

"Well, boy, I need you to come with me." He was firm when he said it.

Mani thought there was nothing to do but go with him. The policeman told him to get in the back of the car. He bent over to climb in.

"Watch your head, son," the policeman said.

Mani thought he was probably a kind man. When he was inside, the policeman turned the car around in the middle of the street and headed back toward town. Mani closed his eyes and thought he could hear his bibi saying something to him about trouble, but it was only the katydids in the trees singing their rising and falling song, the one that sounded like grief.

At the station, two officers interrogated Mani, and a stenographer took it all down. He answered all their questions honestly, truthfully, and completely, leaving nothing out.

"You say you were at the cemetery. What were you doing there?"

"I followed Bennie Hoskins. I wanted to talk to him."

"Why?"

"He was one of the men who burned a cross in our neighborhood in Hatchie Landing. He came to our house and threatened my daddy. I wanted to know why he did that."

"So you knew him?"

"No, sir, but I knew who he was. Maze Wantland and I found him on the tracks twice when we were switching. I moved him to safety. Maze can tell you about it."

"We'll check that out."

"Why did you attack him?"

"He attacked me, and I hit him. He fell and was very still. I think I heard him get up later, but I must have killed him. I didn't mean to. He tried to hit me with a rock or something. I just wanted to talk to him, to ask him why?"

"Why what? You were angry with him. You wanted to hurt him, didn't you?"

"No, I didn't want to hurt him. He hadn't done anything to me, but he hated my daddy. I wanted to know why he threatened him." Mani told them that when he was just eleven years old, his daddy had died. "I wanted to know if he knew anything about my daddy dying in the fire on Tanyard Street." He told them about Bennie Hoskins being in the Hatchie Bottom one night with some other men and how they had swung Ellis Wiggins up onto the fire. He told them all of it, and they said they would check that out too.

"You said you hit him with something. What was it exactly?"

"I think it was a piece of a broken headstone."

"And you followed him to the Supper Club and hit him again with a rock."

"No, sir. I didn't. I didn't go near that Supper Club. I was going toward home when the officer picked me up."

"But you hid in that slough by the river. Why didn't you just go for help?"

"I was afraid. I was afraid something bad would happen to me too, like my daddy and then my mother and Bibi wouldn't have anyone."

"Did you kill Bennie Hoskins?"

"I think so. I guess I did. I hit him."

"Okay, Mr. Hanks. That's all we need." He turned to the stenographer. "Did you get all that?" She replied that she had it all down and would deliver the transcribed statement in the morning.

"Mr. Hanks, we're charging you with the murder of Bennie Hoskins. You'll be kept here in custody."

Mani seemed to deflate. "I understand." He was sorry about losing what opportunities he might have had coming. He was sorry he had messed up. He was truly regretful that he had ruined his chances. He didn't know what else to do. He didn't have anyone to talk to, to ask what to do, so he had told the polite policemen all he could, truthfully and completely, and one of them handed him a tissue when tears rolled down Mani's cheeks. They were not hard on him. They believed his every word.

Chapter 45

Jesse Wickham
Evening, July 23, 1960
Paradise, TN

JESSE FINISHED TYPING the last paragraph of his term paper on Hemingway for English Lit 404. He stretched and began putting away things he had tossed about: a couple of books, some papers, and his jacket. He hung the jacket in the little closet Wynne had cleared for him to use. Inside the closet was another small door that Wynne had said went into the attic crawl space. Jesse opened it and peered into the dark attic. He could see rafters, electrical wires, and a box in the dimness. He pulled the box toward him and lifted it out into the light. It was a small, dusty, wooden trunk. Inside were some letters and three Blue Horse brand notebooks. He was about to open one of the notebooks when the phone rang. He shoved the trunk back into the crawl space.

"Griffin Wynne Funeral Home," he answered.

A crisp voice on the other end said, "This is Ikey Rogers, Madison County Sheriff's Office. We have a body at the Supper Club on Riverside. Can you pick it up?"

"Yes, sir, I'll be right out. Hospital?"

"No, dead body. The coroner has pronounced. Just take it back to the funeral home and keep it for now. Sheriff and a couple of deputies are at the scene. He'll advise as to disposition."

"All right, I'm on my way."

He slipped on the smock he always wore on ambulance calls and grabbed the bag with gloves and extra smocks in it. He pulled onto Chester Street and headed west toward Riverside. He flipped on the rotating red light. No need to use the siren.

In less than ten minutes, he pulled into the gravel parking lot at the Supper Club. There were a handful of people standing at one corner of the concrete block building. Some were smoking and holding beers. They all looked down the slope behind the building now and then, but mostly they talked and joked among themselves. Sheriff Bo Roper came around the corner and motioned for Jesse to back the ambulance down beside the building. He guided Jesse down the slight slope, as if he were directing an airplane into its berth. Jesse opened the rear doors and unlatched the gurney and bumped it over the gravel to where two deputies stood smoking.

"This it?" he asked, looking at them.

"Well, it ain't the circus if that's what you're asking," the one Jesse knew only as Darrell replied.

"Sorry, didn't mean to be ridiculous." Jesse was serious.

"Cut it out, Darrell," Roper ordered. "Here, I'll help you."

"Rattle, get over here and help out," Sheriff Roper ordered the other one.

The four of them carefully lifted the body onto a rubber sheet covering the gurney. Jesse folded it over the body and draped another over. Then he pulled ties from underneath the gurney and tightened them over it all. It gave the cargo an eerie look. Before that, it had just been something under a black rubber sheet. Now it was a dead body.

The four shoved against the gurney. The wheels on the gravel made the body jiggle like it was alive. The few onlookers moved back as if they didn't want to be contaminated by whatever was underneath. Somebody in the back of the crowd told a joke, and everyone laughed.

Jesse asked Roper if one of them should come to the funeral home to witness the unloading of the body. "I mean, since you all are saying this might be a murder. I'm the only one there tonight."

"Sorry, Jesse, but we've got other stuff going right now. Maybe later we can get somebody over there."

"No, it's all right. I'll call Mr. Wynne. I hate to, but he'll come help out." He locked down the gurney and closed the doors. He pulled out onto Riverside and headed toward town.

In a few minutes, he pulled into the bay behind the funeral home. He was unlocking the bay door when the phone rang. He hurried to answer it.

"Jesse, this is Griffin. The sheriff just called to tell me you had a body and might need some help down there. Is that so?"

"Yes, sir, I have the body inside and can manage, but you might want to come down to witness and oversee things since, according to Sheriff Roper, this might be a murder."

"I'll be right down. It'll take me about half an hour. Okay to move the body inside, but don't touch anything."

Jesse went back outside, opened the ambulance doors, and pulled the gurney out. There was a slight incline to the asphalt in the unloading bay. He eased the gurney out and unlocked the lever so the legs would drop down as he eased it out. The wheels thumped down heavily, but held steady. He shoved the gurney toward the bay doors, rolling it inside. He shut the doors and turned up the two window air conditioners to cool the main room. He looked at the clock. Eleven forty-five.

Griffin Wynne arrived at midnight. "Jesse," he called out.

Jesse was upstairs in his apartment, reading, and came right down.

"Mr. Wynne, I'm sorry to make you come out like this."

"No bother, Jesse. Let's see this body and get things settled. I can work on it tomorrow if the sheriff gives me clearance."

They moved the gurney to the embalming room, and Wynne undid the ties. He pulled back the top sheet and looked at the body for a few seconds. "Do they know who this is?"

"No, sir. They didn't seem to know for sure yet. Darrell said they should know by morning. I heard Roper talking on the radio. They think it's a murder."

"I see." He looked for a bit longer, then covered the face again. "Let's move it into the cooler."

They rolled the gurney to the single cooler and opened the door. Wynne pulled a table out, and they put the gurney alongside it. With one at the head and the other at the feet, they lifted the body onto the table, then Jesse shoved it into the cooler. He backed out, and Wynne closed the door.

"Murder is a sad business," he said. "We don't have them too often in our town, thank goodness. I know who he is."

"I heard one of the deputies say it might be the guy who sometimes panhandles around the courthouse."

"Yes, I've seen him sometimes on the courthouse benches or over at the New Southern, outside the restaurant, begging for food money."

"I heard Darrell say he came into the sheriff's office one day, drunk and raving, saying he knew things nobody else knew, and he was going to tell them all someday. Darrell said they locked him up."

"Loyal told me he came into the courthouse one day saying much the same thing." Wynne was silent for a long moment. He looked around the room and down at the floor at his feet. Jesse thought he seemed to drift off. Then he said, "And now, here he is, dead in my prep room."

They walked to the door. Wynne reached for the light switch and turned the room where he prepared the bodies into darkness. Jesse watched him stare into the dark room. Finally, Wynne shook his head, said goodnight, and headed outside to his car.

"Mr. Wynne?" Jesse called after him.

"Yes? Something else, Jesse?"

"Yes, sir. I found a little trunk up in the attic with some papers in it. I put it back. Could I look through it? Does it belong to you?"

Wynne turned squarely toward Jesse. "No. Leave it alone. You shouldn't meddle in the other rooms and spaces, Jesse. Please leave it alone. The papers belonged to a black man named Nathan. They're private."

"I once knew a man named Nathan. He used to work in our neighborhood sometimes. He told us stories. His house burned down one day."

"Yes, I remember. You saw it, and that's when I went to visit your mother to explain what you had seen and to assure her it was all right for you to come up to see the trains. Jesse, the papers are private. I should go up and remove them."

Jesse followed him upstairs to the attic space. Wynne took the trunk, pausing at the top of the stairs. "Unfortunate things happen to good people sometimes, Jesse. Remember that."

Jesse heard him get in his car and start down the drive.

Chapter 46

Griffin Wynne
Late Evening, July 23, 1960
Paradise, TN

WYNNE PULLED ONTO CHESTER STREET, but instead of heading home, he drove to Riverside and turned south past the cemetery toward the Supper Club. He pulled into the gravel parking lot and killed the engine, and sat quietly a moment listening to the night sounds. Inside the club, there was music, strong and frenetic. The excitement of someone just found dead outside had fallen away, and people were dancing, or else they were trying to bury the experience in music and alcohol and dim blue lights. Outside behind the club, frogs croaked in the marshy darkness, some kind of bird or other night denizen called out of the gloom, and the soft night music of insects and unseen animals stretched out in the low marshland.

He saw someone moving in the shadows. At first, he thought it might be Sheriff Roper or one of the deputies, but there was no patrol car around, so he didn't call out. He got out, stood at the corner of the building, and watched a man bent over and sweeping a flashlight over the ground. He picked something up and held it up to the flashlight. Wynne stepped out from the corner and spoke.

"Hello, Malcolm."

"Jesus H. Christ! You scared the bejesus out of me. Who the hell? Oh, Wynne. I didn't know who the heck was out here. Christ, you startled me."

"Sorry, Malcolm. Didn't mean to. I just came down here because," he hesitated, then lied, "my man said a strap came off the gurney when he was here. I was on my way back home from helping him out and thought I'd come see the scene and maybe find the strap. I didn't mean to scare you. It's a stupid idea anyway to try to find it in the middle of the night. I'll come back in the morning."

Malcolm pitched something into an open fifty-gallon oil drum used for trash. "I'm okay, now, but you sure did scare me, though." He laughed a little. "Here, I'll help you look around for it."

"Thanks." A lie even to another liar is an awkward thing. You have to keep it alive and in front of you, or sooner or later it will turn on you.

"We don't get crimes much in Paradise, and I guess I was a little bit curious too." Wynne gave his own laugh.

They walked around the area. When he didn't spot anything right away, he told Malcolm it wasn't a big deal. He walked down to where Malcolm had been shining his light. He swept his own light over the area. There was a stone on the ground and blood beside a crosstie. There was a little blood and maybe something else on the stone. He flicked off his light and turned back to Malcolm.

"Nothing here, Malcolm. I'm sure we'll find it up at the funeral home in the morning, probably in the ambulance. Thanks for helping me look."

Malcolm said nothing, but watched him walk to his car and get in.

Wynne rolled down the window to let in some air. The sound of crickets and cicadas came up to him from the lowland. As he put the car in gear, he heard gravel crunch to the side. He looked out the open window.

Malcolm put his hand on the top of the car. "Anything else, Mr. Wynne?"

Wynne stumbled over his words. "No, ah, well, Malcolm, as I said, we don't get crimes much around here—"

Malcolm interrupted him. "Mr. Wynne, let me save you some trouble. Bennie Hoskins is dead, and you and I both know he deserved to die. Hell, you might even think I killed him, but I'm not admitting to it. I'm telling you he knew too much about a lot of people, if you know what I mean, and I'd keep to my own business if I were you, Mr. Wynne. I may be guilty of a lot of things, but you've got a lot more to lose."

"Malcolm, did you kill Bennie? I need to know."

Malcolm smiled. "Bennie was unstable, Mr. Wynne. He was coming unhinged, and he knew too much about too many people. He knew about you coming to Hatchie Landing that night to pick up that body. Do you remember, Mr. Wynne? Do you know what I'm talking about? How did you handle it? I never did know."

Wynne didn't respond. Malcolm leaned down and spoke in a low voice. "Somebody who knew so much about both of us? Somebody who was crazy? Somebody who might talk too much? Whoever killed him did you and me both a favor, don't you think?" Malcolm crunched away toward the music.

When the door closed behind him, Wynne opened the glove compartment and retrieved a flashlight, and walked to the building corner and shone the light into the oil drum. There, on top of the trash, was a man's tie. He held it up to the light and saw a spatter of blood on it. Malcolm, he wondered? Is this what I saw him toss in?

As he drove home, Wynne thought about Bennie Hoskins waiting lifeless in his funeral home. He could still see him in his Hatchie County Sheriff's Department uniform, standing outside the church the day of Nathan Hanks's funeral. He remembered Malcolm Oakes standing with him. He remembered June telling him about the two men blocking Ellis and Nathan when they tried to register to vote. He had left those people behind in another life. Now they were back, one in life, one in death, trying to get to him again here in Paradise. He resolved not to let them.

Chapter 47

Loyal Hall
Morning, July 24, 1960
Paradise, TN

LOYAL HALL OPENED his *Commercial Appeal* and read the local news section first. The mayor of Paradise had spoken to the Rotary Club. Loyal had been there and had heard the empty speech. The obituaries were next, then a brief entry about a man found dead behind the Supper Club. The man's head was crushed. The bouncer, a man named Malcolm Oakes, said someone found the body out there and called the police. The dead man wasn't identified in the article, but it went on to say he was a vagrant who was seen frequently around town. The article said the reason for the killing was unknown. A black man was in custody for questioning, but no charges were filed yet.

After he washed and put away his coffee cup and plate, the telephone rang. He lifted the receiver. "Loyal Hall speaking."

"Loyal, this is Sheriff Roper. How are you this morning?"

"Fine, Roper, and you?"

"I'm fine, but I'm calling to ask a favor of you. You may not want to do this, but we have a man, a colored man, down here this morning. He has a strange tale to tell, and frankly, we don't know whether to believe him or not. He has admitted to involvement in a killing by the Supper Club."

"I just read about that in the *Commercial Appeal.*"

"Really? They do get their stories quickly. Well, this man's name is Mani Hanks, and he keeps saying he doesn't know anyone who can help him. He's from over in Hatchie Landing, but now he lives and works here in Paradise as a brakeman for the GM&O. He isn't dumb, Loyal. He speaks clearly and seems to believe he's the one who killed the man. He admits to it, in fact. I think he needs a good lawyer, so that's why I'm calling.

"Mani Hanks, name's familiar. Do you remember the man who died in a house fire down on Tanyard Street some years ago? He did some work for me and my sister at the time. His name was Hanks, too, Nathan Hanks, and he was from Hatchie Landing."

"Interesting. I do remember," said Roper. "There is a lot more our man keeps talking about, some of it over in Hatchie Landing years ago, but I'm not sure about all of it. It'll take a lot of digging to get to the bottom of it, if it can be done at all."

"Griffin Wynne and I went over there to Nathan Hanks's funeral. There was a young boy in the family. I remember him. This could be him. I can come down later this morning. Is that okay?"

"That'll be fine. We'll probably charge him shortly. It'll be hard not to since he admitted to killing the man. At least he admits to killing someone. It's our assumption for now that his man and ours from down at the Supper Club are the same, but there is some inconsistency."

"I'll be there as soon as I can. I'm not even dressed yet." He broke the connection and went upstairs to dress.

An hour later, Loyal stepped off the elevator on the top floor of the Madison County Courthouse, where the county jail was housed. The elevator smelled faintly of oil and disinfectant as it rattled and clanked its way upward. The doors opened, and he stepped out into the hallway. The deputy directly ahead looked up from his paperwork.

"Morning, Mr. Hall. The sheriff said you'd be up here this morning to meet with Mani Hanks. He's been real quiet; no trouble from him."

"Good to hear, Johnny," said Loyal. "May I see him now?"

"Sure. Parker's down at the cells. Just go on down."

Loyal walked down the corridor toward the six cells. The deputy named Parker was sitting at a desk. He called out to Loyal as he approached.

"Morning, sir. You here to talk to Mani Hanks?"

"Yes, I am, Parker. Mani Hanks. Thank you."

"Just have a seat here, and I'll bring him out. In fact, you can meet with him in the empty cell over there if you want. There's no need to lock it, being on the third floor like we are. He won't run."

"I'm not worried about it, Parker. It'll be just fine. Thanks."

Parker went around the corner. Loyal heard keys and a cell door being opened and voices. Footsteps sounded along the tiled floor, and Parker's voice got louder as they came around the corner.

Loyal looked at the tall black man with Parker. He wondered if he had stood in the front room with this man and his family. Was his old grandmother still alive? All the neighbors had lined the street as the hearse had passed by. Griffin had slowed the hearse until it was barely coasting over the gravel and dust, pausing in front of each house so they could pay their respects. The image was fresh as if it had happened yesterday.

Mani didn't smile or seem to recognize Loyal. He wasn't shackled or handcuffed. Loyal stuck out his hand and spoke. "Good morning, Mani. I think I remember you from a long time ago. I was at your house in Hatchie Landing when your daddy died."

Mani looked at him quizzically, then said, "Were you one of the white men who came in the hearse?"

"I was, Mani. I knew your daddy back then. He was a good man. I'm sorry about his death. I don't know of anybody who didn't respect him. It was an unpleasant thing."

"Thank you" was all Mani could say.

Loyal turned to Parker and said, "Parker, get me a room somewhere, not this cell here. This man's in a cell enough as it is. Get me an empty office or something."

Parker hesitated a moment. "Okay, Mr. Hall. There's an empty office down here."

"Thanks. I wouldn't expect you to have any trouble from Mani. If he's like his daddy, he's a good young man and probably an innocent man." They followed Parker to the office and waited as he switched on the lights. The deputy returned to his desk at the end of the hall.

Loyal moved two chairs into the open space in front of the desk. He motioned for Mani to sit, and he took the other chair. He looked Mani over. "Are you feeling all right? Anybody tried to hurt you, Mani?"

"No, sir, everybody's been real nice to me."

"Who have you talked to?"

"You mean since I got here? Well, mostly to the sheriff. The one who brought me down here was a policeman from Paradise. I talked a little bit to him and then to another man downstairs, and when I told them about Bennie Hoskins, they decided maybe I should come up here to the sheriff. So I mostly talked to him."

"I see. Why don't you tell me everything you said to him? Don't tell me anything else yet, just the questions he asked you and what you said back to him. Okay?"

"Yes, sir." Mani recounted everything he had said to Roper. Loyal listened without interrupting. He wrote nothing on paper, did not move, and just sat listening.

When Mani was finished with his story, Loyal was silent for a moment. He gazed out into the hallway glare. "Now, Mani, tell me everything you remember about how you came to see Bennie Hoskins, and you can tell it any way you want. You can skip around or anything. I've got plenty of time. I may ask you some questions as you go along. Okay?"

"Yes, sir, that'll be okay." And he began telling all about Bennie Hoskins. They sat together in the cramped office for over two hours, Mani talking and Loyal listening. He told about finding him along the tracks and saving his life. He told about doing it twice. He told about the night in Hatchie Bottom. He told about Bennie coming to their house with other men and how they made his daddy run away to Paradise. He told about his daddy coming home again and how everybody on the street got scared when the men came into the Quarter in the middle of the night and burned the cross. He told about following Bennie and confronting him in the cemetery, fighting, and how he hit him with the stone. Finally, Mani was quiet.

He looked at Loyal and said, "What else do you want me to do?"

Loyal smiled at him. "There's not a thing else you can do, Mani." He explained how things would progress and how the grand jury was in session and would hear his case. They wouldn't be allowed into that proceeding. They would probably return a true bill, meaning that Mani's case would go to trial, but he hoped it wouldn't. He hoped they would find who had really killed the man at the Supper Club.

"But, Mr. Hall, I killed Bennie up in the cemetery. I don't know about him being down at that Supper Club. I left him on the ground up in the cemetery, and I ran away and climbed over the wall and hid out by the river till it was dark. It's what I did. I'm sorry for it, but it's what I did, all right."

"I'm sure you did all that, Mani, but something else had to happen for things to turn out just like this. We're going to try to answer that first, and maybe we can get you free again. I'm going to try really hard to do that for you. Okay?"

"Okay, Mr. Hall, okay. But it's what I did is all I'm saying."

Loyal stepped out of the room and motioned for Parker to come take Mani back. He put his hand on Mani's shoulder. Mani thanked him.

"You take the best care of this man as you can, Parker," Loyal said. "All of you. He's a good man and has had some hard, hard times and a whole lot of unnecessary grief. So you take the best care of him you can. You understand?"

Parker nodded. "We will, Mr. Hall, we will. Don't worry about it." He took Mani by the elbow and nudged him back toward the cell.

Loyal watched them walk the length of the hall and round the corner, then went to the elevator and pressed the down button.

Chapter 48

Griffin Wynne
July 25, 1960
Paradise, TN

WYNNE STOOD IN THE MIDDLE OF THE PARLOR and looked around the way an animal circles when claiming its space. He concluded everything was in order, the tabletops dusted and the lamps all working; the hardwood floor polished, and flowers fragrant and fresh. He insisted on fresh bouquets for the tables every other day. He thought about Bennie Hoskins. There was no one to mourn his death, but Wynne believed each death requires homage, to speak to the wasted life if nothing else, so he had asked Jesse to come as a mourner and offered to pay him extra. He often called college students in cases like this. Jesse had agreed to hurry back right after his last class of the day. On his second turn around, Wynne glanced out the window and saw Jesse hurrying up the sidewalk. He rushed into the parlor. "Give me fifteen minutes to freshen up." He bounded up the stairs to his little apartment and returned minutes later dressed in a dark suit, starched white shirt, and a pale blue tie.

Wynne smiled at the memory of Jesse as a child, knocking on the front door one afternoon shortly after Nathan's death. No one knocks at a funeral home. Death invites everyone. Wynne had opened the door and squatted down, putting himself on level with the child's eyes, "Hello, what can I do for you, sir?"

Jesse had been no more than eight or nine years old, but he had smiled directly into Wynne's eyes and said, "Are you Mr. Wynne?"

"Yes, yes, I am."

"My mother told me you have a train set upstairs."

In that instant, a bond was forged. Here was a mere child who was polite, remarkably articulate, and bold, and who was interested in Wynne's hobby. Wynne smiled at the child.

Jesse had looked down at his shoes. "I was wondering if you'd let me come and see it sometime."

"Well, how about right now? That is, if you have the time."

Jesse's eyes had beamed with anticipation.

"What's your full name?" Wynne had asked as they started upstairs.

"Jesse Franklin Wickham," said the boy, "but people just call me Jesse."

"Well, Mr. Jesse Wickham, I'll call you Jesse, and my name is Griffin Wynne, but people mostly call me Wynne, so why don't you just call me that too?" Wynne had reached out his hand, and the boy had put his small one into his. They shook on it like two adults sealing a deal.

Wynne spent fifteen minutes showing him how the model train operated, then he left him with instructions to watch and not touch until he returned. He had a funeral to prepare for and went back downstairs. He asked Vivian to look in on the boy every few minutes and have him leave after an hour. "Be sure to invite him back," Wynne instructed. "Oh, and I should call his parents to get their permission and reassure them it's all right for him to come here."

Jesse had come back many times after that first afternoon, and they often worked on the layout together. One day, Wynne was painting a small building while Jesse watched the trains move over the tracks in the background. He loved the clicking sound of the tiny wheels over the crossings. Wynne had a wooden whistle that sounded exactly like a train whistle, and Jesse blew it when the train approached a crossing. Wynne stopped what he was doing and smiled at him.

"There's supposed to be a little lean-to on the other side of that building," Jesse said as the train passed a small grocery store on the layout.

Wynne looked up from his painting. "Where is that?"

"Right here," Jesse pointed. "If you want to make all these just like they are in real life."

Wynne didn't recall ever telling him the layout modeled the town of Paradise. "Well, why don't you make me one then?" he said.

Jesse was good at painting the delicate buildings and especially good at landscape details. He was captivated by Wynne's idea of replicating the town, and after that, he would often tell Wynne how a building or a house looked differently from the way Wynne had depicted it. It's true that a child's eye sees differently, and it is not the low angle of the eye. It is a clearer filter in the mind that allows for it.

During his teenage years, the intervals between Jesse's visits grew until, at last, he no longer came to work on the model and run the trains. Wynne missed their occasional brief hours together replicating and debating details, but the trains waited like life itself— ready to roll their small freight around the tracks. Now, here he was again, but this time he wasn't coming to play with trains.

"Thanks for helping out with this funeral, Jesse."

"Thanks, Mr. Wynne, I'm glad I could help out today. The extra money will come in handy."

They went over the details of the ceremony. The man had no family and no known friends. He had died under suspicious circumstances, murdered, maybe. Wynne told Jesse a little about Bennie Hoskins.

The funeral was brief. The minister from First Baptist Church read a scripture, said a prayer, and gave a short homily about death and resurrection. That was it. There was no one to mourn, no one present other than Jesse and Wynne. Wynne stood at the back watching to see if anyone else would come, but he saw no one, not even Malcolm Oakes.

Chapter 49

Loyal Hall
August 12, 1960
Paradise, TN

THREE WEEKS AFTER MANI'S ARREST, Emily called to invite Loyal over for supper. "Stop by the A&P and pick up a quart of milk, a loaf of bread, and some nice tomatoes." The errands were a small price to pay for a home-cooked meal, and the three of them were sitting on the garden porch when the phone rang.

Emily answered. "Loyal, that was Wynne. He called your house and your office, and when you weren't at either place, he hoped he might catch you here. He says he wants to talk to you. He's coming over in a few minutes." She went out to the kitchen, leaving Loyal and Lula to visit.

"How will the trial turn out? How is Mani?"

"Well, the grand jury returned a true bill, of course, and the pretrial machinations are over. I'd say we'll be in trial within a couple of weeks."

"This has all been pretty fast, hasn't it?"

"Yes, but things just happened to work out that way. The grand jury was in session when Mani was arrested, so the district attorney got an indictment right away."

"Who's trying the case for them?"

"Bob Werner is trying it himself. I've talked to him about it, and he's not holding anything back, sharing the information and all. It'll be a fair trial, Bob's a good man. Still, Mani's got a long shot at acquittal at best. My guess is that he'll be convicted. I'm hoping for the best, though."

"But he didn't do it, did he?"

"No, I don't think he did, but he confessed to doing it, and proving he didn't may be just about impossible. If he didn't do it, then who did? The only other person that could possibly be responsible is Malcom Oakes, and there is absolutely no evidence for that. Still, I'm hoping to punch enough holes in their arguments to convince the jury that there is some doubt."

"That shouldn't be hard."

"You'd think so, but don't forget, Mani did confess to fighting with Bennie Hoskins and killing him. And even if I do raise enough questions, it doesn't mean the jury will be convinced, and in the end, that's what counts."

"Not fair."

"It's the fairest we've got. It's a good system, Lula. It's just not always perfect. I'll do my best."

"Who're your witnesses?"

"That's my biggest problem. There aren't any except for character witnesses. I've got his minister back in Hatchie Landing and Reverend Joe Galt over here. Joe Galt doesn't really know him, though, just his family. And that's another thing. I'll try to bring in the family tribulations, you know, Nathan and all, and try to build some sympathy with the jury. Judge will probably call me out on that one, though, especially if Bob objects."

"It seems a shame," Lula said. "He didn't do it, Loyal."

Loyal looked at her. Sometimes she could be blunt and direct. "I don't know, Lula. He insists he must have killed that man. I doubt it, but who knows? I learned a long time ago not to be surprised at anything. Anyway, there is no way to keep that confession out of the trial. He himself says he wasn't coerced into confessing. He repeats that he confessed of his own accord. He actually believes he killed the man."

They heard knocks at the front door. Lula stood. "That'll be Wynne. I'll bring him out here. You two can talk while Emily and I get supper on the table."

Her heels pecked the floor as she went through the parlor toward the front door. Loyal closed his eyes and rested his head against the chair back until he heard them returning.

"Hello, Wynne."

"Good to see you, Loyal. I'm glad I caught up with you."

Lula went off to help Emily in the kitchen. Wynne sat in the glider. "This is a lovely sun porch, isn't it?"

"Yes, it is. Lula said you needed to talk to me. What about?"

"Loyal, I'm—" he hesitated and looked away to the garden. He seemed to drift off, then said, "I don't think Mani Hanks killed Bennie Hoskins."

"Oh? Why's that?" Loyal sat forward.

Wynne explained about going to the Supper Club and seeing Malcolm looking around where Bennie had died. He told of his lie to Malcolm about why he was there.

"What do you think Malcolm was doing?"

"I don't know. He was just looking around, and he was startled when I showed up."

"Well, it's not much. It's not evidence, Wynne. I don't think it will help at all, but it may help me impeach Malcolm's testimony if it turns out to be damaging. I need something, anything to cast some doubt on the situation."

"I think Malcolm had something to do with it."

"What makes you think that?"

Wynne hesitated again. "Just a feeling." Then he told Loyal about the blood on the ground and the stone lying beside the crosstie.

"Well, that's all known fact, Griffin. It's in the evidence the prosecution will use and has turned over to me. Everyone agrees Bennie Hoskins was a drunkard. He was probably drinking that night as usual. We know he was killed by a blow to the head. A stone with blood on it would not be particularly unusual at the scene of an accident, much less such a crime. What I'd like to do is to raise some doubt about where Bennie was assailed. Nobody is going to dispute where he died. It happened beside the Supper Club. The only question is where the blow that killed him took place. Was it at the club? Or was it at the cemetery, as Mani believes? If Bennie was killed at the Supper Club, it would go a long way toward exonerating Mani, provided we could convince the jury he was never there. He says he was hiding in the old riverbed behind the cemetery. It's just his word on it. I doubt the prosecutor can dispute it, but he'll make it sound pretty flimsy at best, and at worst, he'll make it sound like Mani was hiding, which he most certainly was. But proving your stone is the one that killed Bennie would be a tough job. There was plenty of blood on the ground and on other rocks and gravel around there."

"Maybe you could have me as a witness."

"I've already put your name on the witness list. I'll probably call you. We have almost nothing going for us, and your testimony could help."

"You two come in the kitchen and let's have some supper," Emily called to them.

"I'll do my best to raise doubt, Griffin. The question is how? I'll tell the jury about the altercation in the cemetery. They'll know all that, but how can I make them doubt that being the cause of Bennie's death? Your testimony will help, but it may not be enough."

Chapter 50

———◆———

Loyal Hall
September 12, 1960
Paradise, TN

THE DAY BEFORE THE TRIAL, Loyal walked across the courthouse lawn, past the bench where he had chastised Bennie Hoskins for his abusive language, past the Confederate statue, past the memorial to veterans of all wars, and past the water fountain with six fountains bubbling up, where just a few years before people came to drink, whites from the three on one side. The other side had a sign that read "Colored," although nobody, white or black, hardly ever came at all to drink anymore. He went up the steps and inside to the elevator. He pressed the up button and took it to the third floor.

The sound of his shoes echoed as he walked the length of the hallway to where Parker sat at a desk at the entrance to the cell area. "Morning, Parker."

"Morning, Mr. Hall. Do you need a meeting room or will his cell be all right?"

"Give us a room. I need to be sure he's ready for tomorrow. Any problems?"

"No trouble from him at all. I wish all of them were like him. It's too bad he's got himself in this fix. I think he must be a good boy."

"He's a good *man*, Parker. The word is man. Don't use the word boy."

"Well, you know what I mean. I didn't mean anything bad by it."

"I understand, Parker. Just old habits, huh?"

"Yes, sir, I guess."

"Well, it's time to break them."

Parker unlocked the main door and led Loyal into a room outside the jail cells. The smell was antiseptic.

Parker went off down the line of cells and returned with Mani at his side. He wore a clean white shirt and blue jeans that Loyal had brought him from his momma.

"Good morning, Mani. How are you feeling today?"

"Pretty good, Mr. Hall. They feed me well, and except for the lights being on all the time, I can rest some. I wish I weren't in here, though. I wish I could see my momma and Bibi. They're all doing okay?"

"Yes, they're just fine. I talked to your momma and Bibi yesterday. She's some woman, your bibi." He smiled at Mani.

"She sure is. She can cook, and she can tell a tale. I love to hear her tell stories. You get her to tell some stories. You won't forget it."

"I've decided how we are going to do this thing, Mani. We don't have much to go on except your word, and I don't know how this jury will take it if I put you up on the stand to tell it yourself. We can't expect them to believe every word you say, so I'm going to put your bibi on the stand to tell it for you. She can do that part for you, can't she?"

"Yes, sir, she can do that. All I have to do is tell her the truth."

"I may have to put you up there to give the facts since you were there, but the prosecutor will try to trip you up and make the jury feel like Bibi is lying to protect you."

"I didn't mean for him to die. I didn't even know he was dead. I just hit him when he jumped on me. He was slumped up against a tombstone when I ran away from there. The more I think about it, the more I think maybe I didn't kill him, Mr. Hall. I sure hate for Bibi to have to testify for me, though."

"Mani, she is old and very wise, and she looks it. She can tell about all the other things that have happened to you and your family, the events leading up to this one, where Bennie Hoskins died. What we have to do is convince the jury that even though you did hit Bennie, you were just defending yourself, which you were, and you had good reason to be afraid for your own life. We are also going to try to show them that there is no absolute proof that you killed him. He may have been killed by someone else. After all, his body was found down behind the Supper Club, two miles from where you say the two of you tussled in the cemetery off Riverside Drive. We'll try to show them how you and your family have been harassed by officers of the law in another county, and how they made your lives unbearable. The judge might not allow that, though, but the whole idea is to make the jury sympathetic to us and convince them they have no proof you actually killed Bennie. That could backfire on us, though. The jury could conclude that you had motive enough because of all the harassment of your family. Our other real problem is that we have no witness to place you at the cemetery or to prove that you were never at the Supper Club. The prosecutor will try to show that you could have done it at either place."

"Mr. Hall, I'm in your hands, and all I can do is tell the truth, and that's what I'll do. I just hope all the others will do the same when it comes their time."

"Mani, your family has suffered enough. I'll see you in the morning and we'll go down to the trial together."

"Okay, Mr. Hall. I thank you for what you've done for me."

"It's not a problem, Mani. I knew your daddy. He was a good man, too. I can't help but feel I didn't do enough for him when I could have."

"I guess you did all you could, Mr. Hall."

"But I wonder if I could have done something more, Mani." He turned to leave. "You sit here. I'll go get Parker to take you back. You need anything?"

"No, sir, I don't need anything."

Chapter 51

Loyal Hall
September 19, 1960
Paradise, TN

A FEW SPECTATORS WERE SCATTERED about the courtroom: a reporter from the Memphis Press Scimitar, a couple of old men with nothing else to do, folks wanting to escape the heat outside. The witness room was down the hall from the courtroom, small with no windows and uncomfortable wooden chairs with hard, straight backs. The walls were painted a pale institutional green that had peeled in little flakes along the baseboards. June sat holding Bibi's hand. Bibi rocked back and forth slowly as if she were in her rocker on her own front porch. Griffin Wynne joined them. He had been about to sit at the end of one of the courtroom's hard wooden benches until Loyal told him he would have to wait in the witness room. Loyal thought his friend seemed to walk with a burden as he left the courtroom.

The room felt close even though it had been retrofitted with air conditioning. Fans slowly turned overhead. There were floor-to-ceiling windows on either side of the room, but they were fixed and couldn't be opened. The judge's bench was raised in the center. There were fireplaces, no longer in use, on each side of the room. Artifacts from bygone eras were on the mantels. Two small glass cases on either side of the judge's bench contained more artifacts of the county's history: an old steamboat whistle, a Bible owned by a once prominent citizen, photographs of old buildings, some Civil War buckles, and a rusted rifle barrel.

The opening statements were brief. Bob Werner, in his deep and overly loud voice, told the jury about Mani Hanks being taken for questioning, how Mani had told of fighting Bennie Hoskins in the cemetery, and admitted that he hit him with a stone and killed him. The prosecution's case would hinge on that admission and those events that no one disputed.

Loyal briefly told the jury that the prosecutor's conclusion was wrong, even though the events the district attorney had related were facts. The defense would show there was a reasonable doubt that Mani Hanks could have killed Bennie Hoskins.

After opening statements, the judge looked over to Werner, "Are you ready, Bob?" Bob Werner pulled himself up from his chair and stood leaning with his hands on his table. "Yes, your honor." His ruddy complexion and jowly face gave the impression that he was grossly overweight, but in fact, he was just a very big man, heavy boned with a slight paunch. Time and age contributed to the appearance.

"How about you, Mr. Hall?"

"Whenever it pleases the Court," Loyal said.

"Then let's get started." He made a little speech to the courtroom about order, then looked from one attorney to the other. "Let's go, Bob," he said.

Werner introduced as evidence the coroner's report and all the photographs taken at the Supper Club that night. He introduced Mani's signed confession. Then he called as his first witness the Paradise City policeman who had taken Mani in for questioning. The policeman described stopping Mani and then getting the call about the murder at the Supper Club.

"Objection, your honor," Loyal said. "The witness is relating what was, at the time, conjecture."

"We're splitting hairs, Mr. Hall, but I'll sustain."

Werner addressed the witness, "Please just describe the actual events without opinion."

"I stopped and questioned the defendant on the street, and while I was asking him questions, I got this call about an incident down at the Supper Club. The defendant over there," he pointed to Mani, "was muddy and wet, and I was suspicious, so I told him to come with me down to the station, which he did without resistance. He was calm and polite."

"You picked up the defendant on Chester Street inside the city limits of Paradise. Could the murderer have killed Mr. Hoskins down in the vicinity of the Supper Club and then had time to walk to where you encountered him, walking wet and muddy down Chester?"

"I say so. It would depend on what time of day or evening the murder actually occurred."

Next, Werner called Sheriff Bo Roper, who recounted the investigation at the Supper Club. He mentioned having his deputy call Wynne Funeral Home to send an ambulance. He explained that Mani Hanks was transferred to the county jail after it was determined that the murder had occurred outside the Paradise city limits.

Loyal objected again, but this time the judge overruled him. "By this point in time, it was a common belief that a murder was committed, Mr. Hall. You're welcome to show otherwise when it comes your turn."

Werner called Malcolm Oakes. "Tell us what you saw and did that night at the Supper Club."

Oakes recounted the events of the night. He told of someone coming in the door, screaming that there was a dead man outside. "Things went wild all of a sudden," he said. "It's my job to keep order. It's not easy sometimes, but the crowd was into the music, and things were going smoothly until this woman came in hysterical, and everyone went for the door at once. I thought we were going to get somebody killed right there. I yelled for everybody to calm down, and then went outside to see for myself. Sure enough, here was this man lying on his face. He seemed dead to me, so I went back inside and called the sheriff. The rest of the time, I was just keeping order."

"Thank you, Mr. Oakes. That's all."

The judge looked over at Loyal. "Your turn, Mr. Hall."

"Mr. Oakes, did you know this man?"

"Yes."

"So you knew it was Bennie Hoskins. Did you mention that to the sheriff or anyone else?"

"I may have, but I don't remember."

"Did you work with this man at one time?"

"Yes. He and I were deputies to the sheriff in Hatchie County."

"Think carefully, Mr. Oakes. Did you see this man before the hysterical woman came in screaming about a dead man?"

Oakes paused. "Yes, I did. I had gone out for a smoke when he staggered up. I recognized him and knew he was a drunkard. He asked me for a drink. I told him to go away. He persisted, so I went back inside thinking I'd give him something to make him go away."

"Did you give him anything?"

"No," Malcolm lied.

"What did you do then?"

"I went back inside. The man was in bad shape. His head was bleeding."

"Did you offer him help?"

"No, I just wanted him to go away from there. I needed to keep order."

"Was anyone else out and about at this time that could have seen him?"

"I didn't see anyone, but people come and go all the time."

"Mr. Oakes, where were you when this hysterical woman came inside?"

"I was in the bathroom."

"I see. And you had been outside before that?"

Oakes hesitated. "Earlier, yes."

"How early?"

"What do you mean?"

"Just a simple question, how early?"

"Well, I don't remember. I went out to have a smoke when I was sure things were all right inside."

"Was this a long time before this hysterical woman came in?"

"Not too long, but a little bit."

"A little bit. Did you see anybody or talk to anybody?"

"No, I didn't," he lied.

"Really? You just said that you talked with Bennie Hoskins."

"Well, yes, that, but nobody else."

"Did Mr. Hoskins say anything else?"

"He was raving about some black man trying to kill him. He said he was jumped, and he fought back. That's when I went inside to get him a drink. When I came back, I couldn't see him anywhere."

"Did you take a walk around or anything?"

"No, I did not."

Loyal turned to his table and shuffled some papers.

"After the body was found, after things were calmed down, after the sheriff had come and gone, after everybody was back inside having a good time, did you go back outside?"

"Well, yes, I did once."

"Once. Did you see anybody then?"

"No, I didn't."

Loyal turned around. "Really? Did you see Mr. Griffin Wynne?"

"Oh yes, I forgot."

The jury foreman leaned forward. Loyal hoped this was a good sign.

"You forgot. Did you have a conversation with him?"

"Not really. He'd come to look for something. I think it was a strap of some kind off the ambulance or the table, you know that thing they roll the bodies on."

"Gurney, it's called." Some spectators laughed, and the judge rapped his gavel.

"Yeah, that." Oakes was fidgeting. One of the jurors scribbled on a notepad.

"Who was the woman who found the body, this hysterical woman?"

"I don't know."

"You don't know?"

"No, like I said, I was in the bathroom and heard all this commotion. When I came out, people were crowding the front door, and someone told me that."

"I see. No further questions at this time, Your Honor."

Werner stood and looked at the jury. "The prosecution rests, Your Honor."

The judge sat up and put his elbows on the dais. "Are you ready with your defense, Mr. Hall?"

"Yes, Your Honor."

"Then let's take thirty minutes before you begin." The judge left the bench, and the few spectators milled about. Mani asked where his momma and Bibi were. Loyal explained that Bibi couldn't be in the courtroom because she might be called to witness. His momma was staying with her in the witness room. "Don't worry. They are just fine."

The jury filed in and the bailiff called out, "All rise." There was stirring as the judge went to the bench. "Proceed, Mr. Hall," he said.

Loyal called Emily, Lula, Reverend Buster Holt, Reverend Joe Galt, and Maze Wantland as character witnesses, and then he recalled Bo Roper.

"Sheriff Roper, has Mani Hanks caused any trouble whatsoever while in custody?"

"He's been an ideal prisoner: pleasant, willing to cooperate, the best."

"In your investigation, did you interview people at the Supper Club that night?"

"A few that night and others later. I had Darrell Draper, that's Deputy Draper, take down the names of everyone still there that night. We interviewed all of them later."

"Did you talk to anyone who claimed to have found the body?"

"No, no one seemed to know exactly who first discovered the body. Apparently, whoever that person was left before we took down names."

"And no one suggested anyone?"

"No, and I didn't think it important. The body was discovered. We got there right away. There was an arrest and a confession right away. We didn't see a need to pursue it."

"Sheriff, is it possible that the blow that killed Bennie Hoskins occurred at the Supper Club?"

"Objection, Your Honor. The defendant has already confessed to striking the blow."

"Overruled. Sheriff Roper, you may answer."

"It is possible, but there is no positive evidence to that effect."

"But there is no evidence to the contrary either, is there?"

"No, there isn't. However, as far as we could tell, there was no opportunity and no motive that we could find for someone at the Supper Club to have done it."

"Still, there is that bit of doubt," Loyal said while looking at the jury. He got little reaction, but hoped the point was made.

"Thank you, Sheriff."

Loyal then called Jesse Wickham.

"Did anyone help you retrieve the body?"

"The deputies helped a bit at the scene, and Mr. Wynne came to the funeral home."

"Mr. Wynne wasn't at the Supper Club then?"

"No, sir. Not while I was there."

"Thank you, Mr. Wickham. The defense calls Mr. Griffin Wynne."

Wynne took the stand.

"Mr. Wynne, did you go to the funeral home the night Bennie Hoskins was killed?"

"I received a call from my employee, Jesse Wickham, asking for help with a body. I went immediately to the funeral home."

"Tell us what you did while there."

"I viewed the body of the dead man. Afterward, I went out to the Supper Club."

Loyal chose not to ask why Wynne had returned to the Supper Club.

"When you viewed the body, was there anything unusual about it?" Loyal asked.

"Not other than it was unclean, and he had sustained a severe blow to the head."

"Where was this injury? I mean, where on the head?"

"Upper front at the hairline. He had been hit from in front. His forehead was broken."

Werner smiled. Loyal regretted the question. He considered asking Wynne about the bloody stone, but decided not to take the chance. "No further questions, Your Honor."

Werner stood behind his table and drummed his fingers lightly. His round face broke into a broad smile at the jury. For the first time, he moved around his table and strode over to the jury box. He looked at the jury and raised his eyebrows. Then he smiled and turned to the witness box.

"Mr. Wynne, was anyone else around the club while you were there?"

"Malcolm Oakes was there and we spoke."

"What did you talk about?"

"Just the scene and the fact that I was looking for something lost off the ambulance."

"Nothing else?"

"He said that Bennie, the dead man, had come to the Supper Club to find him, and that he'd been beaten."

"So Bennie was alive at the Supper Club?"

"According to Malcolm."

"We've already heard testimony that a person could walk from the Supper Club to the spot on Chester where Mani Hanks was apprehended. So he must have followed him there, struck the blow that killed him, and run away."

"Objection!" Loyal was on his feet.

"Sustained! Mr. Werner, you are leading your witness, and please do not speculate in this courtroom."

"Apologies, Your Honor. No further questions."

Loyal stood again. "A few more questions, Your Honor?" He walked toward the witness box.

"Mr. Wynne, Malcolm Oakes told you that Bennie Hoskins came to the Supper Club to find him. Is that right?"

"Yes, he did."

"Did you see anyone else about when you spoke to Oakes?"

"No, I did not."

"Why do you suppose Bennie came looking for Malcom Oakes?" Loyal knew he was taking a chance with this blind question.

Wynne looked startled and hesitated. "I have no idea. He, Malcolm, said Bennie had been beaten. So I guess he might have been looking for help."

"Did Malcolm Oakes tell you he gave aid to Hoskins?"

"No."

"So anyone might have killed Bennie Hoskins, even Malcolm Oakes, who was there and had opportunity." Loyal looked toward the jury and shrugged his shoulders, palms up.

"Objection, objection!" Werner was on his feet, shouting at the bench.

"Sustained! Mr. Hall. Please don't toy with this court. One admonition should be enough. Both of you know better than to speculate like that."

"No further questions."

Wynne was excused.

Next, Loyal called "Mrs. Melissa Shawl Durber."

Werner challenged, "Your Honor, I've already raised concerns about this witness. She is the defendant's grandmother. She is bound to be prejudiced."

"And we've already gone over that, Mr. Werner. She can testify. You may challenge any remarks, and we'll rule at that time."

"Thank you, Your Honor."

The bailiff swore Bibi in, and she took the stand. "Your real name is Melissa Shawl, but people mostly call you Bibi, is that right?"

"Yes, sir."

"What does it mean?"

"Like I told you a long time ago when our Nathan died, it means Granny in the old ways of speaking."

"Old ways. You are Mr. Hanks's grandmother, then?"

"I almost raised the boy. He's as good a man as you'll find. I don't think he could kill a soul. I don't. He comes from a high place, that's what."

"What do you mean, a high place?"

"It's what his name means. Mani means from a high place. And he came from a high place, and that's where he's heading. I don't know how or what it is for sure, but he is surely headed for something higher up. He's a good man. I know him."

"I know you are worried about him."

"Worried, I've been worried about him most of his life. He was such a sweet child and still is a sweet man, in spite of what all he saw down in the Hatchie swamp when he was a little boy."

"What did he see? Can you tell me about it?"

"No, I can't. He has to tell it himself, but it was bad. I was with him and his daddy, and we saw it together when they were fishing. Man killed down there, a good man by the name of Ellis Wiggins, his daddy's best friend."

"Objection!" Werner jumped up, then said, "No, withdraw that objection, Your Honor."

"I have no more questions, Your Honor," Loyal said.

"Cross, Your Honor."

The judge waved Werner to proceed.

"Mrs. Durber, Bibi, did Ellis Wiggins ever turn up?"

"No, he didn't."

"So he might have just run off?" It was a question.

"He didn't run off. He wouldn't do something like that to Arlene and his children. He wasn't that kind of a man. He wasn't."

"But like you said, he never turned up, so nobody knows if he was killed or not."

Bibi was silent for a moment. "No, I guess nobody can say for sure, but I know it. I saw those lions coming across Kakunga, and I knew. I did."

"Kakunga? What is Kakunga?"

"Kakunga is the line that separates us from the dead. It's like a river."

"And you saw across that line? Saw lions across Kakunga?"

"I saw them, and I saw them when they crossed over."

"I see. Do you often see such things?"

"Sometimes I do. I see wild dogs too. They walk about over there. Once in a while, they come across and cause trouble."

Werner looked at the jury, raised his eyebrows, and smiled. "Thank you, Mrs. Durber. No further questions, Your Honor."

Loyal stood at his place behind the defense table. "Your Honor, one or two more questions."

"Go ahead."

"Bibi, tell us, when do you see these things?"

"Sometimes I have dreams at night, but most times I'm sitting out on my porch reading my Bible and talking to Jesus. I close my eyes and I can see."

"Do you read your Bible a lot?"

"Yes, sir, I do. It's a help to me."

"Do you go to church, Bibi?"

"Course I do. You know that."

Loyal smiled at her. "Thank you, Bibi. That's helpful for the court to know. No further questions, Your Honor."

"Are we all finished then, Mr. Hall?"

"Yes, Your Honor. Defense rests." He sighed deeply and slumped down.

The judge instructed the jury and told them lunch was coming over from Woolworth's. After lunch, they deliberated for only two hours, then the foreman notified the bailiff they had reached their verdict. Everyone gathered in the courtroom.

"Do you have a verdict ready, or do you need more time?"

"We're ready, Your Honor." The foreman handed a piece of paper to the bailiff. The judge read it and handed it back.

"You may tell the court."

Loyal and Mani stood.

The foreman read, "We find the defendant guilty."

"So say you all?" asked the judge.

"Yes, Your Honor," replied the foreman, and sat down and then stood again.

"We don't think he should be put to death, Your Honor," he added.

"That's not necessary for you to say, Mr. Foreman, but thank you anyway for the jury's sincerity and diligence. You're dismissed." The judge rapped his gavel to bring order. "I'll pass sentence tomorrow morning at nine o'clock."

Mani slumped into his chair. The bailiff and deputies came over to the table where he sat, waiting patiently while Bibi and June consoled him.

Bibi put her hand on Loyal's shoulder. "You did the best you could, Mr. Hall."

Loyal hugged her. "I'm sorry. It wasn't enough. I wish I could've done better. I'll appeal, of course, but unless I can find out who really killed Hoskins, it won't fly."

Griffin Wynne left the courtroom.

Mani, June, and Bibi were given a few minutes together before he was led back to his cell. Loyal sat with them after Mani was led away.

"Is there nothing we can do?" June said.

Loyal walked over to one of the fireplace mantels and began to inspect one of the artifacts. "The evidence presented against Mani is really mostly circumstantial, except for the fact that Mani confessed to the confrontation and fight," he said. He explained that since there were no errors in the trial process, their best bet would be to file a motion for a judgment of acquittal. Bibi asked what that meant, and Loyal explained that they have thirty days to file a motion with the judge of the court asking for him to overturn the jury's decision.

"Can he do that?" she said.

"Yes, but it's a long shot. We have to convince him that the prosecutor didn't present enough concrete evidence that Mani was the killer. I also have to convince him that there is at least an equal amount of evidence, circumstantial or otherwise, to indicate someone else killed Bennie Hoskins."

"Can you do that?"

"I aim to try. It means I have to talk to Malcolm Oakes, Wynne, everybody connected to this all over again, and do it quickly."

June wrote to Mani twice each week and sent him a newspaper. Mani always wrote back. They said they loved each other in every letter. He always told her to hug Bibi and tell her he loved her.

Chapter 52

———◆———

Griffin Wynne
September 19, 1960
Paradise, TN

GRIFFIN WYNNE LEFT THE COURTHOUSE as soon as the verdict was returned and drove the few blocks to the funeral home. Vivian looked up from her desk when he came in. Wynne simply shrugged and shook his head.

"What happened?" she said.

"There's little to say. I hoped it would be different for Loyal's sake, if not for Mani Hanks'. But it went like you'd expect, I guess. The young man seems like a decent fellow. His father certainly was. Maybe he did it, but I don't think so."

"You seem more certain than not. How so?" she asked.

Wynne looked slowly around the parlor, then turned back to Vivian and said, "I can't say." He paused. "That man Malcolm Oakes. He's... he's... oh, I don't know, Vivian. I just don't know."

"I understand," she said.

Wynne thought, if only you did understand, but you can't. You'd have to know what I know, and I wouldn't wish that on anyone. Instead, he said, "I think I'll go upstairs and work for a bit if you don't mind." He left her and climbed to the town upstairs.

Later, he came down and sat again in her office. He folded his hands under his chin and, after a quiet moment, said, "I think it's time I retire. Not immediately, but over time. I'll need your help, and we'll make the transition."

"Transition to what?" she said.

"We'll need to find a buyer if we can. I'll stay on if you'll stay until it's done. It will happen when the day comes. And if I die, just sell the funeral home."

"Die? Don't talk like that. You're not about to die."

"It's what to do," he said. "I'll get with Loyal and make a will. There are papers I want him to be the custodian of. If you'll stay on, I'll be sure you are more than adequately compensated, Vivian."

She thanked him and agreed. There were deaths and funerals, and families to minister to, but he spent part of most days working on "the town upstairs" as he now called it. On the highway leading out of town toward the east, he put up a tiny sign with an arrow that pointed east and read "Brushy Mountain 290 Miles." He cleaned all the houses on Tanyard Street and dusted the two little boys he had placed on the curb watching the firemen. He dusted the fire truck, the firemen, and then cleaned and dusted the houses on Institute Street. He went to work on the Riverside Cemetery, adding the stone wall all around, and put weeds in the corners, and added willows and button bushes along the river that appeared to move slowly like a ghost itself behind the cemetery.

One day, he went to his files and removed a folder with the name Bennie Ray Hoskins on the tab. He laid the folder on his desk and turned each page of documentation face down until he came to a photograph. He removed the photograph, took it upstairs to the model train room, and began carving a figure of a man. Over the coming days, he referred to the photograph often as he whittled tiny slivers from the pinewood block in his hands. He spent two days finishing the figure, the overalls, the tattered shirt, its worn shoes, one of which had a hole in the sole, visible because the figure was running. He placed it behind the burning house on Tanyard, beyond the firemen and the little boys sitting on the curb. It was a shadowy figure of a man bent over and running away. He did his best to make it look like Bennie Hoskins. He removed a Blue Horse notebook from a small wooden chest and added notes about his work on the scene, then replaced the notebook.

Chapter 53

Loyal Hall
September 20, 1960
Paradise, TN

THE DAY AFTER THE TRIAL, Loyal arrived at the Supper Club in the late afternoon before opening time. Malcolm Oakes's car was parked in the side lot. He pulled in beside it and went to the front door. It was locked, so he knocked. When he heard nothing from inside, he pounded again. A voice shouted to him to "hold on, hold on, I'm coming." Malcolm Oakes opened the door, surprised to see Loyal standing there.

"Yeah, what do you want?" he said.

"Mr. Oakes, I'm Loyal Hall…"

"Yeah, of course I know. I'm not stupid. What do you want?"

"We need to talk. I'm filing a motion for acquittal in the Hoskins murder trial. I need a few minutes to confirm some information."

Oakes finally stepped back from the doorway. "Acquittal? The boy was convicted. How can he be acquitted?"

"There is a procedure," Loyal said.

"Hot damn, the boy did it. I know he did. Dammit."

"You seem awfully certain, Mr. Oakes. Is there something I need to know?"

Oakes realized he had overreacted. In a calmer voice, he said, "Come on in. I don't have much time." They went into the dim interior and sat across from each other at a round table. The place smelled of tobacco and disinfectant.

"Mr. Oakes, I'd appreciate it if you would go over everything that happened the night Bennie Hoskins died."

"I already told all that. There's nothing more to add."

"I know, but maybe I missed something. How about telling it again for me?" Oakes shrugged and looked around the room. He began recounting the things he had already told. Loyal asked him if he could think of anything else, anything at all. Oakes just smiled and said no.

"Griffin Wynne came down here afterward, didn't he? What did you two talk about?" Oakes straightened in his chair.

"Nothing much," he said.

"Did you talk about how Bennie had died?" Loyal was grasping at straws. "Did you talk about anything that you found?" Malcolm stood up abruptly and took a step away, then turned toward Loyal.

"You need to go. I've got work to do," he said.

"Well, did you find something that you haven't told anyone about? Or did Wynne?"

"We just talked about that strap or whatever it was he was looking for. That's all."

Loyal stood now and went over and backed his lean frame against the bar and watched Oakes. "Nothing else, then?"

"Nothing else. Now you've got to go. I've got things to do."

"Are you sure, Malcolm? Are you telling me everything?"

"Goddammit, I said nothing. Now get out of here before I bounce you out."

"You're not telling me something, Malcolm. If the judge grants this motion, it won't matter because Mani Hanks will be free. But if he doesn't, I can still file an appeal. That's likely to put you in the spotlight again. Keep that in mind." He walked to the door and stepped out into the sunlight. Behind him, he heard Oakes shouting, "The bastard did it. He did it!"

The next day, Loyal called Wynne. "I'm preparing a motion for acquittal, Griffin. I need to get with you to go over again the things you told me before. Did I miss anything? Or is there anything you've remembered that would help? That sort of thing," he said. They agreed on a time the next afternoon.

Vivian was at her desk when Loyal entered the parlor. "Mr. Wynne is upstairs. You can go on up if you want. I think he's expecting you, and he won't mind you coming up. The town is coming along nicely, and he likes to show it off." Loyal mounted the stairs and called out to Wynne when he reached the top.

"Come on in, Loyal." Loyal entered the big room and exclaimed. "My goodness, Griffin. This has grown since I last saw it. Incredible the work you've put in."

"It's my relaxation, my happy place if you will. Sit down. Let's talk. We won't be disturbed up here." He motioned for Loyal to sit in the only chair, and he pulled a small bench near and sat. "What can I tell you?"

"Go over everything you did that night if you don't mind. I may have overlooked something." Wynne recounted coming to the funeral home to help Jesse and the trip down to the Supper Club and his conversation with Malcolm. He omitted finding the blood-spattered tie.

"Is there anything else, anything at all?"

Wynne thought about the tie. If he implicated Malcolm, he would surely talk about the past. Just to get even, for no other reason. Wynne was damned if he did and damned if he didn't. Besides, he really didn't know if it was Malcolm's tie. It could have been anyone's. It may not have been blood at all, or if it was, it could have been from someone in a fight. They happened all the time at the club.

"No, nothing that I can think of," he said. After Loyal had gone, he sat for a long time gazing at the town upstairs. The story's mostly told, he thought to himself. Just a few more facts to put down, and it will be done. Then I'll take care of the rest of it.

PART IV

1975

Chapter 54

Jesse Wickham
April 13, 1975
Paradise, TN

JESSE MULLED OVER what he had learned, all these bits turning up, a fragment here and there like dinosaur bones. Griffin Wynne had spent a lifetime replicating Paradise upstairs, away from the dead and grieving. He had given Jesse the gift of the notebooks. Now he was a servant to them with no choice but to carefully brush away the dust and time to unearth whatever lay beneath.

The pieces almost fit together, those he had gotten from June, Lula, Emily, Loyal, and Bibi. Ellis Wiggins was murdered. There was little doubt about that, but his body had never been found. Some of the men who had killed Ellis were probably connected to Nathan's death. They were present at his funeral ostensibly to keep order. But Nathan's death was ruled accidental. There was no need for lawmen to be at his funeral, no need to keep order. Yet, according to Bibi, some of them were there that day on the street and on the steps of the church.

He drove to the funeral home, let himself in, and went upstairs. The model town seemed to stare back at him. The buildings, the streets, the ghosts of people who had walked them seemed to be hanging in the air above it. Sunlight came through the slits between the window blinds and crept across the miniature town.

Jesse picked up one of the tiny carved boys sitting on the curb on Tanyard Street. They could have been himself and Campo. He replaced it and picked up the little car at the corner. The carving of the running man seemed to be headed toward the car. Jesse blew the dust from the car. Motes rode the currents glistening in the slanting light and settled on the town. He set the car back in its place and looked west toward the replica of Riverside Cemetery, and then back to the car. He looked at the numbers on its tags. What if these were the same numbers Bibi had given Wynne, the numbers from her dream? Knowing Griffin Wynne's penchant for detail, they were not inconsequential.

Jesse opened one of the access doors and crawled toward the hatch near the cemetery to get a better look at it. Standing in the hatchway, he marveled that the tombstones had names and dates. The stone fencing around the cemetery replicated the original stones and more recent repairs. Everything was precise. If you have a whole lifetime to spend, you have time enough to pay attention to detail, he reckoned. As he crawled out, he saw something in the darkness underneath and against the wall. He crawled out and went to the other access door. On the floor just inside was a section of layout that was almost complete. He carefully pulled it out from its storage space and opened one of the window blinds to let in more light. Why was this piece unattached? It seemed to be finished. What did it represent, what place? He puzzled over the larger layout, wondering where this piece might fit, and realized this unattached section was an extension that would have gone next to the Riverside Cemetery section. There was Riverside Drive, the levee through the bottom land, and the Supper Club with its gravel drive and parking lot, a slope along the side, thickets, and marshy lowland there. A tiny crosstie was at the edge of the brush in front of the thickets. An oil drum was at the corner of the building. The little beer sign hung on the front porch beside the door as if its fake neon blue light could illuminate answers.

How on earth had Griffin Wynne created such detail, managed those tiny bottles, the oil drum with something hanging over the edge, and why had he bothered in the first place? He took the drum over to the workbench, where there was a large magnifying glass on a stand. The draped thing looked like a rag, yellow with red marks on it, like splashes. What was it? So much detail that Wynne must have had a reason. "What could it be?" he wondered, this time out loud.

"I can't imagine," spoke a voice behind him.

"Holy—" he caught himself. "You startled me."

"I'm sorry, I didn't mean to," Loyal Hall said. "I went over to see Emily, and she told me you'd been over to Hatchie Landing this morning and thought perhaps you were here at the funeral home looking over the model. I thought you would have heard me coming up the stairs. I didn't try to be quiet."

"It's all right. I was just concentrating so hard on this." Jesse pointed at the piece of unattached layout. "What do you make of it?"

Loyal looked at the section. "I've never seen it before. Where did you find it?"

"Underneath, just there behind that access door against the wall. It's perfect and complete. I wonder why he never attached it?" Loyal shook his head. "He spent almost all of his time modeling toward the end. Maybe he finished this just before he died."

"It's the only section that extends outside the city limits of Paradise. I don't know of any particular significance, though. I'll leave it out for now and come back to it later. I'd like to drive down Riverside and see what that area looks like now."

"Well, there's still plenty of daylight left. We could go now if you like." Loyal hesitated. "That is, if you'd like some company."

"I'd like that, yes. Let's go." He flipped off the lights, pulled the blind closed, and followed Loyal outside.

"I'll drive. Emily said to tell you to come for supper if you wish."

They drove west along Chester to Riverside and turned south, passing the cemetery on their left. In a couple of miles, they came to the spot where the old Supper Club had stood. There was still a turnout from the road where the parking lot had been, but there was no building. The land sloped down toward the lowland and thickets near a stream. Jesse pulled off into the space and cut the engine.

Jesse got out and stood with his hands on his hips. "It's been a long time since the night I was here, but I think this is where it was. What do you think?"

"I suppose this is the place, but it's been gone for so long. Never cared much for it, though it was the only place around you could get a drink and dance in those days."

"It matches the terrain I remember, and on the layout, I guess, but it's hard to tell without the building."

"Yes, I was only here a couple of times. If you're ready, let's head back to Emily's. Supper will be waiting."

Jesse parked in front of Emily and Lula's house on Chester. As they walked up the steps, Emily came to the door, calling over her shoulder, "Lula, Loyal is back and he's brought Jesse."

"Come on in. Come in. We're just finishing up the Sunday paper. Not much news in Paradise these days."

Loyal spoke first, "Emily, Jesse has come across another question he'd like your and Lula's ideas about."

"Oh, good, a mystery, late on a Sunday afternoon. Just the right time for it."

She escorted him to the parlor, where Lula sat reading. Newspapers were scattered about the floor. "Sorry about the mess, it's what we do on Sunday afternoons. Come on in. Sit down. Can I get you something to drink? Tea? Coffee? We don't usually eat a big meal on Sunday evening, but we've got leftovers from lunch."

"How was your interview with Bibi?

"She was just great. She's a marvelous woman. I'm afraid I kept her from getting to church on time, though."

"I knew you would love her. Everybody does. Did she tell you her version of all that happened? You must tell us all about it. We're on pins and needles."

"Yes, she did, and more, even."

"What do you mean by more? Tell us, please. You can do it over supper."

As they sat eating leftover meatloaf and potatoes with fresh tomatoes, and fried eggplant with cornbread, Jesse told them that Bibi had explained how she came to know the names of some of those men who she thought were involved in Ellis Wiggins's death. He explained about her dreams of wild dogs and lions across a river.

"You don't say," exclaimed Lula. "She saw names on their faces? It sounds Biblical."

"They weren't names, but numbers. I think she connects her dreams with reality and makes assumptions that create a kind of new reality. An uncannily accurate one. She told me about a cross being burned on their neighbor's lawn, a family named Wiggins."

Jesse was about to tell them Bibi's story of the cross burning and how she had figured out the men's names when Loyal interrupted.

"I wish I knew enough to get poor Mani out of his predicament. I still feel like I failed somehow."

"Loyal, you don't need to feel bad for anything you did or didn't do," Emily said. "You did a world of good for Mani, Bibi, and June, and you've kept on trying. Mani will be home one of these days."

"Sooner rather than later, I hope," Loyal replied.

"What you mean is, you hope he can get here before we all die, is what. We all do. Bibi would like to see him a free man again before she passes on," Emily said.

"Something may turn up one day. Who knows? God willing," Loyal shrugged.

Lula spoke up. "God is not willing a thing, Loyal. If God had anything to do with it, none of this would have happened in the first place."

The room lapsed into silence. Jesse broke it with a question to Loyal. "Did Bibi ever give you any names, names she thought were people who might have been connected with Ellis Wiggins's or Nathan's deaths?"

"She used to talk about knowing who those men were. As I told you earlier, I was involved with that situation in a different capacity than I was with Mani. Nathan is another story altogether. I wasn't involved at all in that, although I suspected something all along."

"What was that?" Jesse asked.

"I was still with the Bureau then. We couldn't prove it, but there was probably a connection between Ellis's death and Nathan's death. I've said this to June before."

"But you weren't involved in investigating either one?" Jesse asked.

"Not really. I worked the Wiggins case for a while because there was the suspicion of a civil rights violation, but there wasn't enough evidence for me to stay involved appreciably in the matter. After all, there was never a body, so it was technically a disappearance, a missing person. The local authorities did the usual, asked questions, but in fact, there was no evidence at all. Nathan's death was accidental as far as anyone knows. Besides, it was a local incident, not a federal crime. At least none was ever alleged."

Jesse pondered this. "Bibi told me earlier today that she knew the names of some of the men responsible. She really doesn't have proof, but she tells a fascinating story. Those numbers turned out to be license tag numbers. And she saw them on some of the cars that came to the Wiggins house for the cross burning."

"That's intriguing," said Loyal. "If I'd had those numbers, it might have had a bearing on Mani's case, but who knows if the two events were connected?"

"Maybe, maybe not, but fascinating is the right word for it. Could we meet again soon? You may be able to clear up some things I may have mixed up."

"Tomorrow's fine. An old lawyer like me is mostly retired. I don't have many clients anymore, so I'm essentially free most of the time."

They agreed to meet at Loyal's house the next morning at ten o'clock, then shook hands. Jesse turned to the ladies and thanked them again. Lula walked him to the door.

"Jesse, I've always felt that Nathan didn't die in any kind of accident. He died because of somebody. You keep on asking your questions. June will be all right with that." She smiled and embraced him. He felt her old frame, the bones in her back.

"I will, Lula. I'll keep asking until people run out of answers."

Chapter 55

———◆———

Jesse Wickham
April 14, 1975
Paradise, TN

THE NEXT MORNING, Jesse was at Loyal Hall's house on Highland promptly at ten. There was no street-side parking, so he pulled into the narrow drive and climbed the five steps to the porch. He was about to ring the bell when the door opened.

"Good morning, Jesse. Coffee's perking on the stove. We'll set up shop in the kitchen if that's all right with you."

"Thanks. I appreciate you taking this time for me." Jesse pulled out a chair and set his briefcase underneath the table.

"You like cream, sugar?" Loyal asked, bringing two cups.

"No, thanks, just black."

"At this stage in life, the real thing is what I want, no skimping: whipping cream, heavy stuff." He poured a dollop of heavy whipping cream into his cup of dark coffee and sat opposite Jesse.

They sipped coffee for a minute. "Good," said Jesse. "I like it a little strong like this."

"It's the only way to make coffee, one heaping tablespoonful to the cup plus one for the pot. Perk it about three minutes and shut her off. Let it stand for a minute, and you've got great coffee. I don't like these new flavored coffees you're beginning to see around in the stores."

"Neither do I," Jesse said. He took another sip. "Tell me all about Nathan Hanks, anything you know and remember. "

"It was an unsettled time."

"Do you mind if I record what you say?"

"No, go ahead." Loyal waved his hand at Jesse's recorder.

He watched Jesse set up the recorder and turn it on. "Okay, go ahead."

Loyal stared into space and sipped his coffee before he began.

"That was a time when most of those who lived and walked the streets of Paradise, Tennessee, believed this to be as good a place as any to live and die, to hope and dream, to await the final resurrection as Paradise implies. If you had come as most people came, east and west or north and south, by rail or by highway, and happened to turn here, you'd have entered a world whose streets appeared to be free to all yet were barred like a prison to some.

"For those of us within its limits, the fortunate and the unfortunate, the good and the bad, the lovely and the unlovely, this town was our asylum, our reality. Take it from an old man, Jesse, every time and every place is at once hopeful and hopeless. This one was no exception, and by 1946, Paradise was ill at ease. There was hope in some quarters that the lines between the dark-skinned and the light-skinned who lived within our borders and in the hinterlands beyond would blur, but that was just another illusory dream."

"Was Ellis Wiggins's death connected to Nathan Hanks?" Jesse prompted.

"Ellis Wiggins probably died over in Hatchie County, but as I told you, his body was never found. I did the investigation for the Bureau. We never could come up with any evidence. So no one was ever charged. In my own mind, there was a crime, though, no doubt about it."

"And Nathan Hanks?"

"I looked into his death, too. It wasn't a civil rights case, so I had to do it quietly. Nathan Hanks was forced to leave Hatchie Landing. That and Ellis Wiggins's disappearance were connected in my way of thinking, but I couldn't get enough evidence to bring any charges.

That's a hard one to prove anyway. In those days, it was a lot harder. People were closemouthed. What civil rights laws were in place were easily subverted. Even if you could get evidence, it was sometimes hard to get a jury to pay attention to it. There was plenty of intimidation, though. Nathan wouldn't talk about it much. He just took his exile and went home now and then to visit the family. He didn't live very long. He died in a house fire down on Tanyard Street back in the summer of 1948, about two years after Ellis Wiggins died."

"I've come up with some odd scraps of information that raise more questions than answers," Jesse said finally. "Not really information, not evidence, but something."

Loyal sat forward and put his elbows on the table. "How is that? What kind of information? Anyone talking to you?"

"No, no one is talking except June and her family. Bibi told me how she came up with the names of the men who were involved. She claims she had dreams and saw names on the foreheads of lions and dogs walking back and forth." He smiled as he recounted this.

"Well, don't discount anything that woman says, Jesse. I always believed she knew more than she let on. I don't know why she wouldn't come out with it."

"Maybe she's finally decided to. Yesterday, she told me she saw the names on those foreheads. I asked her how she knew for sure, and she said the most astounding thing. She said the night the men burned the cross in front of Ellis Wiggins's house, she saw three of the cars. She saw the license tags and that's how she knew who it was."

"My god. Why didn't she tell me years ago?" Loyal seemed hurt and frustrated at the same time.

"Who knows? That's just what she said. She said she told Griffin Wynne who they were and what the numbers were. Did he ever come to you with that information?"

Loyal was motionless. "God in heaven. He did tell me she had told him something, but he never told me about any numbers. I discounted the whole thing, told him I doubted it would tie to anything. I don't think I even put it in my case notes."

"I found out another thing while I was up in the funeral home the other night, looking over the town upstairs. You know, I used to go up there when I was little. He let me help model some of the buildings. I remember the work he put into modeling that onion dome on the turret on your sister's house. He couldn't get the shake shingles to his satisfaction until one day she gave him an old, worn-out paring knife. He filed it down to a nub, and it was the perfect tool for that one job. His attention to detail was incredible. It's as if his life's work was to model the entire town perfectly as it was in the nineteen forties and fifties.

"Remember yesterday, I showed you the section that I found that's completely finished, but was never attached to the rest of it? Well here's the odd thing about it. There's a model car on that section, parked down on Tanyard Street near where Nathan's house was located. Wynne created a fire scene with a Griffin Wynne ambulance, two little boys sitting on the curb watching, and a man running between houses. There are firemen. There's even a gurney. Everything is perfect.

"I was there that day, Loyal. I was one of those little boys. I don't remember many of those details, but I was there. I remember them bringing a stretcher out to the ambulance, and we never saw Nathan again. We loved that man. We'd watch him work, and he would tell us stories."

"Uncanny!" Loyal whispered.

"That model car is perfect, too. It has a license tag on it. I wrote down the number. Would it be possible to find out if that was a valid tag number and who that car belonged to? That is, could we find out if it was on a real car back then?"

"It might be possible. We'd have to guess at the year unless that's on the tag too, and get who it was registered to, but that wouldn't prove anything. It simply says that Wynne used a number on a tag that happened to match a car that belonged to a certain person."

"But couldn't it point us in a direction?"

"Maybe, but that's all it would do," Loyal said.

"I'd like to know. Can you check it out for me?"

"Sure, I can try. You've got me hooked."

They considered it over their coffee.

"What makes me think that Wynne is trying to point us in the right direction," Jesse said, "is that he also put cars in the Supper Club parking lot in the unattached section I found. One of those cars has the same number on its tag."

"Well, there you go. If I were defending someone, I'd argue that's proof enough that this tag number on a model car is meaningless. It's just what an old man would do when he was modeling. He wouldn't bother to make up new tag numbers; he'd just use the same one, or maybe he forgot he used that one before. Maybe he made several model cars and made them all alike and put them on the layout in more than one place. It's what I'd argue. And I'd win the argument too. I'll check it out, though. You get me the number."

Jesse gave Loyal a scrap of paper. "Tennessee 231-715, and there are two more numbers. None of the cars in the Supper Club lot have numbers except for the one I just gave you and these two, Tennessee 621-819 and Tennessee 621-772."

Loyal studied the numbers. "I'll check them out and see what I can find. It may be too far in the past. Do you know what year it was?"

"No, I'll look at the model, but I don't think it gives a year. If it were near the year those incidents occurred, it could have been any year from 1945, or a year or two before, until the year Nathan died. The one at the Supper Club, though, I don't know about that one. That's what makes me think that Wynne was trying to say something. The fire on Tanyard Street happened in 1948, and the Supper Club incident happened in 1960. The format of tag numbers had changed by then. Wynne must have been trying to show a connection by giving the same tag number to two car models in different years. He was too much of a perfectionist in all other details."

Loyal pondered that. "Damnation, son. You could be right. You should have been a detective. It wouldn't be like him to overlook a detail like that. I'll see what I can do. Let's just see what happens."

Chapter 56

Loyal Hall
April 15, 1975
Paradise, TN

FOR LOYAL, THE COURTHOUSE was a sweet kind of place. He loved the terrazzo hallways, the brass cuspidors unused anymore but still in place beside doorways, the oak doors that led into courtrooms and offices, the stains and oils of thousands of hands on door faces, the smell of something substantial, the smell of humankind aspiring to the enormous task of order in the pursuit of life, liberty and happiness, the smell of the rule of law, he liked to think.

He had loved the courtroom work, both as an agent of the FBI and as a lawyer after he left the Bureau. So many criminal cases, mostly petty by comparison to what went on in larger cities. He spoke to people as he went down the hall toward the vehicle registration office. Those who knew him reached out to shake his hand; those who didn't merely nodded. Some were officials, and most were citizens who had come to the center of law to record some piece of business, the myriad declarations of democracy.

He went to one of the brass-grilled windows at the county clerk's office and stood in line like any other citizen. Mary Childress, one of the clerks, saw him and smiled. She motioned for him to come around to the door and to the back. He excused himself from the people in front of him and went to the door. Mary welcomed him inside. Everyone knew him. He waved and spoke to the room in general.

Carl Manley, the county clerk, came from his office with his hand stretched out and greeted him warmly. "What brings you to us today, Loyal?" he asked.

"I need help looking up some old information, Carl. I have an old license tag number and was wondering if you had a way to look it up and see who it might have belonged to."

"Well, tag numbers belong to cars, not to people." He laughed. "But we can sure try and see what we find. What year is it?"

"That's a little bit of a problem. It could be as early as 1945, give or take, to no later than 1949."

"Give or take," said Carl. He looked at Loyal and raised an eyebrow. "Come with me." They went down the hall to the elevators with their walls of golden oak and brass handrails made shiny by countless hands. A cuspidor sat unused in a corner. Carl pressed a button, and the old machine clunked and shook slightly as it descended to the basement.

Downstairs, they stepped out into a more utilitarian atmosphere than the one on the floor above. Gone was the oak trim, replaced by plaster walls above terrazzo floors. Loyal followed Carl to the end of the wide hallway, where he opened a metal door. Inside, shelves of cardboard file boxes were arranged in rows. Each shelf was lettered and numbered. Each row was marked as to what it contained. Each box was identified. There were shelves of court records, shelves of land and property records, and shelves of motor vehicle records. Carl led the way down one row and back up the next. He paused halfway along the second row.

"Roll that ladder over here," he instructed as if Loyal were an employee.

Loyal did as he was told, smiling at Carl's efficiency.

Carl climbed the ladder and read over the labels on the boxes before him. "Nineteen forty-five, let's start there," he said. "Here we go." He tugged at the box and ran one hand beneath it. "Get ready to grab this. It may be heavy, Loyal."

Loyal reached up as Carl slid the box out and lowered it to him.

"Take it over yonder to that table. We'll have a look for your old number."

Loyal did as he was told again. He set the box on the oak table and removed the lid.

Carl came up beside him. "Here, better let me do this." He ran his index and middle fingers across the tops of the folders like a person walking. He pulled a file and laid it on the table, and began to flip page after page of printed numbers. Next to each number was another number. "These here,"—he pointed—"are the reference numbers to the actual vehicle. The first number is the tag number. Later on, we started associating the tag number directly with the actual vehicle identification number. We didn't do that early on because the ID numbers were put on the motor block, and thieves could file them off. It's harder nowadays. Anyway, we'll have to take this number and go to another shelf to get your car." Carl wrote down a number that was opposite the tag number Loyal had given him.

"Before we find out who owned this one, can we check 1945 and see if that tag was still on the same car then?"

"Sure, help me move this ladder." Carl climbed again and hefted a box to Loyal. His fingers made their journey over the tabs as before and extracted a folder.

"Here it is. Probably the same person. See, it's the same cross-reference number. Let's go take a look."

They went down the rows and turned into another aisle where shelves were filled with large black ledger books. Carl pulled a small library stool over to the shelf in front of him and stepped onto it. He pulled out a book and handed it to Loyal. "Let's take a look." Carl quickly riffled the pages to the cross-reference number for the tag. "Here it is, my friend." He grinned and pointed with his hand palm up, as if to say, You aren't surprised that I found it, are you?

The entries were by cross-reference number, model year, make, description, owner, and vehicle identification number. Loyal read the entry. *1939 Chevrolet coupe; two door; black; Malcolm Leroy Oakes.*

"Well, well, well," said Loyal.

"Interesting?" asked Carl.

"Oh, very interesting." He looked sheepishly at Carl and asked, "There are two more numbers. May I look for those, too?"

"Let's see them." Carl wrinkled his forehead as Loyal showed him the numbers.

"Nope, afraid not. Those numbers are from another county. See, the leading digits are different from this other one. I could do some checking, but don't get your hopes up. Each county keeps its own records. Some retain them for a long time, like we have, others don't. Also, the systems in each county were different in those days, not standardized numbering like we do today. Give me a little time. Once I find out which county we're talking about, it'll be easy to find out whether they still have the records."

"Call me when you find out. Could I get a copy of this page and check the 1949 book just to be sure it's the same person?"

"Sure." Carl retrieved the book and verified that the car was still registered to Malcolm Oakes. "Do you want a copy of this page too?"

"Oh, yes."

"Okay, come along. We just got a new copy machine installed upstairs. It's a dandy compared to those thermal machines. You couldn't keep a record printed on thermal paper very long before it faded away. Used to scare me to death that we were losing good records that way. The fact is, the print just faded away. This is real paper copying. I nearly drove everybody crazy till I got it approved. Now everybody in the courthouse uses it, and wants one for their own department. The mayor says I stirred up a mess when I bought it." He was grinning from ear to ear as if he had just conquered Everest.

Carl clutched the books to his chest as they went back upstairs. He made a copy of the pages and gave them to Loyal. They shook hands and visited for a few minutes, then Loyal thanked him and left after speaking to each of the clerks. His heels made a rhythm as he walked the terrazzo toward the front door.

Chapter 57

Loyal Hall
April 15, 1975
Paradise, TN

AT HOME, LOYAL CALLED JESSE to tell him what he had found, and they agreed to meet at Emily's in an hour.

As Loyal was getting out of his car at Emily's, Jesse pulled in behind him.

"How did you find it?"

"Let's settle inside and I'll explain. Not much to it, really. Carl Manley did it, actually. He's as much a stickler for detail as Wynne was, except in a different way. I'd say he's managed to catalog and save every record that's come into his care. He went right to it. Damnedest thing you've ever seen."

Emily directed them to the parlor. "Lula! Loyal and Jesse are here," she called down the hallway. Within minutes, Lula came in, and behind her was June. They all settled in. Loyal chuckled and said, "I feel like the king's messenger."

"No kings around in this room. I just dropped by for a few minutes. I've got to get on home to Bibi. Nice to see you two again." The others chimed in with comments of their own.

"June, you might want to stay for a minute and hear this. It's flimsy, but it does point in a certain direction. Jesse has come up with this information. Give him all the credit. All I've done is twist an arm down at the courthouse."

"I doubt you've twisted very hard. You're not the type, Loyal," said Lula. "Anyway, tell us." The doorbell rang as she spoke.

"That will be Vivian," said Emily. "I called her. I thought she ought to hear about it, too."

Loyal spoke when Emily returned with Vivian. "This is not the breakthrough you're thinking. It's not even much help, if at all. It just tells us in a circumstantial way that our suspicions may have been right all along. We just didn't know where to look."

"Anything helps, Mr. Hall," said June. "Even if we can't get Mani out of prison, for us and him to know that someone else killed that man will be a relief. I think he can manage to stay there the rest of his time if he knows he didn't do it and if he knows the rest of the world understands he didn't do it. It'll be a big help to him just to know."

Loyal chuckled again. "I'm afraid you've all gotten your hopes up for a long and exciting tale, but it's not that way. Jesse, tell them what you found and what you suspect."

Jesse recounted the scenes on the train layout and told about the unattached piece he had found underneath. He told them about the cars and the license tag numbers. "Loyal has verified whose car that one tag was registered to back in 1945."

The others looked at Loyal with anticipation. "It was a 1939 two-door black Chevy," he said.

"And?" spoke Emily. "Loyal Hall, you can drive a person to absolute distraction. If I weren't already nearly dead from age, I'd be there because of you. Now quit tantalizing and tell it."

"It was registered to Malcolm Oakes," he said, and waited.

In unison, Vivian and Lula asked who Malcolm Oakes was.

"Malcolm Oakes was a deputy sheriff in Hatchie Landing back when Ellis Wiggins was killed," June said. "He was still a deputy when Nathan died. He and some other deputies came to his funeral."

"That's nice," replied Vivian.

June replied, "No, it's not nice, dear. They weren't there to pay respects. They were there to remind us to stay in our place."

"Here's what may have happened," Jesse said. "We all believe Ellis Wiggins was murdered, though his body was never found. Malcolm Oakes and others were involved, maybe responsible for it. June says they came to Ellis's funeral to be sure nothing got out of hand. When Nathan decided to come back to Hatchie Landing, they got worried again. At least I suspect Malcolm and someone else did, and one or both of them took matters into their own hands and—" he paused and looked at June. "I'm sorry, June, but they may have killed Nathan."

"How do you know that?" she asked.

"I don't. But why would Griffin Wynne put so much detail that describes Bennie and Malcolm into the town upstairs? Why would he put the same automobile tag number on two different vehicles even though the two were in different time periods and couldn't have had the same number?"

"I hear all you say, Jesse, and it may be true, but tell me this," June asked, "does this connect to Mani? What good will it do him?"

Jesse looked at Loyal. "Loyal, you'll have to connect the dots on that. We know that Mani confronted Bennie Hoskins. Maybe everything is just like Mani described it, and he and Bennie scuffled, but Bennie got up and ran away while Mani was hiding out down by the river, thinking all along that he had killed Bennie. What if Bennie went down to the Supper Club to talk to Malcolm? What did you tell me he said at the trial, Loyal?"

"Malcolm testified that Bennie came to the Supper Club, and he found him hurt and drunk outside, raving about some black man who had jumped him and fought him. He said he went inside to get Bennie a drink to calm him, and when he came back out, Bennie wasn't there. They finally found him dead behind the building."

"What if it was Malcolm that killed Bennie?" asked Jesse. "What if he decided Bennie was too big a risk since Mani had recognized him, and Malcolm decided to kill him, and if it got blamed on anybody, it would be Mani? Could you make that case, Loyal?"

"Well, I could try, but I'll be honest with all of you. There isn't a snowball's chance in hell that anyone will buy it, especially at this late date. Remember, the record shows that Mani confessed to Bennie's killing. This is a wonderful story, but I'm afraid that old dog won't hunt, as they say. At best, we could try again to establish, contrary to Mani's contention that he killed Bennie in the cemetery, that if Bennie was found dead behind the Supper Club, then it wasn't Mani's blow that killed him. But remember, I tried that at trial, and the jury didn't buy it. They bought Malcolm's story instead."

They talked about it for the next two hours over supper and came to no certain conclusions. Finally, Vivian said she had to go home. Loyal and Jesse agreed to meet again the next day.

On the way to their cars, Loyal said, "Jesse, how about showing me that train layout?"

"Sure. Right now, if you like."

They drove the short block to the old funeral home and parked behind it. They went upstairs, and Jesse flipped on the lights.

Loyal marveled at the layout. "I'm amazed every time I see this. The detail is amazing."

Jesse directed his attention to the area around Tanyard and the unattached section he had left on the floor near where it would be if it were attached.

"Look. The old car is parked here at the curb on the corner of Tanyard and Institute. There's the man running between houses. Take a look at him. Does the figure look like anybody you know?"

Loyal looked closely.

"It's okay to pick him up," Jesse said. "Just put him back where he was."

Loyal turned the figure around in his hand. He put it back. "It could be almost anybody. It does look a little like I remember Bennie Hoskins, but then it looks like a lot of other people I remember, too. Sorry, Jesse, it's not much help."

Jesse pointed out the area around the Supper Club on the unattached section. They both got on their knees and looked closely. "There are people standing around here in the parking lot," said Loyal.

"I guess those are supposed to be the people who were there when I arrived that night."

"You were there? You never told me that."

"Yes, I was working as the night and weekend ambulance driver for Wynne. I got the call that Saturday night. I guess that's when they arrested Mani, too."

"It was. Tell me what you saw. What did you find when you got there? Who do you remember was there?"

Jesse told him all he could remember about the night and picking up the body, about the deputies, Darrell and Rattle, being there, and how they helped him load the body. He told about Wynne coming to help him when he got back to the funeral home. He recounted Wynne's story about going back down there that night to look around again and running into Malcolm Oakes.

"Did Wynne say why he went back down there?"

"He said he was just curious. I remember he told me he made up a story about losing a strap off the gurney when he ran into Malcolm. In hindsight, I assume he wanted me to know what he had said in case Malcolm ever asked me about it. I'd never even run into Malcolm, but that's what I figure he meant."

Loyal stared at the scene on the floor before them. "These people are all at the corner of the building facing the same way. I wonder why?"

Jesse looked at the people again. "There were always curious onlookers at accident scenes, sometimes a lot of hysteria. I remember as I was pulling out of the parking lot, after we had loaded the body, Darrell and Rattle were still down there looking around. A woman came out of the front door. A man was with her, and she was upset. He was trying to calm her. I wasn't paying much attention; I just needed to get out of there. I remember they stood on the porch, and now and then she pointed down beside the building. The man had his arm around her. They came out into the parking lot as I was pulling into the road. I don't know whether they got in a car and left or what."

"Do you know who it was?"

"Just some woman with a man. I guess she was upset over the events and wanted to go home."

Loyal studied the layout. "I wish we could find someone who was there. Someone who saw what happened or saw things right afterward."

"Didn't you find any witnesses for the trial?"

"Oh, yes, we got names from the sheriff and ran them down. We called the ones we thought could help, but it didn't."

"Did Darrell and Rattle get the names of everyone who was there? Are you sure you got all the witnesses?"

"Oh, I'm sure we didn't get them all. Some had already left, in fact, when the deputies arrived."

"If we could find someone who was there but who wasn't identified as a witness, for whatever reason, that might shed some new light on things."

"I don't remember missing anyone, though. We might be able to get the records and check through them again."

"Would they still exist? In that much detail?"

"Oh, I expect so. It may take a little doing, but you know, the newspaper might be able to help. They ran stories about the incident and the trial. See what you can dig up."

"If they archived those old editions, we can search them. I'll start tomorrow morning."

"Mind if I join you?"

"Not at all. I'll be there by eight o'clock."

Chapter 58

Loyal Hall
April 16, 1975
Paradise, TN

THE MICROFILM ROOM at the *Paradise Sun* was a small space with spartan furniture. Jesse showed Loyal downstairs to the archives and showed him how to look up issues by date and subject in the catalog and how to retrieve them. "Just leave the items you pull in this box. Someone will file them later."

"Sure. Thanks."

Loyal found the year 1960, and pulled all the issues within a week of Mani's arrest. It was hard not to get distracted by the trivia of old times. There was an article about the Court Alley Café with pictures. He remembered some good evenings spent in that little tavern after court, celebrating wins and commiserating over losses. There were some good men in there, even though in those days, only white men. It was a mixture of white collar and blue collar every night, a clean, well-lighted place, as Hemingway might say.

In one article headlined "The Supper Club Murder," the reporter had done a good job of finding people who had been at the Supper Club that night. There was a woman named Peggy Hamilton who was quoted as saying *it was awful, it was our anniversary, and we were there to celebrate and have a good time, then this killing happened. I'll never forget it.* Loyal pondered this. If she was celebrating an anniversary, then she was probably married. That wouldn't mean a thing nowadays, but back then it would have. He wondered if she was still around the area.

He didn't remember that name from the trial. He wrote the woman's name on a yellow pad. He noted a few other details from the article, but found nothing else of interest in any other articles that he didn't already know.

He returned the films to the box as instructed and climbed the steps up to the newsroom. "Thanks, Jesse, for setting this up. There's a name I'm going to try to find. I'll let you know whether I have success or not." At home, he paged through the phone book looking for the name Hamilton. There were four of them. One was outside of town in the Cotton Grove community. The others were in town. He called the first one and asked to speak to Peggy. "Ain't no Peggy here," was the only response, and then a dial tone.

He dialed the second number and when a woman answered asked to speak to Peggy. "Who's calling?" she asked.

"This is Loyal Hall. I'm calling for Mrs. Peggy Hamilton. Is this the correct address and phone for her?"

"Who are you and why are you calling?"

"My name is Loyal Hall," he repeated. "I'm a lawyer and I defended a man accused of murder here in town a few years ago. I still think he is innocent, and I think the Mrs. Hamilton I'm seeking may have some knowledge of the events of that night and could help. I'm sorry if I've caught you off guard. If you wish, you can hang up and look me up in the directory and call me back at my home or my office."

There was a long pause. "I'm Peggy Hamilton. Are you calling about the night that man was killed at the Supper Club?"

"Yes, in 1960. That's the one I'm calling about. I defended the man named Mani Hanks, who was accused of it. Could I come talk to you for a few minutes about it?"

"No, I don't think so, but we can talk over the phone if you want to."

"All right, then. May I ask you some questions?"

"Sure. I don't know whether I know anything that will help you, but go ahead. I've only got about twenty minutes. I'm a nurse and have to be at work in an hour and a half."

"Thanks. Let's see. Okay, did you actually see the killing that night?"

"Jesus! Of course not. Ask a sensible question."

"I'm sorry. I don't mean to offend you. I guess that's the lawyer in me. Why don't you tell me what you did see?"

"No, I'm not going to tell all that, because if I did, then I'd be telling you what I was doing out there in back and I'm not about to do that."

"What can you tell me then?"

"Don't ask me what I was doing, okay? I was out back, that's all. With my husband. It was our anniversary and that's a fact. You can check it out. All of a sudden, we saw this scruffy man come around the corner, and Malcolm Oakes was with him. Malcolm was shoving him toward the back and talking mean to him. I assumed Malcolm was doing his job as a bouncer at the club. Anyway, he and the guy talked and seemed to get into an argument. Then Malcolm went back inside. My husband and I went back inside, too. I don't think Malcolm ever even knew we were out there. Later on, someone else came in screaming that there was a dead man outside. She was hysterical, and we all went outside to see, and sure enough, there was a man there. He was dead all right. I'm not a nurse for nothing."

"Did you go to him? That is, since you are a nurse?" He realized it sounded accusatory, and he didn't mean it that way.

"I tried to, but my husband held me back. He said, 'The guy's already dead, honey.' He wanted us to go, and he started trying to get me to leave, but I wouldn't. I thought I should go check the poor thing out. Maybe he wasn't dead after all. That's when Malcolm came out again."

"Anything else you can remember?"

"You know how it is in a crowd like that. People get all abuzz with the excitement. There was a lot of talk for days. We went to the club a lot in those days. It was the only place you could get a drink in a dry county. I heard later that someone else saw Malcolm go out before that with a bottle of whiskey. I asked the bartender, and he told me Malcolm did take a bottle outside that night, but he couldn't remember whether it was before or after the killing."

"This has been a big help. Thank you. Who do you think killed that man? Do you think it was someone at the club, or was it someone else?"

"Lord, how should I know?" The woman was silent for a moment. "I always wondered whether Malcolm had something to do with it because he was arguing with the man."

"What were they arguing about?"

"I couldn't hear. I really couldn't. They weren't talking loudly, but they were definitely arguing about something, or at least Malcolm was fussing at him about something. We were kind of around on the other side of the building, sort of making out, you know. We were young. We were still just kids, even if we were married."

"I understand. Of course. So you think maybe Malcolm did it?"

"No, I didn't say that. Malcolm wasn't a nice man, if you know what I mean, but I don't know that he would do something like that. Maybe he would. I don't know. He was there. He went inside, and some say he came back out again. I didn't see him come back out until it was all over."

"Thank you so much, Mrs. Hamilton. I may call you again. I may even ask you to testify if I can get a second hearing, a second trial. Would you do that for me, for Mani Hanks, if he is really innocent?"

She hesitated. "I might. Call me if you get some more information, okay? My husband won't like it, but you can call me if you think you've got a case. I've got to go to work now." Loyal was still pondering what she had said when Jesse called.

"Loyal, I've been up looking over the layout again. We missed the man sitting in the car!" He sounded excited.

"What man in what car?"

"In the model on Tanyard Street, the car parked beside the road, there's the man running between houses, and there's the car. A man is sitting in that car. Can you believe that?"

"Fairly easily, as a matter of fact. Why are you so excited about it?"

"Loyal, the man sitting in the car shows that Wynne knew someone was waiting there for the running man. He said they drove off together, didn't he?"

"I don't know. Did he?"

This brought Jesse up short. He had been so sure of the fact. Where had he learned it? "Wynne must have told me about that. He wants us to connect Bennie and Malcolm with Nathan's death."

"That may be so, but your man in the car doesn't do it. Besides, connecting the two in that way only makes it worse for Mani. It gives a sure enough reason for him to have killed Bennie."

"I guess you're right. I don't have an answer for it." After they hung up, he tried to weave all the bits of information they had into a whole, but no matter how he arranged them, he couldn't string them together.

Chapter 59

—◆—

Jesse Wickham
Evening, April 16, 1975
Paradise, TN

IT WAS RAINING AS JESSE DROVE toward his apartment, thinking about what Loyal had said, and the street lights reflecting off the wet pavement seemed to add to his confusion. I'm tired, he thought. Maybe after a good night's sleep, it will all make sense. The parking slots near the front awning of the building were taken, so he parked as near as he could and ran through the rain, jumping over puddles on the pavement. He showered, still trying to make sense of what he had learned. Maybe I'm trying too hard to prove a particular point. A good reporter will let the facts impress him instead of the other way around.

The greenish glow from the clock display told him it was after midnight. He thought about his conversation with Loyal Hall. What was he missing? He got up and switched on the bedside light, squinting in the brightness, and opened Nathan's little trunk and removed the notebooks. He had already read through those in Nathan's hand. When he had flipped the pages of the ledger, it had appeared to be filled with entries related to the monument business and later the funeral home, with a few journal entries written by Griffin Wynne, which he had already read. On the inside covers of the ledger were sleeves for documents, and in the back cover, there was a sheet of paper written in Griffin Wynne's neat and precise script and signed by him without a date. Astounded, Jesse read it.

In 1940, I came to Paradise to escape, to cut away and leave behind a single, sordid moment in my life. I spent the remainder in creation, but never far from death. Life is a weave of circumstances, and nothing illustrates it better than the way my life and the life of the black man, Nathan Hanks, entwined. Like me and all the rest, Nathan Hanks came to Paradise with a dream, an exile nurturing a small hope. Of course, there were others in the warp and weft of it, Nathan Hanks's family, my own sister, Loyal Hall and his sister, the boy Jesse Wickham, and those men I ran away from and whose actions you might say were the first thread in the story. But who can ever say when and where a story begins; who can tell the whole story of a life? It's like a tapestry. You can't always tell from the face of it how the images relate. Sometimes, you have to turn it over to read the weave. The story brushed against me again and again, the way a soft breeze in the morning rustles the leaves, then lies down in the burning heat of the day, only to return in the evening to whisper and caress the low places. It was a constant memory touching my shoulder, reminding me that what is real and what is dreamed are inseparable. Even so, I could never tell the whole story, and I could never tell it in words.

~ Griffin Wynne, Paradise, Tennessee

He tried to reinsert the sheet into the sleeve, but it caught on something. He pulled out a sheet of paper folded over a thin envelope. On the envelope were the words *To Whom It May Concern* in the same hand as before. He opened the envelope.

To Whom It May Concern,

I attest that Ellis Wiggins of Hatchie County was lynched on or about the twenty-second day of June in 1946. I know this because I lived in Hatchie County before I came to Paradise in 1940. Prior to that time, I was briefly a member of the Ku Klux Klan. I know the names of others who were members. Some of them may have been responsible for his death, but I do not know. I learned of Ellis Wiggins's death from a man named Malcolm Oakes, who was a Deputy Sheriff in Hatchie County.

In the evening of June 22, 1946, I was called to Hatchie Landing to pick up a body and bring it to Paradise. It was purported to be the body of an unknown person, and I was asked to make final arrangements and conduct the burial in Paradise. All papers were in order. Copies of those papers with specific instructions for their opening may be found in the care of my good friend Mr. Loyal Hall. However, unless he is the one reading this, he has no knowledge of their contents.

The person who called to request that I transport the body was Malcolm Oakes. Oakes was one of the men I associated with in the Klan in Hatchie Landing until 1940. He at first refused to allow me to open the casket to witness that a body was in fact present. I insisted, and he relented. It contained a body that had not been properly prepared for burial. I demanded an explanation. Oakes insisted that I needed no explanation and that all paperwork was in order. I asked the identity of these remains, and he answered that this was an unidentified person and the County would not incur any additional expense for preparation. The paperwork he handed me attested to the fact that this was a person of unknown identity.

I was skeptical and told him I didn't think I should move this body. He put his hand on my shoulder and told me that my help was needed in this. When I asked him why, he told me the man in this casket had to do with all the trouble in Hatchie Landing. He told me about Ellis Wiggins and that someone had killed him. I asked him who had killed him, and he said he didn't know. Then he looked at the casket and said, Maybe that man did it. I asked him what happened to Ellis Wiggins's body. He told me that he and Bennie Hoskins had seen to it. He told me the only thing needed from me was for me to handle the body in this casket so that there would be no more trouble. He reminded me that I was a loyal member of the Klan and was bound to do my duty. I told him that I was not a member and had not been since I left Hatchie Landing. He only smiled at me. In the end, I returned with the remains to Paradise, a shaken man.

Later, while making the man's body decent for burial, I discovered what I believe to be Ellis Wiggins's burned remains in the lining of the casket. I am ashamed that I was afraid of Malcolm Oakes's implied threat. I am ashamed that I went on to conduct my part in the cover-up of Ellis Wiggins's death, but that incident changed my life completely. I never again associated with those men, and I rejected all they stood for.

I believe Ellis Wiggins came to me that evening in the casket of the unknown man, and I arranged a proper burial for him. I do not know the names of the men who were actually responsible for his death. I suspect many, if not most, of them are dead themselves now. I shall be dead soon enough myself. I am old and tired. Life has its way of wearing on us and preparing us for the end. I go gladly and pray that if there is a God and a heaven, I'll be received there, broken soul that I am.

None of this relieves me of responsibility. It does not absolve me of guilt. I am not innocent, but I truly am sorry for my part. I would beg for forgiveness from all who have been hurt, but I cannot find it in me to risk that. People close to me for whom I care greatly would be immeasurably hurt. I will not do that publicly or privately.

I also attest that Mani Hanks is innocent of the killing of Bennie Hoskins. Malcolm Oakes killed Bennie Hoskins. I know this because he confessed to me on the night of Bennie Hoskins's death.

Malcolm Oakes died less than one year later of a gunshot wound outside the Supper Club. I was pleased to be the one to administer that deadly wound, but that was arrogance. He was a flawed man. But isn't each of us flawed in some respect? Aren't we each capable of willful hurt?

What happens inside us when we decide the life of another man is worthless? No one has that right. I did not. To do so is to put one's self above the other, and that is arrogant. If there is an unforgivable sin, it is arrogance because an arrogant man cannot say I am sorry and forgiveness requires two parties: the one to say I forgive and the other to say from his heart, I am sorry. Without those two, there is no forgiveness. Strangely, it was a black man who taught me that. Reverend Buster Holt preached the sermon at Nathan Hanks's funeral, and he spoke to that effect.

I have put aside arrogance, and I have forgiven myself and tried to live a good life, but I cannot create forgiveness for myself. I am truly sorry, and I beg forgiveness, but I will never know whether my own forgiveness becomes a reality.

In all good faith and from a wounded conscience, I say these things.

Griffin Wynne, September 29, 1965

Chapter 60

Jesse Wickham
April 17, 1975
Paradise, TN

THE NEXT MORNING, BEFORE SEVEN, Jesse was on the phone with Loyal explaining what he had found. He read him the letter from Griffin Wynne. Loyal was silent for a long minute. "Come on over and bring the notebook and the letter. I'd like to see them, especially the letter. I'll have a fresh pot of coffee on, and I can fix us some breakfast."

"I'll be over as soon as I can. Breakfast isn't necessary. I have a couple of stops to make first." Jesse drove to the funeral home and went upstairs to the model. On hands and knees, he examined the Riverside Cemetery replication. In one corner was a wrought iron arch. Wrought into the arch were the words *Blessed be the poor for yours is the Kingdom of Heaven.* Behind the arch in the corner of the cemetery were gravestones, some with names and others with none. "The potter's field," Jesse whispered. He looked closely at the markers. There, in the southwest corner, was a tombstone with no name and the date June 22, 1947. In front of the stone was a small object that Jesse at first took to be part of the grave marker. He blew the dust off and looked closely. The initials E. W. were clearly carved on the object.

He turned out the lights and went downstairs. He paused at the small office that once was Wynne's, and smiled. "If the town upstairs is what I think it is, you are amazing, Mr. Wynne," he said, "simply amazing."

He drove to the Riverside Cemetery and walked to the back, turning to his right among old stones—some leaning, some chiseled with age, some hardly readable—until he saw one that stood straight and was almost clean of lichen. The inscription read, *Here lie the known and the unknown.* In front of the tombstone, a small rectangular granite box was set into the base. Its lid was sealed tightly. On top were the initials E. W. Next to that grave was another with a stone inscribed with the name *Bennie Hoskins* and the date of Bennie's death.

He pondered these facts and Wynne's letter and the ledger papers as he drove to Loyal's house.

"Did you bring the letter?" Loyal asked him.

"Yes, it's right here in my briefcase. You may read it, Loyal, but I can't let you have it."

"That's all right, Jesse. I don't want it. I just want to see it for a minute. Here, I've brought something that Wynne gave to me in 1974, not long before he died. I handled his legal affairs from 1955 until he died. They weren't complicated. He gave this to me, as he put it, *to keep in case anything unusual ever happens to me.*" Loyal held up an envelope. A folded piece of paper was clipped to it.

He thumbed the paper. "This is his instruction. It's specific."

Jesse waited.

"Instructions to Loyal Hall. Upon my natural death, please destroy this. However, if anything untoward should happen to me, you may open this envelope. I treasure your friendship even in death." Loyal laid the envelope on the table. The clip left a brown imprint on it. "I think I should open it, don't you?"

"Why didn't you destroy it when he died like he asked?"

"I don't know. I really don't. His reference to our friendship was one thing, I suppose. When he gave it to me, I put it away in my law practice lock box at the bank, but when he died, I couldn't bring myself to destroy it. More than once, I started to open and read it, but always felt I'd be violating his trust. The other day, I brought it here. I almost opened it the other night after we left Emily's house."

Jesse looked at the envelope. It was similar to the one he held in his own hand. "Yes, I think you should."

Loyal opened the envelope and removed the letter. The wording in Griffin Wynne's hand was identical to the one Jesse held. "I'll be damned," Loyal said.

"Me too," added Jesse. "Why do you think he wrote two identical copies of this with instructions to destroy one, but not the other?"

"There's no way to know, is there? Maybe he needed to have someone know about it after all, someone to forgive him, and he chose you. Maybe he thought this would benefit someone else someday, and in fact it has, hasn't it? I'll be able to appeal Mani's sentence now. With all the old papers still at the funeral home, it will be easy to authenticate this as Wynne's handwriting."

"What will happen?"

"Who can say? The Appellate Court can hear the new evidence and order a new trial, or it can simply reverse the earlier decision. The latter would be the best for Mani. But if not that, then we have enough evidence to win a new trial if it comes to it."

"That's wonderful, but Loyal, I've discovered something else."

"What?"

"I think I've found Ellis Wiggins."

"What do you mean you've found Ellis Wiggins?"

Jesse explained what he had found on the model and at the cemetery.

Chapter 61

Bibi Durber
Late Fall 1975
Petros, TN

BIBI DREAMED THE NIGHT BEFORE they went to pick up Mani. This time, only one lion walked about on the other side across the water, and it was looking away toward the far hills. At last, it padded away through the trees, and all she could see were thick trees and low plains that were soft and green between the river and the hills, and sunshine glancing off the water. She remembered her own bibi telling her about the plains in Africa that stretched far off toward the blue hills. Trouble had walked out of her dream.

Loyal drove over to the Quarter from Paradise early the next morning, and they drove all day. Such a long journey. June sat in the front seat next to Mr. Hall, and Bibi sat in the back watching the rain all the way from Nashville to a place outside of Knoxville. Mr. Hall had gotten them a motel, but they wouldn't take Bibi and June. Who could believe that? Times were changing fast, but there was still a way to go. Mr. Hall told the man it was a new day. He swore he would see him in court someday. The man thought he meant to hurt him, but Mr. Hall didn't mean any such thing.

Loyal called up somebody, then told them he had them a place to spend the night in a lady's home. It wasn't too much more driving to get over there, and they were all fed and in bed by ten o'clock. It stopped raining during the night, but Bibi was so tired she didn't know it.

The woman who put them up was Jewish and a little bitty thing, and she had a pretty menorah on her sideboard. Her family was killed in the war. She told them a sad story about it. Trouble just keeps on walking around in the world.

They left her house early. Bibi thanked her, and they hugged. She put her hand on Bibi's face and looked in her eyes. Not many people ever looked deep into Bibi like she did. She knew what the lady was looking at, and it made her feel better about all their trials. She knew she knew what they'd been through, but even though Bibi tried, she couldn't imagine what the lady had been through. She just didn't have a way to pull something like that into her mind, except the part about losing family. She knew about that part. Bibi felt like saying something, but all the two of them could do was hold on to each other for a minute.

Mr. Hall drove them over to a place called Petros, where they were to meet Mani when he got out. There was a tall ring of mountains all around them. You knew it was a hard place to be, and Bibi felt sorry for those men shut up in there. Some of them had done really bad things, but still, she was sorry for them. Sorry they had messed up like they did.

Mr. Hall went inside with one of the guards to get Mani and bring him out. Another guard stood with them while he was gone. The morning was cool, and a breeze blew down from the mountains across the yard where they waited. Bibi asked the guard if the mountain had a name. He told her the mountain was called Brushy Mountain, and that's why the prison was called that name.

The sky over the mountain wasn't like she thought it would be—blue, and she would be happy, but it wasn't that way. Gray is what it was, and tired is all she could feel after all those years. You'd expect something dramatic after what they all went through together—Bibi, June, Mani, and poor Nathan, dead all these years. But it wasn't like that. She was cold. June slipped her coat on Bibi's shoulders, and they waited out there a long time. They wanted to be there when they brought Mani and Mr. Hall out. They wanted to see them even though there was the chain-link fence and the sharp coils of wire, and only that one little gate for them to come through. They wanted to see them as soon as they came out.

Mr. Hall had seen them through it all from beginning to end, and Bibi appreciated that. She supposed nobody could have done more even if they tried, but it wasn't nearly enough. It wouldn't have mattered anyway. It was just one of those things you have to live through to get it over with, one of those things that isn't going away, so you have to live it all the way through. Then it'll be done for you, but it'll still be out there somewhere. It'll catch somebody else one day, somebody just like you, and they'll have to live it through too. You can't understand if you haven't lived through something like they did. No, you can't understand it even if you try, even if you hurt for them like a lot of people did, even if you try to imagine it, you can't. You have to live it, that's what.

Mani and Mr. Hall came out the door and into the yard. There was a guard beside them, but he wasn't guarding. He was talking to Mani and smiling, but Mani just looked straight ahead and walked with his long stride across the yard toward that little gate. Mr. Hall wasn't talking either. Bibi saw that the poor guard was trying to be polite as he escorted them across, and Mani and Mr. Hall understood, but she thought, What does it matter after all that time? What does it matter if somebody tries to be nice after something like that? It doesn't, that's what. Mani and Mr. Hall did appreciate the guard smiling and saying those polite things to them. Mani told them later that the guard was a nice man and wished him good luck. But it doesn't matter after you live through something like they had lived through. It's like one more snowflake in a snowstorm. It doesn't make a difference.

Chapter 62

Mani Hanks
Late Fall 1975
Hatchie Landing, TN

MANI HAD DREAMED OF THE TRIP HOME the whole time he was locked up, although there were times he was sure it would never happen, and yet the four of them—Loyal, June, Bibi, and Mani—arrived back in Hatchie Landing at six o'clock in the afternoon, tired and worn. They had planned to stop in Paradise and have supper with Emily and Lula. Mani was looking forward to seeing them again after such a long time, but Bibi felt tired and frail. She wanted to get home. Emily said they would plan a celebration in a few days. Mani could hardly believe he was seeing the Quarter when they drove in. It hadn't changed much; some houses were freshly painted, some needed it, and there was no dust from the newly paved street. He half expected to see a patrol car follow them in, but nothing like that happened.

June settled Bibi in bed, and they sat around the kitchen table and talked for a while until Mr. Hall said his goodbyes. June asked him to tell Emily and Lula that she would be over to see them in a few days. He would and promised to lend his weight to help Mani get on at the railroad again. He knew Mr. Padgett, the general foreman at Iselin, and had spoken to him already. Something would work out.

The next morning, Mani was enjoying the wonderful feeling of waking up a free man in his own bed in his momma's house when he heard June crying quietly. He went into the kitchen barefoot. She was sitting at the table with her face in a towel.

"Son, it's your bibi. She's passed in the night."

He took June in his arms and held her for a while, and then he went to see Bibi. She looked peaceful, just like she was asleep. He called out to her quietly, but she couldn't answer, though he felt like maybe she did. She had stood beside him all that time, and now that he was home, she could rest. He touched her face and told her he loved her, and it was like he could feel her reminding him to walk to that high place she had hoped he would find. Maybe he would someday, but he didn't know what it might be or how he could get there. Life doesn't give you a clear path to walk.

He heard June telling Mr. Hall over the phone what had happened. "Mr. Hall, she was holding on until we could get all this trouble settled. That's what kept her alive all these years, way past her time. She lived for yesterday. She could finally rest in peace. Grieve for losing her, but don't be sorry. I went in to check on her before I went to bed, and she was awake. She told me to call you today and tell you that she was happy, and to thank you again for all that you did for us. She called Mani in and told him to keep reaching for his high place. Mr. Hall, she knew she was about to go, but I didn't realize it. It wouldn't have mattered even if I had. She would have gone on across anyway. I will let you know about the arrangements as soon as I know. I'd appreciate it if you would tell the others the news."

By the afternoon, they had everything settled. They would bring Bibi home the next day so people could sit by. Buster Holt would preach the funeral sermon at the Quarter Town Zion Church in Hatchie Landing the day after. It rained all night, and a cold wind blew from the north, but the sun broke through in the morning before the service began.

The hearse turned into the Street, drove slowly down to the end and turned around, and came back to the house and stopped. All the men came out of their houses and stood along the walk just like when they brought Nathan home. Then some of them brought Bibi's casket into the house and set it in the front room right where Nathan's had sat. That brought tears to Mani's eyes. The Sisters had brought in food and decorated the house with flowers. They weren't fresh, blooming flowers from the garden like Griffin Wynne had done for Nathan's, but they were lovely.

The Sisters arranged chairs so people could sit by awhile, and they put Bibi's Bible on a little table beside the casket so folks could see how worn and used it was, and know how much she studied it, even though they all knew how much she loved the old ways and kept them alive in her stories. Mani told the Sisters to bring the children by later so he could gather them around Bibi and tell them some of her stories, and they did that afternoon. They sat on the floor beside Bibi while he told them the story his daddy had told him when he was little about the Whydah bird with its long, long tail and how all the animals had begun to try to learn to talk to one another. One little girl wanted to know why the Whydah bird chose the butterfly's language to learn first.

"It was just like the whydah bird said, because it was simple and beautiful. You see, everybody's language is that way, simple and beautiful, only we don't know it, but the Whydah bird knew it, and he knew that the only way the other animals would ever figure it out was for them to learn it by doing it. Just like all of us. We have to start somewhere, and when we do, we'll see how easy it is to understand someone else."

Mani sat in one of the chairs beside Bibi the whole day. He thanked her for never giving up on him. He never knew what it meant to be loved until he came out of the gate at Brushy Mountain and saw her frail old body standing there like it was a bent old oak tree living there just for me. She lifted up her arms to him even before he got out of the gate.

Before the day was over, Buster had come by and sat with them, Arlene came down all the way from Chicago, Loyal Hall brought Emily and Lula over from Paradise, and the Sisters and the Brothers came and went all night long.

Chapter 63

Rev. Buster Holt
Next Day
Hatchie Landing, TN

THE NEXT MORNING, several of the Brothers arrived at nine o'clock. The service was to be at ten and the burial at the Hallowed Ground afterward. June and Mani spent a long time at the casket saying their goodbyes to Bibi. They each touched her face and told her they loved her, and June promised her that they'd keep on loving each other, too. Then the Brothers closed the casket. June asked one of them to take Bibi's rocking chair from the porch and put it up front at the church right beside her casket, and they did. More of the Brothers and Sisters lined up along the walk when the hearse came, and they carried Bibi outside. There were people all along the Street as she rode away to the church.

Buster spoke eloquently of Bibi. He told of her life and her heritage, which was the heritage of them all no matter where they came from. This woman represented them all. She had shown them what the real promise was. It wasn't a promise to possess the land. It was a promise that those who loved could overcome anything. Her life was the proof that this was true. The Sisters were in tears, and the Brothers said amen. Buster then raised some questions.

"Bibi's life was a picture for us all to see, but we couldn't see it good, and it makes us wonder at the burden she bore," he said. "Our trouble was her trouble, and she showed us how to live through troubled times. She bore up when Ellis Wiggins disappeared. She bore up under Nathan's death. She bore up when her Mani was taken away. She bore up, and she didn't hate."

Then he asked, "What really killed Ellis Wiggins? What really killed Nathan Hanks? What really killed Bennie Hoskins?

"Notice I asked *what*, not *who*. No one really knows the answer to the who, though we have some notions. It may be that some folks knew at one time, but they're all dead now. The rest, the living, only have suspicions. It certainly isn't satisfying to anyone, but that's simply the way it is. But *what* killed them is the thing I'm talking about, and the answer to that is hate, pure and simple. Someone hated Ellis Wiggins enough to kill him, and that started the whole progression. Or did that hate exist already; was it there from the beginning, maybe the beginning of time? Who knows the answer to that either? It spilled over into Paradise and killed Nathan Hanks, and it flowed on down to the other side of the river, down beside that Supper Club where it killed Bennie Hoskins. Mani Hanks went to prison for that killing, but he didn't do it, and everybody knows that now. It may have killed Malcolm Oakes and maybe others that we don't even know about. But our Bibi bore up under all that hate swirling around her, and she showed us how it's done.

"So what do you say about something like this? How do you explain it? I can tell you that a trouble like this doesn't happen just one time. Once it happens, it lives on. Like a disease, it infects other folks and no one knows when or how, and no one knows when it began or when it will end. But a trouble like this is complicated. There is some room in it for just about anything.

"Bibi would say this is the question you've got to answer for your own self... Is there room for forgiveness? There are some who believe so, and there are some who say that retribution is the only response. But isn't retribution just like the crime itself? Can you really tell the difference? To turn on your enemy, you have to become like your enemy. You may save your life, but you will lose your soul. Your only salvation is to forgive, even if it may cost you your life. Our Bibi lived that.

"Something breaks inside you if you decide to turn on another person. Something breaks in all of us, and without forgiveness, the break will never heal. Without forgiveness, we all remain broken. Anyone who preaches forgiveness has to know that forgiveness is not a one-sided affair. There is the side of the damaged, the injured, and the wronged that must be willing to say, *"I forgive."* Then there is the other side, the side that inflicts the damage, the wrong that must say, *"I am sorry. I repent."* Without both of these, Brothers and Sisters, without the *"I forgive"* and the *"I am sorry,"* there is no forgiveness. Brothers and Sisters, do you hear what I'm saying to you? You can forgive when you are hurt. You can say I'm sorry when you are the cause of the hurt. But forgiveness doesn't happen until both those things come together. Hear what I say."

The Brothers said amen, and the Sisters said amen.

The church was silent then and still. No one sniffled or wiped a tear. Faces everywhere were lifted up. Buster moved over behind Bibi's rocking chair and set it to moving slowly back and forth.

"So what makes the loss of our Bibi so hard to bear? Is it because we've lost the beacon that led us through the hate that rose up and murdered Ellis Wiggins? Is it because hate is so senseless, or is it because it infects so many others? Hate broke something inside Bennie Hoskins and Malcolm Oakes and all the others who were with them the night Ellis Wiggins died. Once it broke, their only salvation was forgiveness, and maybe none of them knew how to ask for it. They couldn't heal the broken thing inside themselves, and it finally killed them both. But who on the other side ever offered forgiveness? No one went to them to say it. So who is the guiltier then?

"As Bibi used to say, *All the dead are on the other side, some good and some bad. We all will go there one day. Until we do, until that old lion, Death, pad-foots across and taps us out, we have a choice. We can live or we can die.*

We can do right or do wrong. We can hate or not. Our souls can be whole or they can break in two.'

"Some say Malcolm Oakes told people about Ellis Wiggins and Bennie Hoskins, but they turned their backs on him. Bennie Hoskins never got the image of Ellis Wiggins out of his mind, and Malcolm never got the image of Bennie Hoskins out of his mind. It finally broke both of them. They died out there in the night somewhere near Paradise. They never knew to ask for forgiveness, and they never knew how to say I'm sorry."

Buster gestured toward the slowly moving chair and continued. "If Bibi were sitting alive among us right now, she would tell us about another one of those lions walking back and forth. She would tell us it had a name on its forehead too, just like Death and Trouble and just like Sorrow. But when this lion comes across, the others slink away because they can't stand up to this one lion whose name is emblazoned on its forehead just like theirs. And she would tell us this one lion's name. Brothers and Sisters, she would whisper its name." Buster's voice dropped low. "She would whisper, *Forgiveness.*"

"Brothers and Sisters, nobody knows for sure how old our Bibi really was. But Melissa Shawl Durber, June's momma and Mani's bibi, the little girl called 'Dream Freedom' by her own bibi, walked with us for over a hundred years. She lived through hard times, and she lived with happiness. She knew happiness isn't always found. She knew sometimes you have to make it.

"She made her own happiness, and she passed it around. She was a good woman. She knew what it meant to say *'I forgive.'* She knew what it meant to say *'I am sorry.'* She said, *'I am going to live.'* She said, *'I am going to do what is right.'* She never broke in two. And folks, Melissa Shawl Durber, our Bibi, walked to freedom. She walked into the Promised Land where she waits for you and me."

Mani stood beside Bibi's chair on the little porch in the cool of a morning some days after the funeral, after the grieving clothes were packed away in so many chests of drawers or set into the shadowy recesses of closets and the things grieved for had become sweet memories and the living were once again able to relive them with some joy beyond their sense of loss even though their eyes moistened at the sudden intrusion of remembered things. A gentle breeze across the porch set Bibi's chair to rocking as Buster had done at the funeral, and in that moment, in that breeze, he was certain he heard her voice.

"It took me a long time to understand that none of us is so good that we can say those wild dogs aren't us. No, sir. I saw them in that dream a long time ago, and I can tell you. No matter who you are, there is one with your name on it, too."

Epilogue

By 1948, Paradise was gathering all manner of people unto itself, some good, some bad, most in between. The town's streets and shops, the churches, and the governments were simply receptacles for them. We all come to a place as exiles in some manner, seeking shelter, hoping for peace, rarely completely happy. The town's citizenry, who, for the most part, were only observers to this secular diaspora, would occasionally welcome one of these as its own, content to leave the remainder to drift the perimeter of its formalities and informalities, exiles forever.

Like the real town of Paradise, Griffin Wynne's model was a receptacle for memory, an archive of stories, and he was the archivist. For years, he recorded in exquisite detail its streets and houses, its rail yards and graveyards. I remember his hands, blue-veined and wrinkled, would glide like boats sailing deep waters, as if sensing time's heft and wallow. He would pause now and then to reconsider a portion of his work, then move on, fingertips touching like calipers measuring depth and thickness to a precision beyond physics, beyond the actual, not looking so much as drifting over his town, as if to enter on his own terms, no distraction, no impediment, striving to reach an understanding between mind and matter. One day, satisfied there was nothing more he could do to alter the inevitable, he bent close as if to blow away the dust one last time like God breathing life into clay, and left it, the replica of Paradise, to wait for the right conjunction of time and space.

~ Loyal Hall, as told to Jesse Wickham,
Paradise, Tennessee, 1975

THE END

www.ingramcontent.com/pod-product-compliance
Lightning Source LLC
Chambersburg PA
CBHW070425170726
48291CB00002B/367